A portion of the proceeds generated by the sale of this book will benefit
Ministerio Amor y Esperanza in Nejapa, El Salvador – fearlessly reaching the
forgotten youth of El Salvador with Christ's love.

Find out more: www.maeelsalvador.org

ELI–THE PHENOM'S STORY

A HISTORICAL NOVEL OF THE 1946 BASEBALL SEASON

WRITTEN BY: MARK ZIMMERMAN

Illustrations by Allen Markovic.

Cover design by Anna Zimmerman.

Printed in the United States of America

First Printing, 2022

ISBN 978-0-578-37917-3

"I don't care how
long you've been around,
you'll never see it all."

BOB LEMON,
CLEVELAND INDIANS (1946–1958)

 JUNE 1946 22

The cool breeze was moving easily through the car. It was a perfect morning for the first day of summer. That Great Lakes humidity that soaked you even before you put your shirt on was nowhere to be found as Cy Slapnicka tried to concentrate on the road in front of him.

That wasn't easy at the moment.

Twelve hours earlier, he had left a hastily-called meeting of all the scouts employed by the Cleveland Indians. In a smoke-filled room at the Hollenden Hotel, Slapnicka and his fellow scouts found themselves in a circle – some seated on chairs, some on the bed, some sitting on the window ledge.

In the center of the room was the Indians' new owner, Bill Veeck.

Slapnicka stroked his chin as he drove, thinking about his new boss.

He'd heard the rumors weeks ago about William Veeck Sr.'s son coming to Cleveland, but paid them little mind. The rumors of baseball teams being bought or sold were as numerous these days as the number of World War II vets scrambling for jobs.

In the last week though, he'd heard about Veeck scrambling from bank to bank in downtown Cleveland, with Hal Lebovitz of *The Cleveland News* right alongside. The team Cy worked for was for sale, and although it seemed ridiculous to all the scouts, the now former owner – Alva Bradley – had no idea how that happened.

Cy slid the Ford sedan off the highway and into the parking lot of his favorite diner when he was headed for the rolling farmlands south of Cleveland.

As he opened the screen door, the smell of the onions on the grill hit him hard.

"Hello, Cy!"

"Hi, Helen."

"Usual…?"

"You know it."

"'3 Pigs', Norm!"

"Cy's here?"

"Hey, Tom."

Tom swung his head around the corner from the kitchen, his apron already stained from the breakfast rush.

He lifted his eyebrows, "Sounds like you have a new boss."

"Yep," said the scout, "it does appear that way."

"Whattya know about this guy–what's his name–Veek?" Tom was instantly a fan who needed some inside info.

Slapnicka shrugged. "Worked with his dad with the Cubs. Got a loan to buy a minor league club in Milwaukee, turned it around with Casey Stengel as the manager, and made a nice profit for his investors. Went to the South Pacific with the Marines, and got his leg smashed by an artillery piece."

"Wait a minute," Tom said as he moved back to the grill, "isn't he the guy that-"

"-Tried to buy the Phillies a few years ago?" Slapnicka said.

"Yeah... said he was going to stock the team with negros." Tom's voice trailed off. He reached for the Swiss cheese as the ham started to sizzle.

"You're right, Tom. Veeck – oh, you say it with a short 'e' – had all his investors lined up, and he was ready to buy the club. But, he told Judge Landis about his plan, and The Judge cut it off right there. No sale. No Negro League all-star team playing in the National League."

"Hm." Tom tore off a sheet of wax paper to wrap the sandwiches.

"Nope. The old Judge wasn't ready to break the color line just yet," Cy said.

Tom grabbed a paper sack and snapped it open. "But those Dodgers didn't wait 'till the Judge's body was cold before they signed that boy Robinson."

"And Robinson's tearing up the International League right now in Montreal." The scout nodded, "He's going to be in Brooklyn next year, mark my words."

Tom's eyes narrowed as he handed Cy the bag of sandwiches. "Is that why this Veek-"

"Veeck."

"-Veeck fella is sending you out on the road this weekend?"

There was no way Slapnicka was going to answer that question honestly.

"No, Tom. That's not what I'm driving through Ohio looking for." Slapnicka spun toward the register to change the subject as fast as he could.

"Hey Helen, did you fill my thermos?"

"Sure did," she replied with a genuine smile. "What would you do without us, Cy?"

"Heaven knows, Helen," the scout said – moving quickly toward the screen door. "See you on the way back through, Tom."

"Take care, Cy!"

Slapnicka couldn't get in the car fast enough. It roared to life, he slipped it into gear, and rolled back onto the highway headed south.

He didn't answer that question from the diner's owner because of the usual reason – having a hot prospect that he just couldn't talk about.

He didn't answer the question because... he had absolutely no idea what he was driving toward Newark and Zanesville to see. He knew there were some promising young men to look at, but these weren't high school and college kids. He heard about some industrial leagues filled with veterans just back from Europe and the Pacific... longshots. The longest of longshots.

As he drove into Wayne County, and the hills began to gently lift and turn the big Ford, Cy had no idea what – or who – or how he was supposed to do what he had been told to do at the hotel the night before.

Cy's mind drifted back to last night's meeting as he drove, with the realization that he was literally going to search for a needle in the haystacks of the Ohio countryside.

THE NIGHT BEFORE

The Hollenden Hotel, Cleveland | 8:00pm

Bill Veeck entered the room and tossed a cane against the wall by the door.

"Hello guys, I'm Bill. I know most of you because I saw you all in the stands in Milwaukee."

Heads nodded around the room.

"I also know you because of all the free beer you drank at my park."

Smiles, with some hearty laughs and winks followed that line.

Veeck paused for a moment, then plunged in.

"Guys, as of noon today, my syndicate and I are the owners of the Cleveland Indians."

The room went silent.

"Oh, c'mon, I'm not here to fire you. I need all of you more than ever, but I'm going to need you immediately, and every day until further notice."

The young, sandy-haired, ex-Marine now had everyone's attention.

Veeck pursed his lips, then continued, "I think we all saw where the ballclub's at when we looked at the morning papers?"

"Sixth." A few voices in the room muttered.

"That's right," Veeck said, "we are two months into the season, and we're 17 games behind Boston. Our lineup isn't producing runs. The only reason we're sixth is the pitching staff. We won 3-out-of-4 from Mr. Mack's A's, but the most we could draw for those games was 16,000... for a Sunday doubleheader... in a 70,000-seat stadium."

Veeck looked around the room.

"Can I get a chair guys? This is about the time of day this foot really starts throbbing."

One of the scouts got up, and passed his wooden chair to the new owner. Veeck spun it around with a flick of his hand. He was tall and thin, his wiry frame showing beneath a half-unbuttoned sport shirt. He sat with his legs on either side of the chairback, tilting his smashed right foot back on its heel.

A few of the scouts stared at that useless right foot. The man in the center of the room could have probably got out of going to the South Pacific, but chose to go. Respect was replacing the unease that was in the room a few moments before.

"Sorry guys, I started a little fast there," Veeck said. "Just so we're clear from the start, I'm Bill. Just... Bill. 'Mr. Veeck' was my dad. My door will always be open to you. Hell, it'll be open to everybody. The first thing I'm doing when I get to the ballpark tomorrow, is take my office door off its hinges, and put it away. When you need me, you've got me."

Bill smashed out the butt of the cigarette he'd been smoking when he entered the room, and rapidly lit another.

"Yes... 'when you need me, you got me'," Bill said again, "but right now, I need all of you. You all know about Milwaukee, right?"

Heads nodded, with a few smirks.

"Fireworks, Ladies' Days, cow milking contests, morning games for the third-shift workers in the defense plants," Bill said, as his voice kept rising. "But we also played some damn good baseball. All of those things I did with the Brewers, I'm going to do here. We've got a huge ballpark over there, and we can fill it."

Some of the scouts' eyebrows raised.

"But, not yet. Where are we again?" Bill asked.

"Sixth place," a few more of the scouts answered.

Bill pressed, "And how far back?"

"17 games out of first," came the reply.

"I need 'hope'," Bill said as he spread his hands.

"The pitching-" one scout offered.

"Is fine." Bill said, "Feller is back to what he was before the war, Harder is giving us everything he's got left, Gromek's done fine. We're in good shape there, guys. But we just can't *hit*. Boudreau's hitting .300 again, but he can't knock anyone in if there's no one on base. We're going to get him some help, but we can't trade for the help we need with what we have on hand."

One of the scouts asked, "Well, if we can't do it this year, are we going out to hunt down possibilities for '47?"

"Like I said guys, I need 'hope', but I need it *now*," Bill clarified. "To answer your question; 'Yes', we need to identify the players and the trade partners that will get us into contention in the next three years. I'm going to have one team going, one team playing, and one team coming. We'll be making lots of moves in the months to come, but – we need 'hope' right now."

"Where do we get that?" another scout asked.

Bill said, "That's why I need all of you. Immediately."

Feet shuffled in the room. Some of the scouts exchanged an 'is he nuts?' look out of the corners of their eyes.

"Tomorrow morning. Hell, tonight if you can get on the road – I need all of you to get back to your circuits, and start asking questions. High school graduates, college kids-"

"We've seen and cross-checked, Bill-"

"Then see them and cross-check'em *again*. Then, look for the vets who've just returned. Industrial leagues, Legion ball, I don't care where you find him."

"Him?" Slapnicka asked. (And was surprised to hear his voice.)

"'The guy who's going to bring me *hope*', Cy." Bill smiled at the veteran scout. "Cy, I need you – all of you," he spun in his chair and looked at the men looking back at him as he lit another cigarette, "to find me that guy who we can get here to Cleveland right away. The unique guy who will get fans in the seats for the rest of this year, get them excited, keep them excited, and give them hope going into the winter, when we can really make some moves. Maybe he's a war hero, maybe he's got one arm like Pete Gray, maybe he's not out of high school yet – like Nuxhall-"

"-or Feller." Slapnicka said.

"Or Feller." Veeck smiled at Cy. He wheeled back to the rest of the room, "Maybe he's a negro, maybe he's not a 'he'-"

That got everyone's attention.

"-or maybe he's even a midget." Veeck laughed. "But, there's a special player out there who can put butts in the seats, and one of you has to find him for me. *Immediately.*"

Slapnicka's voice got tight, "C'mon Bill, that's-"

"Impossible." Bill finished the sentence. "Yeah, I'm saying: 'Hi, I'm Bill, you still have your jobs with the Indians, but right now, I need you to drop everything and find me an all-star before the All-Star Game'."

The entire Cleveland Indians scouting staff sat staring at Bill Veeck in silence.

"Thanks, guys," Bill said. "Good luck."

The scouts remained seated around the room.

"We're done," Bill added."But when you find him, call me from wherever you are. I'll get there the next day at the latest, and I'll bring a few of you with me to cross-check if I can. We've got 14 weeks left in the season. We can't catch Boston or the Yanks, but we can give the fans a reason to come, and to come back... the rest of this year, and next."

One by one, the scouts began to leave. All stopped to shake Bill Veeck's hand and offer their congratulations.

As he reached to grab his hat, Cy Slapnicka felt a hand on his shoulder. He turned, and faced his new boss.

Bill looked him in the eye, "Slap, I need a miracle."

"Yes you do, Bill."

"You can find him Cy," Bill said, "just like you found Bob Feller ten years ago."

"He wasn't hiding, Bill," Slapnicka said, "You can't hide talent like that."

"This guy's out there somewhere," the owner smiled, "he'll be right under your very sensitive nose... sniff him out."

The veteran scout exhaled long and slow, wiping his brow.

Bill Veeck smiled, "I've been looking forward to working with you, Slap. You're as good as they come. You find'im, and I'll sign'im."

Cy Slapnicka turned right out of the doorway, and trudged toward the elevator.

The next few tomorrows were going to be long days.

JUNE

Somewhere in Holmes County

Cy was lost. Not on the highway. He'd driven this path in search of many a young bat and arm. His big Ford could have driven itself to any sandlot in Ohio.

The scout was lost in his thoughts.

It is impossible, he thought – working a toothpick around his mouth.

Ultimately, it was hunger – not intuition – that stopped the car.

When Slapnicka got the phenom he was supposed to find out of his head for a second, the toasted ham and cheese sandwiches in the grease-stained sack in the seat next to him jumped back into his thoughts.

It took a minute for Cy to find a spot by the side of the road, but he felt the crunch of the gravel under his tires, took the car out of gear, slowed to a stop, and yanked on the brake.

The hills and farmland of Holmes County, Ohio stretched out in front of him like a painting. The summer songbirds were everywhere, the sky was a blue that gradually deepend as your eyes scanned upward to take it all in, and the sounds –

The sounds of baseball.

Down the embankment to his right, a ballgame was underway.

Cy had motored through this area enough to know that every Saturday afternoon, the young men of the Amish community blew off steam with some pretty lively ballgames.

The expanse below him made for the perfect Amish ballfield.

Bordered in right field by corn that was definitely waist-high or better, the field was carved out of the farmland around it by a winding ditch of a stream that ended in a watering pond for the farm's livestock.

Because of the awkwardness of getting horse-drawn plows in and out of that flat peninsula of land, the plot was put to the best use by the families that surrounded it:

A ballfield.

Slapnicka was a bit awestruck by the grass infield, and what appeared to be evenly-graded dirt between the bases. The backstop, he noted, wasn't going to move anytime soon. Eight-inch diameter posts supported perfectly cut and mitered planks, all encased in a tight, chicken wire screen.

The dugouts were hardwood, and just as solid as the backstop they were attached to.

Plain, black Amish buggies were everywhere – parked at rails on both sides of the field, with the horses still hitched. None of the horses were actually tied off, Cy noted. Their reins were just draped casually over the rails.

The ballpark was surrounded by fans.

Huge families stretched out on giant blankets, with baskets of food dotting the grassy slope, and along the foul lines.

Groups of long-bearded fathers cheering on their sons.

Mothers resigned to the fact that the small children not in the game would sort themselves out at the end of the afternoon, and find their way back to their families' buggy.

The younger women were trying very hard to not watch any particular young man in the game closely... while each was watching the particular young man she was trying not to look at directly very closely.

And more than one of them – more than likely – were watching the same young man.

Cy realized that his presence had been noted.

Amish children were turning to their parents and pointing at him.

Old Amish men peering up the embankment, were looking at him, and shrugging their shoulders at each other.

The action on the field even paused between pitches, as the players on the field, and on the bench cast their eyes at the "English" – the intruder at the top of the hill.

Slapnicka lifted his fedora, and tilted his head toward them, then offered a small wave.

It sufficed.

The attention of the fans turned back to the game, but not without occasional glances with furrowed brows. Cy's unwanted presence was annoying.

Cy smiled as he took in the scene. The patterns of baseball so familiar, yet in this unique setting, notably different. The players on both sides were all wearing white shirts, grey pants, and black suspenders. Even their bowl haircuts rendered their appearance completely uniform. The only true differences between the young men were in height and weight.

Can't tell the players *with* a scorecard, Slapnicka laughed to himself.

Ready for his second toasted ham and cheese, Cy turned, and reached for the sack behind him.

It wasn't the sight, but the sound that made his eyes wide, and his head snap around.

There was a crack – and then a sharp echo off the opposite hill – a sound that got the attention of everyone present.

The veteran scout knew the sound well.

Williams, Greenberg, Gehrig, Foxx... Josh Gibson and The Babe... they could produce a sound like that.

But who...?

The young men playing center and right field had given up the chase, and were pointing skyward. Cy – too late to pick up the flight of the ball, glanced back toward the infield. The young man had rounded first, and pulled up into a home run trot halfway to second.

The scout's head turned again as he tried to focus on the corn growing beyond right field.

He saw two stalks snap backward from the ball's impact. Then a few more shook as if struck about ten feet from the first impact.

His head swung back to see the batter cross home plate.

Tall. Maybe six feet. Muscled, but not *thick*. Those forearms and wrists. Blacksmith...?

Behind the backstop, the old Amish men were roaring with laughter, approximating the arc of the ball with their hands.

Slapnicka realized right away – they've seen this before.

Cy's head swung back toward the outfield. A young boy disappeared between the corn rows, headed straight for the ball. His straw hat was the only part of him that could be seen. The scout's mind was racing – everyone here is familiar with what just happened... no one is excited – at all.

The tiny straw hat disappeared for a second, then the boy popped up from the corn, holding the ball aloft for all to see.

How far...?

The scout was now making the mental calculations he'd made for years.

So many sandlots, so few fences.

Slapnicka looked at the diamond.

If it wasn't 90 feet between the bases, it was darn close.

400 feet...?

He thought of the bleacher wall at the lakefront stadium – a 460-foot poke, just like the scoreboard at League Park.

He looked again at the spot the little boy was returning from with the baseball...

No... can't be...

Cy ran his mental math again. Trying to make sense of it.

The sound of the contact.

The sound of the ball shredding corn leaves.

The straw-hatted kid holding the ball above his head.

450 feet...?

His eyes came back to the game seconds later. His brain followed seconds after that. The half-inning had ended, and his gaze fell upon the hitter instinctively.

The young man was basically what a scout sees as "perfection" in his mind at the beginning of a baseball season. Even though he was wearing the plain clothes of his Amish heritage, Slapnicka saw the classic physique – the wrists and arms he'd seen at first glance, and the lower body – the place where the power came from.

Cy glanced at his watch.

1:30, and he was due to see that factory league game in Newark at 4 o'clock.

He had 30 more minutes.

The inning was progressing, but it was the scout who drew another round of attention from the Amish – on the field and off – as he worked his way down the slope.

He had to get a closer look.

They were visibly frowning at him now. Every step closer Cy drew to the right field line drew another disapproving look.

In the next 30 minutes, the young man glided at least 100 feet to pull down drives by players on the opposite side who also harbored a pretty fair amount of talent. But this game belonged to the young man whose every move was now being visually measured by the veteran scout.

As his turn came around in the order, the other team brought in a new pitcher.

Cy noticed the speed right away. More like Harder than Feller, but certainly fast enough for Class C pro ball. The accuracy of the pitches were definitely not professional grade.

It appeared to be a bit personal now. Cy had the impression that the other team had been worn out quite enough by this blond young man, and the solution seemed to be throwing pitches as hard as possible in anger, and seeing if he could hit them.

The strong young hitter let two high and wide ones alone, but once again – on what Cy figured was the '2-0 pitch' – that sound of "perfect contact" between bat and ball echoed off the side of the hill.

"Good Lord..." the words were out of Slap's mouth before he realized it.

An Amish woman on the blanket next to Cy covered the ears of her young one. The "English" was obviously about to blaspheme.

This one was a power alley pull. Hit lower, but harder, than the first.

The scout snorted a laugh as he saw the left-fielder in "the pose." Just like a major leaguer whose pitcher had just been crushed, the teen didn't even turn his head. He just kept his throwing hand and glove on his knees and stared down at the grass by his feet.

Cy saw the splash in the cattle pond, as the families surrounding the field laughed and cheered again. Then, the scout heard it – loud and clear:

"ELI!"

His teammates were whooping, and whistling now. The normally reserved older men behind the backstop were doing the same – much to the horror of their wives.

"Eli..." the scout whispered to himself.

As the inning ended, Cy brought an audible gasp from the crowd as he walked to home plate. The stares of the Amish had turned from annoyance to astonishment as the English in the fedora stepped on home plate, pointed himself toward left-center field, and began walking in long strides toward the pond.

The players – as stunned as the fans – could hear the odd man counting each stride as he walked, oblivious to the scene he was causing.

Slap reached the pond quickly. He couldn't believe his own ears.

"155, 156, 157, 158... 159."

The boy who retrieved Eli's first home run, now held the second in his right hand.

"Can I see that ball, son?"

The Amish boy's eyes went wide, and his face turned white.

"I just want to see it for a sec."

The child dropped the ball at Slapnicka's feet. And ran away crying.

Cy turned to look back at home plate.

159 paces. A yard-a-pace.

477 feet.

Damn.

Then, the scout realized what he was feeling as he squeezed the ball in his hand.

The give just under the cover.

The ball was soft.

Not mushy, but there was enough give in it that a major league umpire would toss it in the BP bag.

The kid hit an imperfect ball perfectly. And drove it about 477 feet. Lordy.

"...English..."

But, what did it mean? These Amish pitchers were big and strong, but nowhere near as accurate as the pros. Slap checked his watch. There was no way he would make it to Newark and Zanesville now... mainly because Cy had to see more... of Eli, the center fielder who was now looking directly at him from about a hundred feet away. And was laughing at him.

"ENGLISH!"

Slapnicka looked at the left fielder, who made the universal gesture meaning "gimme the ball."

Cy zipped a throw to him. Chest-high with some mustard. Not bad for an old guy.

The ball snapped into the Amish outfielder's mitt. The left fielder raised his eyebrows, and he exchanged a glance with Eli in center, who nodded to the scout with the smallest of smiles.

Two more pitchers emerged from the other team's bench to face Eli in the innings that remained. Neither one was successful in getting the kid out. In what Cy figured out was the bottom of the sixth, an outfielder laid down to stop a screamer from reaching the corn, but before he could jump and get the ball to second, Eli was standing on third.

In the eighth, the pitcher threw one big curve, and won a moral victory.

After fouling off two fastballs, the pitcher tried to sneak another curve past Eli.

It almost worked.

Slap, who had now worked his way behind the backstop – to the continuing annoyance of all – recognized the spin as the ball emerged from the pitchers' hand.

Eli saw it just a split-second later.

He adjusted mid-swing, and sent a soft liner over the shortstop's head. Three players sprinted for the gapper, but it was no use, and they all knew it. The second baseman stepped off the bag before Eli arrived – standing – with a 180-foot bloop double.

As the game wrapped up, Cy was a ball of nervous energy.

The teams exchanged handshakes, and laughed about who would get the first pick when the bat was tossed next Saturday.

Slap stared at Eli as he walked away from the bench. The young Amish ballplayer sensed it, and returned the look with a nod.

"Eli."

"Yes."

"My name is Cy. May I ask your last name?"

"No, you may not." The voice came from behind the scout.

"I'm sorry..."

"You should be," the older man with the beard said, "you caused quite a scene, English. Uninvited. Speaking to married women. Stopping our ballgame to walk across our field."

"I meant no insult, Mr.-"

"Weaver. Elijiah Weaver."

"My apologies for my behavior, Mr. Weaver. My name is Cy. Cy Slapnicka."

The Amish elder was measuring him. "And you are still here why?"

The scout nodded to the young man standing at Elijiah's side. "I was hoping to have a word with this young man."

"My son. And *why?*"

"He's a fine ballplayer, Mr. Weaver. I hoped I could speak with him about that."

"Go ahead."

"I hoped I could speak to him alone about that."

"You may not," the elder Weaver spoke. With finality.

"Eli Weaver," the scout looked him in the eye, "my name is Cy Slapnicka."

Slap offered his hand. A very firm handshake was returned without a word.

"Eli," Cy continued, "I am a regional scout for the Cleveland Indians."

The young man stared at the scout.

"The Cleveland Indians are a major league team, son. I'm sure you've heard our games on the radio."

"We don't own a radio. We don't have electricity. We are plain people," Eli said.

Cy winced. "Yes. I'm sorry. I do know that-"

"I know about the Clevelands. I read the sports page when I am in town. Booder-oww and Keltner -"

Elijiah was anxious to get home, dinner was cooking. "Enough talk. Come, boy."

"Mr. Weaver, I would like to ask another question of your son."

"And I would like to go home and stop talking with a rude English."

"With your permission, sir?" Slapnicka knew he was on thin ice, and he didn't want to blow it before it had a chance to begin.

"Hurry."

"Eli," the scout's eyes met the young man's, "if I can have your father's permission, I would like to take you to Cleveland for a... tryout."

Eli's eyes were wide. He didn't seem to be breathing.

"A what?" Elijiah sputtered, "where???"

"I would like to take Eli to Cleveland, to our ballpark, and have some of our coaches work with him for a day. To see if he is as fine a ballplayer as I'm suspecting he might be."

"And what is the purpose of such a thing?" The elder Weaver couldn't imagine...

"That I might become a baseball player," his son said quietly.

"And who will help me with the second hay cut?" Elijiah sensed disaster.

"If I am good enough, father, I will be paid well. Isn't that right?"

Slapnicka nodded. Eli continued, "The money could end the debt with your brothers."

Smart kid, thought Slap.

Elijiah was turning red, "And you will be away from our people again? No."

Cy turned to Eli's father. "Mr. Weaver-"

"NO."

"Father. We could ask the elders after church tomorrow," Eli said softly.

Wow, he's good. The scout was more impressed by the minute.

Cy matched Eli's quiet tone, "If that is what I must do, I will certainly-"

"It has nothing to do with what you must do, English," Elijiah said tersely. "This question is only to be asked by our people to our people."

"I understand, sir."

"No. You don't. Come, boy. We go."

"Mr. Weaver," Cy's voice rose just a touch, "when may I call at your house tomorrow?"

The father stared a hole through the scout, and walked to his buggy muttering. Eli–through landmarks and some sketchy road names–gave Cy the directions, but asked him not to come until after dinner.

"I need to call my boss, to see if he can come join me," Slapnicka said, "but... there are no phones here."

"In town," the young ballplayer replied. "Just a couple of miles down this road."

"What town?"

"Mt. Hope."

JUNE  22

League Park – Cleveland

It had been a full day for the new owner of the Cleveland Indians.

Bill Veeck was awake with the sunrise, walking one end of League Park to the other, peeking behind every hot dog stand, opening every door to every stall in every bathroom.

Behind him dragged a long line of custodial workers, and the line got shorter every time Veeck stopped, stooped, and began pointing underneath counters, and emerging from a souvenir stand, pointing, gesturing, and leaving a few more to clean in his wake.

Then, swooping up and down the steps through the box seats, he snatched up a crushed paper cup here, a hot dog wrapper there –

"Is it going to be like this every day?" one of the workers said under his breath, as he ran with his broom and pan to a pile of cigarette butts Veeck was waving him toward.

As the gates opened, the sandy-haired owner took on the role of ticket-taker. Bantering with every fan, complimenting the ladies' hats, nodding at some of the trade suggestions, and exclaiming a loud, "Oh come on, you're **nuts**!" at others.

Hal Lebovitz of *The Cleveland News*, who had followed Veeck from one Cleveland bank to another in the days leading up to the purchase of the club, shook his head in amazement.

"Was he like this in Milwaukee?"

"Every day," came the reply of Harry Grabiner.

Grabiner was Veeck's right-hand man. Lebovitz' question launched him into his mental file of Veeck stories.

"In Milwaukee, he ripped out a bunch of seats to put in a barber's chair so the fans could get a trim and a shave at the ballpark." Grabiner laughed, "Do you know how important the lighting is in the ladies' rooms? ...and how there need to be more of them than men's rooms?"

Lebovitz shrugged his shoulders, and shook his head.

"You're not married, are you?" Grabiner smiled. "Bill is on a crusade," Grabiner explained to the reporter. "He's in a war for every dollar he can get out of a fan's pocket."

Harry and Lebovitz arrived at the open-air press box above home plate.

"Baseball is king... right now," Grabiner said, "but this post-war economy's teetering on the brink of recession. Bar owners have televisions in their joints back east. They'll be in people's homes soon, and that's going to make our job – competing for entertainment dollars – tougher every day."

A couple of reporters looked up from their typewriters as Grabiner kept rolling. "We're going to make good use of that big stadium downtown, but even there, we've got competition soon – Paul Brown's football team is less than three months from their first game."

Lebovitz nodded.

With the game action underway, Lebovitz looked down from the press box at a disappointingly small Saturday crowd.

"We can change this," Harry said, nodding toward the field, "and Bill knows that we don't need a winning team to put people in the seats-"

That turned some reporters' heads.

"-but we'll need a winning team to keep them in those seats." Harry nodded along with his own words.

When a bad call at first base went against the Indians, a huge howl of protest erupted from the box seats behind the bag.

The reporter glanced up from his notes.

Leading the sniping at veteran first base umpire Ed Rommell was none other than Bill Veeck.

Lebovitz caught Grabiner's eye down press row, and tilted his head toward the rhubarb.

Harry Grabiner sidled over to the reporter with a broad smile.

"He's one of them," Grabiner said, "just a fan, like everyone else. When he worked for his father with the Cubs, his dad tried to flag him away from getting too close to the fans. It's about the only time he's ever disobeyed his father. This is what Bill lives for. He wants them to feel like they're a part of the operation."

Hal scribbled in his notebook, and looked down at Veeck with a smile.

"You haven't had a chance to be with him for his 'tour of the bars' after the game, have you?" Grabiner asked.

Lebovitz looked at the team's business manager with a blank expression.

Grabiner winked, "How well do you hold your beer?"

"Not well," said the reporter.

"Good. He'll need you to drive."

"Harry," stammered Lebovitz, "what-?"

"Oh, no," Grabiner assured him, "Bill holds his beer in legendary fashion – but he does tend to lose track of time when he's schmoozing with fans at the bar. Now, tonight he told me he's going straight to the stadium at the lakefront right after the game. He's got to get that park looking sharp. Big gate for the doubleheader tomorrow."

The Indians won 4-3, and Lebovitz' suspicions about the crowd were correct: a little over 8,000. With Ted Williams and the first place Red Sox in town, that was not a good sign.

Hank Edwards had won the ballgame with a 2-run shot over the tall screen in right field, but Lebovitz was headed to the locker room with more questions for Veeck than for the Tribe's right-fielder.

The door to the clubhouse banged open, and the owner came through that door like he was shot out of a cannon.

"Ready to go downtown?" Veeck asked.

"I've still got to file my story," Lebovitz stammered.

"We'll swing by the paper. Finish typing on the way."

As Veeck strode toward Lexington Avenue, the reporter followed - checking to make sure he had everything with him.

It was obvious the Indians' new owner was ready for Cleveland.

As the cab pulled up to the curb, Veeck almost leaped inside, waving for the reporter to hurry.

The thought sitting in Lebovitz' mind at the moment was: Is Cleveland ready for Bill Veeck?

JUNE 22

The lights of the giant stadium on the shores of Lake Erie were all lit. As Clevelanders drove by on this Saturday evening, it seemed a large steamy mist was rising from inside the ballpark. Baseball fans knew that the Indians had played that afternoon on the east side. They also knew that tomorrow's doubleheader was scheduled for the big ballpark by the lake.

The cleaning frenzy Bill Veeck had presided over that morning at League Park had now more than tripled in size in this 70,000-seat stadium.

Once again, the new owner walked the concourses and ramps, using a bullhorn to direct the men with the firehoses who were spraying down every exposed inch of the ballpark. The mist, rising up toward the arc lights created a shining fog inside the huge stadium.

The P.A. system crackled to life, calling Veeck to the loading dock where tens of thousands of hot dogs awaited unloading. They would be cooked in the morning, then handed to every fan who came through the turnstiles. Boxes containing souvenir baseballs for the kids, and buckets containing flowers for the ladies were being distributed to each of the stadium's five entry points.

Veeck knew he might have a gate near 50,000 tomorrow, and he was going to make his first Sunday as the Indians' owner a memorable one. A day that fans would talk about with their neighbors when they returned home that evening.

The best promotions are always the unannounced ones, Veeck smiled to himself as he climbed the steps in Tower A to his new – albeit unfinished – office.

The smile quickly turned to a sharp wince halfway up the last stairwell.

His foot was killing him.

Veeck had driven himself hard since 6am, and now he was paying the price.

As he turned the corner to the final flight of stairs, he heard his phone ringing.

No matter who this was, Veeck thought, he has to wait 10 more seconds. As he flopped into his chair, he snatched the receiver from the phone's cradle.

"Yeah, it's Bill."

"Bill? It's Cy."

"Slap! What did you find me in Zanesville and Newark?"

"I never got there, Bill."

For the next five minutes, Cy Slapnicka recounted what he had seen on a Holmes County ballfield just hours before. His boss was alternately skeptical, mesmerized, and amazed by what he was hearing.

"Can you get here tomorrow afternoon?" The scout asked.

"I've got a 50,000 gate tomorrow, Cy."

"This kid might help you get a bunch of gates like that, Bill-"

"You're speaking my language, Slap," Veeck laughed. "But... can I go back a bit here? What was that word you used a few minutes ago...?"

"...Amish...?"

"Yeah, that's the word," Veeck said. "What do you mean 'Amish'?"

"They're a religious sect, Bill. They speak German in their homes. They ride in horse-drawn buggies, and they all dress the sa-"

"Pennsylvania Dutch?" the owner said.

"Exactly," Slapnicka replied.

"So, if the kid's the goods, we're going to offer him a modest amount to sign, and that's probably going to be more money than he's ever seen in his life," Veeck said.

Cy paused. "It's not that easy, Bill."

"Why not?"

"When you come out here tomorrow, you'll see."

"He's 19 and married with five kids?" Veeck asked.

"No," said the scout, "he's 19, he's doing a lot of the work at his dad's farm-"

"We'll get them a tractor-"

"AND," Cy interrupted the interruption, "this decision may have to be made by the family's church."

"Can you put his father on the phone?"

The scout exhaled into the phone. "They don't have phones, Bill. They're *Amish*."

Not much made Bill Veeck speechless.

"Bill...?"

"Slap..."

"This is not going to work the way you're used to doing this," Cy said. "You can't just walk into an Amish home, sweet talk the mom, wife, or girlfriend, whip out a check with some zeros on it, and sign the kid's name on the dotted line. These people do things their way, at their speed, and they really don't care what we think."

The owner searched for anything resembling the right question, "You're telling me that this will *not* be the kid's decision?"

"Yeah," Cy exhaled. "At best, we'll be talking to the dad."

"At best...?"

Slapnicka drew in another breath. "I'm afraid so. There also may be a council or some people from the church."

"Dammit Cy." His foot was killing him, and now Veeck suddenly had a headache, too. "Why did you have to find a religious one?"

The game had ended hours ago. Hal's story had been filed. But, he had to call his boss about the phone conversation he's just had with the Indians' new owner.

"477 feet???" Ed McAuley's voice rose to a squeak on the other end of the line.

"I'm telling you, that's *exactly* what Slapnicka told Veeck," Hal Lebovitz replied.

"...and you got this from...?"

"Straight from Veeck," Lebovitz said. "I'm going with him out to Holmes County tomorrow to check this out."

"That's not your story, Hal," his boss said. "That's not your beat."

"Veeck called *me*," the young reporter snapped back. "He wants me to come with him."

"*Wait a minute*," McAuley said, "Veeck's not going to be at his first Sunday doubleheader? I called the ticket office two hours ago. They're expecting 50,000!"

"That's what I'm telling you. Veeck thinks Cy is about as infallible as they come. If Cy says this Amish kid walked on water, I think Bill would dig a pond in the outfield. C'mon Ed, you're covering the doubleheader anyway, and it's my day off." Lebovitz was pushing hard.

There was a hesitation. Then a sigh.

"All right, Hal. You sniffed him out when he was hobbling from bank to bank. He's your story as much or more than anyone else's," McAuley surrendered. "Please remember you're a reporter, not a PR guy."

"Yes, mother."

"...and you're a real smart aleck. Good luck."

"I'll file what I have as soon as I can. Talk to you tomorrow."

Lebovitz dropped the phone back into its cradle thinking that his days covering high school sports might be coming to an end.

JUNE

Holmes County – Somewhere Near Mt. Hope

Hal Lebovitz of *The Cleveland News* had never chased a story more than 25 miles from Cleveland before. Now, driving through Amish country with a cloud of dust trailing behind him, he and his passenger were the object of long Sunday afternoon stares as they passed every farm.

"Here's the road!" Veeck said. "Turn right."

A minute later Bill had Hal slow the car.

"This is it. 'Weaver'."

Then, Lebovitz looked down the road another hundred feet.

"That one says 'Weaver' too, Bill."

In fact, six of the next eight mailboxes read 'Weaver'. The string was only broken by a 'Miller', and a 'J. Miller'.

Veeck looked up to the next place as the road crested.

Cy Slapnicka was waving.

At another mailbox that read 'Weaver'.

The driveway was arrow straight, a quarter-mile of double-rutted buggy-width dirt, ending at a large white farmhouse with an even bigger barn.

The cows wandered toward the three men now standing at the end of the driveway, eyeing them from behind the barbed wire surrounding their lush, green pasture.

Bill Veeck couldn't have been further from his element. "Now what?"

"We wait," Cy Slapnicka said. "They know we're here."

"I can't see anyone moving up there." Hal Lebovitz pointed at the farmhouse. "Are you sure?"

"You can't hide cars on Amish roads, Bill," the scout replied. "Especially on Sunday."

The reporter raised an eyebrow and looked at the scout, "477 feet?"

Slapnicka gave Lebovitz the lowdown on the young Amish phenom, while Veeck shook his head. "Explain to me again exactly why we can't dazzle him with cash, and take him to Cleveland?"

"We're asking for a family's livelihood, Bill," Slapnicka said. "Eli is probably his father's right-hand man. He's technically an adult, and the farm is going to be his. The family – and most likely there are more than two generations living in that house – is dependent on everything that happens in these fields, and that barn."

Veeck's brow furrowed. "But when you signed Feller, you were taking his father's future away, right?"

"Bob's dad had tractors and electricity, Bill," Cy said. "These folks don't. It's all about sweat equity – every day."

There was a wave of a hand from the farmhouse.

"Eli?" Veeck asked.

"Eli Weaver," replied the scout.

As the three men walked up the driveway, Bill Veeck realized that the things that made him such a great salesman when it came to signing players – money, pride, and fame – may not be of any use to him in the next hour.

"Eli." Slap reached out his hand.

"Cy."

"Eli Weaver, I'd like you to meet my boss, Bill Veeck. He is the team President of the Cleveland Indians."

"Hello, Eli." Veeck smiled.

"Bill."

Slapnicka pointed to the third member of the party. "Eli, this is Hal Lebovitz of *The Cleveland News*. He is a sports reporter."

"Reporter?"

Hal smiled now. "Young man, I hear you might be quite a story."

A look of confusion crossed Eli's face.

"But we'll talk about that later," Lebovitz said.

The noise of adult conversation, and children playing filled the backyard.

But, as Eli brought the three guests around the corner of the farmhouse, the noise vanished.

At picnic tables. At the horseshoe pit. At the sandbox.

Silence.

The horses at the buggy rail turned their heads to look.

Eli's father broke the silence, "I see you are back. And I do not like why," making things more uncomfortable.

"Come inside." Elijiah Weaver said. "The sooner we talk, the sooner you leave."

Inside the screen door was a spacious kitchen, with windows on two sides. From there, the men were escorted to the living room.

Two elderly Amish men were waiting for them. Both with long, gray beards. Both with stern expressions.

"Our Deacon and our Bishop," Elijiah said curtly. "Sit."

Cy, Bill, and Hal did exactly as they were told.

"Our Deacon and Bishop know why you come," Elijiah said, not even looking at his three visitors. "Now," the elder Weaver turned to his spiritual leaders, "please tell them 'no' and send them on their way."

"A moment please," said the one on the right. "Introductions."

"I am Cy Slapnicka, a player scout for the Cleveland Indians."

"Yes," said the older man, "you are the one who interrupted our ballgame yesterday. I remember you." He pointed at the reporter. "And you?"

"Hal Lebovitz, sports reporter for *The Cleveland News*."

"From a newspaper. Hm," the Bishop snorted.

"And you?" the older Amish man asked.

"My name is Bill Veeck, I am the President of the Cleveland Indians." Veeck smiled, "Call me Bill. And may I ask your name, sir?"

"Josiah Miller." The older man said. "I am the Bishop for this group of families on these farms you see around us. The Deacon with me is Edel Miller."

The Deacon nodded, but said nothing.

"Now," the Bishop began, "could you please explain to me what is so important about young Eli that would attract your attention?"

Cy glanced at Veeck and tilted his head slightly in the direction of the three Amish men.

Bill Veeck cleared his throat. The Bishop's hard stare scared him a lot more than the loan officer at Society Bank a few days ago.

"Bishop," Veeck began slowly, pointing at Slap, "Cy is one of the best scouts in baseball, and he saw something in Elijiah's son yesterday that made me drive two hours from Cleveland to meet Eli for myself. With your permission, sir," he looked at Elijiah Weaver, "and your permission, gentlemen," he looked straight at the Bishop and the Deacon, "I would like to take him to Cleveland to try out for a spot on the Cleveland Indians roster."

Eli almost gasped out loud, but held it in.

"NO," Elijiah Weaver said flatly.

"Well, he's got that word down," Veeck whispered to Cy... a little too loudly.

"Wait." The Bishop stroked his beard. "You wish to take Eli to the city to play a game?"

"Not a game, Bishop," Veeck said, "just a tryout."

"What is the point of a 'tryout', English?" the Bishop smiled. "We know Eli is the best of our ballplayers."

"English...?" Veeck looked to Slap.

"You. Us. We are 'English'," Cy said softly. "Or 'Yankee'. They could call us 'Yankees', too."

Veeck rolled his eyes at that thought. "I'll take 'English'." He pressed on with the Bishop. "If he's good enough, we would pay him to play baseball for the Cleveland club, and we will pay him well."

"What is... 'well'?" The Bishop's beard was getting a good stroking.

Veeck thought quickly. "At least $100 per week. Perhaps more."

"Hm." The Bishop raised his hand. "And what work will he do for you during the week?"

"That will be his work, Bishop." Veeck had never heard a question like that about anyone he was trying sign before. "The Cleveland Indians Baseball Club will pay him to play baseball for us."

The three Amish men spoke very quietly to each other in their German dialect. There were heads nodding yes and no.

The Bishop straightened in his chair. "Veeck."

"Just Bill-"

"Bill Veeck. We are plain people. People of faith," the Bishop stared but spoke slowly, and without anger, "but, we are not fools. How can you pay someone to play a children's game?"

"Bishop, I-" Veeck had a thought, and turned to the reporter. "Hal, do you still have yesterday's sports section?"

Lebovitz produced the creased and well-read newspaper section, and laid it on the table in front of the Amish men.

"There," Veeck pointed to the box score, "we played yesterday in front of 8,526 paying customers."

"Paying?" The Bishop looked up – incredulous.

"Of course." The new owner said, "That's how we are able to pay the players."

"Eight thousand people have the money to spend to sit and watch grown men play a child's game...?" The Bishop started to laugh. The Deacon followed as if on cue.

Veeck smiled, "Yes, Bishop. And this afternoon, at the stadium in Cleveland, we may have 50,000 there to watch the games." Veeck pointed to the picture showing the crowd behind the Indians dugout cheering as a run was scored. "To me, there is nothing more beautiful than a ballpark filled with people on a summer day."

The Bishop looked at the baseball man. He rose from his chair, and walked to the window. He turned to Veeck. "To me, there is nothing more beautiful than what is out this window. Our fields. Our barns. Our people." He paused again.

"*If* Eli were to go with you-"

Elijiah Weaver could barely contain his anger, "Who would harvest our corn? Who would drive the team for the second and third cut of hay? Who will shoe the horses? Who will be sure the milking is done twice a day? His *mother*?"

"Elijiah," the Bishop said softly.

Eli's father turned his anger to Bill – "Who, Mr. Veeck?"

Veeck thought quickly, "With what we would pay him in his contract, you could easily hire several day laborers to do those tasks." Veeck could feel his chief scout staring a hole in him from the other side now.

"No, Mr. Veeck. We do not 'hire' workers." The Bishop shook his head. "Our families work together. We are in the fields together, we build together, we worship together, we live together, and... we die together."

The Deacon finally spoke – in halting English. "Do you undershtand?"

Bill Veeck understood. He had never been on the defensive in negotiations before, because he had always been talking with his players, or other club executives on an 'apples to apples' basis. He had no counter for the Amish way... other than his money – and that was obviously no good here.

At that moment, coming over the window sill, was a blond-haired boy with a classic Amish bowl haircut. He couldn't have been more than 7 or 8. Cy recognized him right away from the ballgame in the field the day before.

"Bishop! Oh, Bishop!" the boy yelled, "Eli must go! He will be better at baseball than any English anywhere! You have seen him play for yourself, and you said yesterday what a fine player he was! He should go!" He repeated the final phrase in his native tongue for effect. Eli's mother had already rushed in, grabbed him by the ear, and led him from the presence of the men.

"He should **go**!" the boy yelled before the screen door slapped shut.

Eli looked at Veeck, then at his father, then the Bishop.

"May I speak?" Eli said respectfully.

Veeck brightened, "Yes, I'd like to hear-"

"Shut up, Bill," the scout said through his teeth. Veeck sat down.

"Father," Eli said, "I have had many opportunities for rumspringa, but I refused."

Veeck tried to mouth the word to Cy, but the scout put his finger to his lips, and patted the owner on the knee with the smallest of smiles.

"Go on," Eli's father said. He feared what was coming now.

"Until now," Eli said firmly.

"I'd like to go. With your permission," Eli said, "and certainly with yours, Bishop?"

The Bishop stroked his beard again. "It is unusual. This is not the customary way, or for the customary… *reason*. But you are still of age, and unbaptized." The Bishop looked at Eli's father.

"I have already lost him for a year to the English because of the war." Elijiah Weaver shook his head.

"What just happened…?" Veeck whispered to the scout.

"Eli just got himself what you couldn't get him, Bill," Slap whispered back. "*Rumspringa* is usually a time when a young man 'sows his wild oats' among the English, but it looks like Eli's come up with a new twist."

"How can I file a story without a phone?" Lebovitz asked.

The Bishop looked at Eli's father, and then the Deacon, before he cleared his throat and spoke. "Mr. Veeck, I must ask if you do – *employ* – Eli, you would allow him to return to his farm in October to complete the harvest with his family."

"The way we're playing, he'll be very available in October," Veeck deadpanned.

JUNE **2 4**

Cleveland Municipal Stadium

Eli emerged from the Indians clubhouse, and stopped cold on the second dugout step.

The green carpet of grass. The vastness of the space. The scoreboard. The flags. Over 70,000 seats surrounding him...

Bill Veeck paused from raking the dirt behind first base. "Eli! Are you ready to hit a little?"

"Yes, Bill."

Veeck could see the kid was nervous. "Well, you sure look the part."

The Indians' clubhouse man had issued Eli a cap, the three-quarter length undershirt ("No jersey. Not yet," Veeck told the clubbie), baseball pants, belt, sanitary socks, and stirrups. Eli Weaver cut a sharp, muscular figure as he stepped onto the field. He paused at the edge of the grass, though, and looked down at his shoes.

"Whatsamatter, kid?" the owner asked.

"Well... it's these shoes." Eli scuffed at the dirt. "Never worn anything like 'em before."

"Oh, yeah." Veeck had never considered that the kid had never worn – let alone seen – a pair of spikes. "Lemme look at the bottoms."

The young man lifted each foot and pointed it toward Veeck.

"Good thing he gave you some used ones," Veeck said. "Those spikes are worn down a bit. Hopefully they won't be much of a bother."

"Do I have to wear them?" Eli asked.

"Ballplayers do." Veeck nodded.

"Hm." Eli looked at his feet with some doubt.

"Let's get you up to the plate." The owner looked into the outfield. "Mel!"

Mel Harder had been tossing with a batboy. The veteran right-hander turned, nodded, and ambled in toward the mound. After zipping a couple in toward the bullpen catcher behind the plate, he nodded and waved.

"Go ahead, Eli," Veeck said, "see what you can do."

Eli Weaver nodded, and as he walked toward home plate, he saw Cy Slapnicka and Hal Lebovitz sitting in box seats by the dugout. It occurred to the young Amish man that two days ago, he hadn't met any of these people. He had never been in an automobile for more than five minutes. And, he had never been this far from home.

He did however, have a bat in his hand.

The pitcher had a baseball in his.

That much was familiar.

Eli felt his feet settle into the powdery dirt at home plate.

That was familiar, too.

He raised his eyes toward the pitcher, and his hands tightened slightly on the bat handle.

Most of the time, whenever we watch any sport, we have no idea when something significant is about to happen. Seeing something we've never seen before is such a surprise, so unexpected, that we often miss the start of the moment where our perception of the possible changes.

It was a simple batting practice fastball down the middle. Veeck was waving directions to one of his cleaning staff at the back of the lower deck. Like his scout two days before, the owner missed the sight of the swing, but not the sound of the contact.

The pure sound of bat barrel perfectly meeting baseball echoed in the empty stadium.

Veeck wheeled and picked up the low arc of the ball over the outfield. It never seemed to rise, but sailed toward left-center weightlessly. Within a few seconds, it skipped off the grass berm in front of the bleachers, and short-hopped the fence.

Veeck stared at his scout. Slapnicka gave a single nod.

Eli was still in the box, bat cocked, ready for the next pitch.

Bill Veeck had measured his new home park two days before – to make sure of the accuracy of the numbers painted on the concrete façade. He knew what he had just seen.

"460 feet," he whispered to himself.

The next ten offerings by his veteran pitcher met variations of the same fate.

Now, it was Lebovitz who was staring at Slap. The scout poked the reporter with his elbow.

"We're just getting started," Cy said. "Let's see what happens next."

"Mel!" Veeck yelled out to the mound, "how you feelin'?"

"Fine, Bill," the soft-spoken Nebraskan shrugged at his new boss.

"Let him see some 'gamers'."

Harder nodded.

Eli sprayed the next ten pitches from gap to gap. A few found their way into the left field grandstand.

"Just a few more, Mel." Veeck extended two fingers on his right hand, and wiggled it by his hip.

"Here we go," said the scout. Slapnicka had been waiting for this.

Ted Williams and Joe DiMaggio, arguably the greatest players of the era, had said repeatedly that it was Mel Harder's curveball that was the single hardest pitch for them to hit. Now, the Cleveland righty was going to let it fly against this young, strong right-handed hitter.

Eli's knees buckled, and his head twitched back from the coming impact.

The sound of the ball smacking into the catcher's glove was the next thing that got Eli's attention. The bullpen catcher held it where he caught it – on the inside corner – for a few seconds, just to give the rookie a long look at what had happened.

"You okay, kid?" the bullpen catcher laughed, lifted his mask, and spit some tobacco juice at Eli's back foot.

"Hm." Eli pursed his lips, and looked out at the pitcher.

Harder's next pitch was a fastball, high and tight.

Eli Weaver hit the dirt.

"Whatsamatter, kid?" the catcher was enjoying himself.

Veeck, still standing by first base leaning on his rake, knew that what happened in the next two minutes would decide whether he stayed in Cleveland, headed west to play some Class C, or got a bus ticket home to Holmes County.

Harder then went back to the curve.

As the ball left the pitcher's hand, Eli saw the turn of the wrist. Even though his body's momentum was already edging forward, he left his weight on his back foot. Even though his hands had also started forward, his wrists didn't begin to snap.

It wasn't indecision.

It wasn't hesitation.

It was an adjustment.

Bat barrel met ball.

365 feet later, the ball banged off the right field grandstand wall, and ricocheted toward center field.

"He learns quick," Hal Lebovitz said as he opened his reporter's notebook again.

Cy Slapnicka looked out at his new boss again, and thought he detected a slight smile on Bill Veeck's face, and it seemed like he was trying to hide it.

The next ten pitches were a game of cat-and-mouse between the veteran pitcher and the young hitter. However... by the last few pitches, it seemed like the younger man was taking on the role of the cat.

"Hey, Mel! Can I throw a few?"

Another pitcher pulled off his jacket and jogged toward the mound.

"Oh, boy," the reporter said.

The scout smiled.

Veeck's eyebrows raised.

Bob Feller reached into the wire basket for a baseball.

"No warmup. Let's go." He motioned to the young man to step back into the right-handed batter's box.

Feller's high leg kick and body turn meant the baseball would appear out of his pant leg. Or shirt sleeve. Or both.

Eli heard the ball more than saw it.

His bat didn't come close.

The Heater From Van Meter.

The Iowan on the mound smiled, and reached for another baseball.

This time, a small grunt came with the release of the pitch.

Eli got the bat moving a little quicker. The ball was grazed by the wood as it passed through the strike zone, and spun back into the screen behind home plate.

The next grunted fastball from the All-Star pitcher came even a bit quicker than the first two.

This time, Eli made contact, sending a grounder into right field. A sharp single.

Now, it was Bob Feller's turn to stare.

Bill Veeck was smiling now. And wishing he'd sold tickets for this.

Feller now rocked into his motion, and let a fastball with even more heat come from his right hand.

This time, that distinctive sound of bat and ball could be heard all over the ballpark again.

This time, Bill Veeck saw the impact.

This time, the bullpen catcher stood.

So did the scout and the reporter behind the dugout.

Bob Feller turned toward the bleachers.

The sight of the ball landing in the front of the far-off bleachers was accompanied by the sound of the rattle of it bouncing off the wood planks and concrete.

Feller turned back around and glared at Eli.

"Uh-oh," the scout said quietly.

"Bob's mad now," said the reporter.

Another dozen pitches.

Feller would establish dominance.

A few sharp swings from Eli would snatch the momentum back.

Finally, from the corner of the Indians' dugout, came another voice.

"Thanks, guys. Take 5, Bob. Hey Bill, can I talk to you for a second?"

Lou Boudreau, Cleveland's shortstop – and manager – walked out toward Veeck.

"Eli," Veeck said, "why don't you head out to the outfield and show us a few throws into second and third."

"Okay."

As Eli jogged out to right field, he passed Feller – who was walking toward the dugout. The veteran gave the kid a quick nod and a polite tip of the cap, which the young man returned.

For the next few minutes, the manager and the owner stood, watched, and talked, as the coach with the fungo bat put the young Amish man through his paces. Eli caught balls on the move in front of him, sprinting side-to-side, and with his back turned on the infield. From the right-center field fence, his throws to second and third were on the fly, and belt-high one-hoppers.

"So, what level do you plan on starting him?" Boudreau asked.

"Right here, Lou," the owner said.

"You're serious."

"We're in sixth place, Lou." Veeck said. "We're first in the league in pitching, and last in the league in hitting."

"Don't let that kid get away, Lou."

The owner and manager didn't realize that Feller had been listening from the top step of the dugout.

Boudreau stared at Feller and Harder. The veteran starters stared back – nodding at their manager.

"And a 19-year-old kid is going to get us to the Series?" Boudreau's voice raised an octave.

"You and I both know the reality of our situation. You know I'm not saying that," Veeck said, "but all I am saying is that we need something – someone – to put fans in the seats while we retool this roster for where we want to go."

"So, I don't have to start him?" the manager asked suspiciously.

"No. Not yet," Veeck said. "Give him a chance in situations where he's not going to hurt us, but has a chance to help us – and himself. That's all I ask. If he belongs here, we'll know soon enough."

Boudreau looked down and shook his head.

"Lou," Veeck spread his hands, "if he goes bust, he goes home. There aren't enough people coming to the games to notice – and the guys in the press box are barely awake after hitting the commissary."

Boudreau looked out into right field as Eli uncorked another throw on the fly to third. He thought for a moment.

Across the field, players were beginning to wander into the visitor's dugout.

"Hey! Eli!" the manager called, "good job! C'mon in here!"

Veeck looked at his manager.

"No sense in the Yankees seeing anything we don't want them to see," Boudreau smiled. "At least not yet."

MONDAY NIGHT
JUNE 24

Cleveland Municipal Stadium

Bill Bevens had cruised for the Yanks, surrendering only three scratch singles to the Indians. But, Allie Reynolds had scrambled to hold down the Bombers as well, and New York held a slim 1-0 lead going to the bottom of the 9th.

It had been a quiet evening for Eli. He walked into the equipment room, and was issued his uniform. Boudreau had tried to explain to the clubhouse assistant that the new rookie was a little "different", and might need a little help with certain things.

Like carrying the ball bag, and the veterans' bats from the clubhouse to the bench. Vince, the clubhouse assistant who was only a year older than Eli, assured him that as a rookie, there were chores he'd be expected to do for the veterans... every day.

Otherwise, Eli was the perfect rookie: seen and not heard. Before the game, each of the coaches came by to introduce themselves. To varying degrees, they had each heard a slice of Eli's story. Two of them who were not at the park early that day viewed Eli with little more than curiosity.

The other, Buster Mills, who saw Eli's batting practice first hand from the outfield, sat with him for a while, and helped him understand what was expected of a major league rookie.

Buster had been a player/coach for Cleveland, but on that day, Bill Veeck asked him to become a full-time coach, and to give his 38-year-old legs a rest. Mills never told Eli that he had taken Buster's place on the active roster that day. Instead, the Texan made it his mission to be the voice in Eli's ear. Although he knew almost nothing about the Amish and their ways, it was pretty obvious that Eli Weaver was going to need some extra attention – on and off the field.

The game moved quickly. Even though it would not end in total darkness, as dusk took over from daylight, the arc lights on the roof shined brightly down onto the field.

Eli was a bit awestruck.

Even though there were only 19,000 in the ballpark that evening, it was infinitely more people than the young Amish ballplayer had ever seen before. Add to that the calls of the vendors, the smells of the hot dogs and popcorn, and the glare of the lights...

Eli was less than 100 miles from his farm, but was in another world.

How could he have not known of these things?

The futility of the night – of the season so far – was wearing on Boudreau. As had already happened all too often in the first three months of the campaign, another outstanding pitching performance had been wasted. Allie Reynolds was about to be 2-9 on the season, and he didn't deserve it.

As Les Fleming went up to bat, the Indians' player/manager looked down his bench. Everyone was hitting lousy right now, including himself. Boudreau was up third this inning, and if he could just get up there with someone on base, he'd have a ghost of a chance of catching up with one of Bevens' mistakes.

On the second pitch, Fleming topped a roller to Rizzuto for the first out.

We're not even making solid contact, Boudreau thought. If someone could just stay back on that breaking ball-

Boudreau's eyes fell on Eli Weaver.

"Pat," the skipper yelled, "take a seat! Eli – grab a bat!"

Eli's face went white.

Buster Mills was right there. In Eli's ear.

"All right, kid. Show 'em what you got. You've been watchin' this fella all night. He throws 'em up there just like Mel did this afternoon, right?"

"Yeah."

"Then do to that ball what you did to the ones Mel threw."

"Okay."

The home plate umpire took a few steps toward the Tribe's bench. "C'mon Lou, you got somebody?"

Veeck was sitting with some Indians fans behind the Yankee dugout thanking them for their faithfulness, when he saw the umpire ask Lou for a hitter.

Would he...? Veeck asked himself.

A second later, he saw Eli reaching for a bat in front of the dugout.

Lou, you're a *helluva* guy. Veeck thought.

"...and so, with one out here in the ninth, manager Boudreau will call for a pinch-hitter, before player Boudreau can come to bat. It would appear that... number 17... a young man by the name of... Eli Weaver is coming to the plate. Bob, what do we know about this young fella?"

"Not much, Jack. We do not see any minor league records for young Weaver, but he is only 19 years old, and hails from Mt. Hope, Ohio. We understand the Indians' new owner, Bill Veeck, just signed him after a tryout this afternoon."

"Well, Lou Boudreau has sure put this young man in a pickle... it's the bottom of the ninth, and the Clevelands have barely nicked Bevens this evening... just three singles off the Yankee righty. Bevens' first delivery FOULED into the seats beyond the third base dugout... that cost a gentleman the rest of his bag of peanuts... no one seems to be the worse for wear down there... Weaver... tall, strong young fella... broad-shouldered... the 0-1 – INSIDE! And friends, Bevens the veteran, welcomes Weaver the rookie to the major leagues... young Weaver picks himself up, dusts himself off, and climbs back in there... some catcalls headed Bevens' way, but that's baseball, friends... now the 1-1... LINEDRIVECAUGHT! Ohhhhh, my!!! Weaver hit that one a TON! A BULLET into the glove of Johnson – and the Yanks third baseman somehow holds on for the second out!"

"Jack, that's the hardest hit ball of the night... on either side!"

"And Johnson has tucked his glove under his arm and is holding his left hand gingerly as he walks to the outfield grass... MY did Weaver put some mustard on that ball!"

Lebovitz didn't wait to see Boudreau make the final out. He was headed down the ramp toward the Indians' clubhouse. Bill had asked him to get to Weaver in the locker room first after the game, and deflect attention away from the rookie if any reporters came around.

Hal realized that this kid might attract *a lot* of attention. And probably before he would have a chance to deflect it.

TUESDAY
JUNE

League Park, Cleveland

Buster Mills was waiting for Eli in the hotel lobby, and took him to the counter at the diner on the corner to get him breakfast. "How ya' doin', kid?"

Eli looked at his coach and new confidant. "It is... hard."

"Hard?"

"New things." Eli shook his head. "Too many people. Horns honking. Noise all night. Lights. Radio. Toilet."

Buster clicked his tongue. "Guess I hadn't thought about all that. I read a little bit about your people when I came to play here. Never saw more than a couple of you at the train station. Hal, the reporter fella, told me about your farm last night before the game. Sounds like a hard life."

"A hard life?" Eli smiled. "No Buster, not a hard life. It is *our* life."

"I grew up on a farm, too," the coach said, "'course we had a tractor. And a toilet... and lights."

The two men had found some common ground. They spent breakfast talking about crops, planting, harvesting, and rain – or the lack.

Buster enjoyed his breakfast. Eli knew nothing was fresh – the eggs, the sausage, or the bread for the toast.

"I'm not sure I can do this." Eli shook his head. "It is too much. When I talked myself into this, it was the baseball I wanted."

"Then keep your mind on the baseball," the coach said. "Let me and the boys on the ballclub help you with the rest."

"The 'boys' do not like me."

"You're a rookie Eli," Buster explained, "all rookies carry the ball bag, tote the bats, and do whatever the veterans tell them to do. Trust me, word got around pretty fast about what happened in early battin' practice yesterday. You keep hittin' baseballs like that, the veterans are gonna like you right fine."

"But, I am different from all of you."

"Eli, let me try to explain... Bill Veeck may be thinking about more than what you can do on the field." Mills looked at the rookie sitting across from him, "Do you understand what a 'promoter' is?"

Eli looked puzzled.

"Bill's job is to put together a team that can win every day," Buster tried to choose his words carefully here, "but, he also wants to give the fans a good 'show'. And, because of who you are, and what you are, he might do some things that will make the fans... notice you more."

"So, am I a ballplayer, or part of a 'show'?" the rookie wondered out loud.

"Well... both, I guess," Mills shrugged.

Eli looked annoyed. "So, I'm like the bearded lady at the county fair?"

Mills laughed. "Something like that."

Eli shook his head and looked out at the busy street where drivers were beeping and gesturing at each other at the intersection. He shook his head again.

"Too different."

Buster leaned in, "You listen to me, son. Your teammates ain't your family back home, but you play hard every day, and we're gonna be your family here and now. We take care of each other, Eli. If you have a problem with the newspaper fellas, the radio people, the newsreel cameras, you just let us know. Tell you what – just scratch your chin like you're thinkin' about your answer, and one of us will be over to help right away."

"We'll see," the young ballplayer said.

Mills walked Eli a couple blocks east of the hotel and showed him which streetcar would take him to League Park.

Eli looked out the window as the electric railway car made its way down Payne Avenue. The sights and smells of factories. The cars weaving in and out of traffic in front and behind the streetcar. Everywhere he turned his head he saw something he had never seen before. Something he knew he had to write home about.

The factories subsided quickly, and Eli passed homes that seemed to be attached to each other. Tiny gardens caught his attention – growing things in the middle of all this noise, he thought. Children playing catch or pickle-in-the-middle in the street. A game of baseball in a side alley among the parked cars.

It's baseball – Eli thought – but how can they play without room to run?

The streetcar stopped, and the doors swung open.

"League Park," the driver barked. "Your stop, kid?"

"Yes," Eli replied.

"You with the ballclub, rookie?"

"Yes," Eli looked at the driver curiously. "How did you know?"

"Who else would be riding away from downtown in the morning on this line?" The driver smiled, "Beat them Yanks. See you on the way back downtown, maybe."

Eli immediately liked League Park better than the giant stadium by the lake. Less than one-third the size of its younger cousin downtown, League Park felt tight and tucked away like his mother's linen closet.

Of the 16 major league teams, only the Cleveland Indians had two "home fields". The mammoth downtown stadium was about 15 years old, built at the beginning of the Depression. League Park first saw baseball action in 1891, when its location at East 66th Street and Lexington Avenue sat at the eastern edge of the city that had discovered the profits of steel, and would soon learn the power of petroleum. Rebuilt as one of the country's first concrete and steel ballparks in 1910, it was beginning to show its age.

Eli sat in the small clubhouse and put on his uniform slowly... and began to feel the guilt from his upbringing again, The bright red and blue flannel on the cream-colored jersey, pants, and stirrup socks. Not the "plain" clothing of his people, he worried.

Then, as his hands froze on the buttons of his jersey, he stopped and looked at the lockers surrounding his.

In each stall hung a jersey, pants, and stirrup socks. Just like his. It occurred to Eli that here – in this locker room – at this ballpark – he was going to be dressed just as "plain" among his teammates, as he would be if he were with his people in the hand-mowed pasture where he grew up playing. As he finished buttoning his jersey, Eli smiled and wondered what the Bishop would think of his new idea of "plain."

He was earlier than his teammates, and wasn't sure what to do next, so he headed for the dugout, spikes clicking on the concrete floor.

"Eli! Hold up a minute." Inside a small cubicle off the hallway sat his manager.

"Yes?"

Boudreau looked him in the eye. "If I put you in the starting lineup today, can you hit me some more balls like that one you got a hold of last night?"

Eli smiled. "I'll do my best."

"I'm sure you will." Boudreau nodded, looking at his lineup card. "Right field. Batting seventh."

Eli watched his manager write "Weaver" below the name "Keltner" on the card in front of him.

"Did you have breakfast with Buster Mills?" Boudreau asked. "He'll be here in a couple minutes. I want you to go with him out to right field so he can show you how to play the wall."

As players began milling on the field to warm up and take batting practice, Eli was in right field for 20 minutes taking balls off League Park's 39-foot tall wall. Buster Mills, fungo bat in hand would lash baseballs into each of the three sections of the wall, with each section producing a different ricochet, or bounce, depending on whether the ball struck the loose metal of the sliding door which opened to the area where the streetcars congregated after the game, the tighter metal above it, or the wood-framed section atop the wall, just below the metal screen.

"It's more than where it hits," Buster said, as he whacked another liner over Eli's head. "It's *what* it hits – listen for the sound."

The ball cracked into the hardwood, and sprang back over Eli's head.

"Don't worry, yer learnin'!" Buster yelled. "Now listen to this one!"

Another liner – this one lower – headed for the area just above the metal door. The impact made a dull thud. The baseball dropped straight down to the dirt in front of the door. Eli was on it in an instant.

Mills knew he had an excellent student. In the final five minutes of his workout in front of the wall, Eli was sensing the flight, the height, and the impact almost perfectly.

"Good job, kid."

"Thanks for the help, Buster," Eli smiled. One of his first smiles in the last 48 hours.

"Betcha didn't play balls offa walls like that on the farm," the coach laughed.

"No," said Eli, and he smiled again, "the liners over the barbed wire fence by the cow pasture made you think pretty quick, though."

"I'm sure they did!" smiled Buster.

Bob Feller worked around some trouble in the top of the first.

The Yanks' Tommy Byrne was not as fortunate.

Within a matter of minutes, he was in deep trouble.

"Well friends, the Indians have opportunity knockin' on their front door right here... 3 runs home, 2 men on, and still only one out. Now, here comes the young man from Mt. Hope, Ohio, Eli Weaver... his second major league at bat, and his first major league start-"

"Jack – take a peek at Johnson at third for New York (laughs) it looks like he learned his lesson last night at the Stadium... the Yankee third sacker has backed up well behind the bag, giving Weaver a little more respect today-"

"Young Mister Weaver hit a line drive that almost came out the other side of Johnson's glove last night... Let's see what this encounter brings... Byrne needs a double play ball right now... and that first pitch to Weaver... is way outside – ball 1."

"He can't find the handle on that breaking ball, Jack."

"The stretch... and the 1-0... swung on by Weaver, and OHHH LORDY!!

WAY – WAY – WAY BACK!!! DiMaggio looks up – and IT IS GONE!!!"

"He hit the SCOREBOARD, Jack!!!"

"He hit the scoreboard indeed, Bob! Above and to the left of the 460-FOOT marker!"

"Have you ever seen the like???"

"AMAZING!"

"The flash bulbs are poppin' as Weaver crosses the plate... and he is getting some excited greetings on the Cleveland bench!"

"Yankee player/manager Bill Dickey is on his way to the bump... and Tommy Byrne is headed for an early shower! One-third of an inning, and six runs home for the Indians!"

Bill Veeck was standing behind Hal Lebovitz in the press box, and grabbed him tightly by the shoulders as he yelled with joy.

"No cheering in the press box!" smiled Lebovitz.

When he ran out to right field to grab his glove for the top of the second, the few fans down the right field line applauded, and waved their hats at the young man. Eli sheepishly returned a small wave. As Eli added a single and an RBI double later in the game, many of the 6,000-plus in attendance had relocated to the right field seats. It was clear that they had found a new hero. And, in the midst of a growing group of fans was the new owner – adding his cheers to the many.

In the 9th, with Cleveland in command, and Bob Feller finishing another fine outing, New York second baseman Joe Gordon lashed a liner to right. As he approached first, Gordon heard the thud of baseball and loose metal. Knowing the ball would drop to the base of the wall without a ricochet, he cut the bag sharply and headed for second.

Eli, the pregame student, froze for a moment as the ball went over his head, but then lit out for the wall at full speed. Hearing the thud, he began to slide as he reached the right field wall – 290 feet from home plate. As he felt his right foot hit the door frame, his momentum began to bring him upright as he grabbed the ball in his right hand at the base of the wall. In one motion, he unleashed his throw to second.

Ten feet from the bag, Gordon stumbled as he started to slide, then scrambled to a stuttering stop.

"What the hell...?" was all the Yankee All-Star could think to say.

Lou Boudreau stood at the bag with the baseball in his glove. Waiting for him.

"Sorry, Joe... you're out," Boudreau laughed as he tagged him with a tap on the 'NY' above the brim of his cap.

Gordon turned with his hands on his hips and stared into right field.

The Indians infielders, including Feller and catcher Jim Hegan, were laughing with their gloves up to their faces.

And in the right field stands, a full-blown celebration was underway, with Bill Veeck as acting drum major.

The Indians had soundly defeated the Yankees, 8-3.

Bob Feller was now 12-5 after fanning 13 Bombers on the day.

For the Yankees, Joe DiMaggio was 4-for-5.

But, the reporters had converged on Eli.

And he was stroking his chin.

A lot.

Buster Mills tried to help, but it was Veeck who came to the rescue –

"Guys, let me tell you what this kid has done down in Holmes County..." Bill proclaimed as he stepped in front of Eli's locker.

Mills got him into the trainer's room as quick as he could. One place in the clubhouse that was off-limits to the press.

"What did they want to know all that stuff for, Buster? What do they care where I'm from, or where I played, or what I ate this morning?" Eli was a bit dazed.

"This is how it is, kid," Mills said in a calming voice. "People listened to the game. They're gonna git the evening newspapers, and tomorrow morning's papers, too. You're news."

"It's like this every day?" the rookie asked.

Buster snorted a laugh. "You keep playin' like that..."

Eli stared at him.

"Kid," Buster put a hand on his shoulder, "shower up, and we'll get the streetcar back downtown."

Eli walked with Buster across the infield toward the now opened right field gate.

Mills put his hand on Eli's shoulder. "That's a pretty darn good start, kid."

Eli smiled. "That was fun."

"Fun?" Buster laughed. "That was the New York Yankees you just took apart, son. That's supposed to be work."

A streetcar was waiting on Lexington Avenue.

But, as the coach and player walked through the opening in the outfield wall, Buster saw that streetcar ride would have to wait.

"ELI!!!"

From every direction, Eli Weaver was surrounded by the Knot Hole Gang – the kids from the neighborhood who lingered on Lexington Avenue waiting for home run balls. Sometimes, they turned them in for a free general admission ticket for the rest of that game. Sometimes, they kept their prize to use on their neighborhood sandlot – where the ball was treated with respect – since it came from League Park.

Right now, they grabbed for his hand, and pounded him on the back. The young man looked for Buster. "What do I do?" he mouthed.

Mills waved and smiled.

"Have you ever hit a ball that far before, Eli?"

"What kind of bat do you use?

"That throw to get Gordon was great!"

"You showed them Yankees a thing or three!"

The kids escorted him to the streetcar. A smiling face greeted him at the door.

"Looks like you had a pretty good day!"

The same driver that brought him to the park in the morning waved Eli and Buster into the car.

As the streetcar pulled away, headed downtown, Eli's newest fans waved.

"See you tomorrow, Eli!"

"Good game, Eli!"

Eli Weaver smiled and stuck his head out the window. "See you tomorrow!" He looked at them out the back window of the streetcar until it made the turn toward Payne Avenue.

"Just keep my mind on the baseball," Eli said softly.

"That's right," Buster nodded.

The New York Spaghetti House – Cleveland | 7:00pm

As Eli ate, he peppered Mills with questions about his new life:

How do I stand during the National Anthem?

What do I say to the fans in the right field stands?

Why do reporters need to know what they want to know?

What do I do with this money they hand me every day?

Do those folks in the stands know as much about baseball as they think they do?

Did I put my uniform on the right way today?

The rookie shook his head. "Do I have to wear that... 'cup'?"

"Well," Buster struggled to stifle a smile, "do you want to have children someday?"

Eli stared at him.

"Put down your fork," Buster said.

Thirty seconds later, the young man had a new respect for personal protection.

The chatter from Eli continued. He described in detail every pitch he faced, situations he'd seen in the game, and what every Yankee hitter was trying to do when they came to the plate.

"Well, if I'd a'knowed you could talk this much, I woulda' brought some ear muffs," the veteran laughed.

"Sorry, Buster," the rookie said, "I'm a little excited."

Mills smiled. "That's all right, kid. I would be too, if I were you. You had a helluva day!"

"Buster! I knew I'd find you here!"

Eddie the newsboy ran between the tables with a copy of each of the late editions under his arm.

"Thanks, Eddie. Keep the change."

"Thanks, Buster!" The kid's head spun to Eli with his eyes widening.

"Hey... you're Eli Weaver! I'm Eddie!"

Eli looked at Buster, then back to the boy with a smile. "Hi, Eddie. I'm Eli."

"Oh boy, you sure beat up on those Yankees today!" Eddie said. "Y'think you can do it again tomorrow?"

"If Boudreau puts me back in there, I'll do my best."

"Swell!" The boy was starstruck. "See ya soon, Buster. Great to meet-cha, Eli!"

Buster turned to the sports section from the News to see Hal's story first.

'WEAVER'S WALLOP SPANKS YANKS'

Mills saw the huge photo that splashed across the fold.

A smiling Eli Weaver was perfectly framed as he crossed home plate, reaching for Lou Boudreau's outstretched hand.

Eli Weaver saw the photo of himself.

And his face went white.

WEAVER'S FIRST HOMER DENTS THE LEAGUE PARK SCOREBOARD IN 8-3 ROUT OF YANKS

The Mt. Hope livestock auction | The next morning

Elijiah Weaver was focused.

His hogs were drawing prices they deserved. His ewes had already brought some excellent bids. The auctioneer paused for announcements about next week's sale, and Elijiah looked around the pen.

Several faces that were looking at him, looked away quickly.

A moment later, he distinctly saw the Steiner men point at him. They did not turn away. They stared hard at Elijiah.

In an instant, at his elbow, stood the Deacon.

"And this is the 'modesty' shown by the Weavers?"

The Deacon literally threw a newspaper into Elijiah's lap.

Elijiah looked down... at his smiling son. Reaching for the hand of a stranger.

An English.

And Elijiah's face went white.

Jake's Diner – Zanesville | 8am

Cy Slapnicka waited for the Rexall to open before he got breakfast. He'd heard the score from League Park the evening before at the industrial league game he was scouting, and went to grab a paper as soon as he was up and moving this morning.

The local paper carried capsule stories and box scores from all of yesterday's games, but at the top of the sports page was the wire photo of a smiling Eli Weaver reaching for Lou Boudreau's outstretched hand.

The eggs and hash had rarely tasted so good.

And Cy's face went into an ear-to-ear smile.

Tower A at Cleveland Stadium | 8am

The newspapers hit Bill Veeck in the chest, and woke him from a sound sleep.

Ada Ireland was standing in his office doorway. She always did have a good arm. "Are you going to make a habit of this, darlin'?" she asked her boss.

"I like my office couch," Veeck said, trying to wake up, "it's comfy – especially when my hotel room is full of acquaintances looking for a free place to sleep."

"Your kid got a lot of ink this morning," Ada said as she moved about the room picking random items up off the floor. "Hope he doesn't get a big head."

Veeck shook his head as he opened one of the local dailies that hadn't been too kind about his efforts to purchase the Indians. "Not likely," Bill said, "the Amish are different than we are. Not motivated by the same things."

"Mmmm, hmm." Ada looked at her boss again. "This Weaver kid might just find he likes it here on the 'outside'."

"Yeah," the owner said with mock annoyance, "then I'll have to pay him more."

Ada shook her head. Bill had only been working out of this room for four days. How could he have made it look like a tornado had come through here already? This is going to be just like Milwaukee, she thought... only on a major league scale.

"Hey Ada, grab your pad," Veeck said. "We need to map out some ideas to help Eli's story along a bit."

Bill Veeck spread out three local sports sections in front of him. Each paper's photographer had caught Eli's heroics from the day before at a different angle. And each paper had splashed them prominently on the front of their sports section, each trying to outdo their competitor's catchy headline.

And as Veeck's brow furrowed, his face slowly broke into a sly smile.

The John Miller Farm –Mt. Hope | 11am

Every time Rachael Miller entered a room at her aunt and uncle's house, all conversation stopped. All. Morning. Long.

Did they honestly think she couldn't hear what they were talking about?

As she threaded her needle, the muted back and forth chatter continued from the sunroom.

Eli.

A picture in a newspaper.

Immodesty.

Becoming like the English.

Rachael sighed. Loud enough, she hoped, to be heard in the other room.

The conversation paused. Then resumed.

69

Eli had been courting Rachael Miller after dinner on Sunday evenings, and had become a regular at her house a quarter-mile away. While she didn't fully understand why he felt the need to leave, she trusted him. Eli had told her that his using the term *rumspringa* was only about being able to see if he could measure up, to succeed at baseball he had only seen in the newspaper when he went into town... *nothing else.*

Oh, she thought... the newspaper.

Rachael went outside to gather some flowers to take back home for her mother. She made sure to let the screen door slam extra hard, so that her gossipy aunts could talk more about whatever it was that Eli had supposedly done. Once she had a nice bouquet for her mother, she re-entered the house – re-slamming the screen door crisply so they knew she was back inside. Then, she looked for what she really wanted to bring home.

The newspaper.

She found the section with the photo of Eli tucked deep inside.

Rachael's happy gasp brought her hand straight up to mouth.

So handsome.

But... a *photograph.*

A graven image.

How could something so wonderful, be so *evil?*

She quickly and neatly folded the section with Eli's photo and shoved it deep into the pocket of her apron.

The rest of the newspaper wrapped her mother's bouquet.

Later that evening, after her family had retired to their rooms, Rachael pulled her apron from its place – hanging on the closet's doorknob. She reached deep into the pocket for the treasure she had brought home from her aunt and uncle's that day.

In the conversations she had overheard, Rachael understood the wrong.

Eli's photo had been taken.

Normally, this was no more than an annoyance for the Amish. The discourtesy of the English, who really didn't understand the sinfulness of their actions.

This time however, it was more than the photo. The fact that it was so big, and so prominent... and so *public*... Rachael did feel that hollow feeling, too. Like something had been *stolen* from her – from Eli – even if it was just a photograph.

And yet...

Eli looked magnificent.

On the darkened side of the room, Rachael's younger sister opened her eyes. "Why did Eli leave?"

Rachael continued to stare at the newspaper article.

"To play baseball games with the English."

"Is that all?" the little girl asked.

Rachael thought for a second. "I think he wants to prove that he is their equal."

"Are you mad that he's gone?"

Rachael sighed, "I don't know."

"Are you happy for him?"

Now it was getting annoying. *"I don't know."*

Then, Rachael realized her sister wasn't trying to be a pest. "When I ask mother and father about Eli, it just seems to make everyone upset."

There was silence for a moment. Then, from the darkened corner of the room came one more question.

"When will you know...?"

Rachael sighed. "When he comes home... *if* he comes home."

She pulled the shears from her sewing kit, and carefully cut out the story, and the photo.

She took a long look at him in the candlelight, folded the newsprint, and placed the story and photo inside her prayer book.

Rachael said a short prayer for Eli – even though she wasn't quite sure what to pray for – and blew out the candle on her nightstand.

JUNE 26

Eli had seen his bunk a couple of cars forward but had no idea of laying down just yet.

The speed at which he was traveling was unnerving.

In less than a week, he had passed from the age of horse-drawn buggies, to the automobile and streetcar, and now to this huge moving machine that rattled and clacked its way through the broad, flat countryside outside his window.

Eli's mind wandered back to this afternoon.

He hadn't struck out in a game since he was... 6?

Today, those Yankee pitchers had struck him out *twice*.

It was almost as if they refused to throw the ball over the plate.

He was thankful to Buster for pulling him onto the bench next to him after the second strikeout. By his next time at bat, Buster told him that he would whistle on the bench before the pitch, to help him not swing at curveballs. That helped Eli scrape out a hit through the infield.

Then, his last time up, he figured out that Buster might have been doing something he shouldn't do to figure out which pitch was coming, and asked him not to whistle. Eli figured out quickly in his last time up, that the Yankees not only didn't want to throw the ball over the plate, they didn't want him to hit the ball at all.

And so, he walked. There was no such thing playing farmball. You just stayed at the plate until you hit one, and for Eli, that rarely took more than two pitches. His father had always told him it was because the other pitcher just wanted to get it over with.

His father.

Had he seen the photograph in the newspaper?

Eli hoped not, but feared so.

Would they come try to take him back home?

How could they?

How could they even find him?

He was on a train. Going faster than anyone he knew could imagine.

To Chicago.

Chicago?

Mills said that Chicago was much bigger than Cleveland.

Eli couldn't believe that one.

Mills said the Chicago was 300 miles from Cleveland.

300 miles...

And that the train would arrive there in a little over five hours.

These English sure had some crazy ideas.

The photo.

A few minutes earlier, he'd sat and talked with Veeck and Boudreau about the photo. He tried to explain to them that his people felt that photographs were a violation of God's commandment about not keeping or holding any "graven image" – not just a 'false idol' – but photographs of themselves, or their families. It just wasn't permitted.

At first, Eli couldn't figure out the reaction of the two men. As he explained his problem with the photograph, the two just looked at each other like it was something they'd never thought of. Finally, Bill told Eli that he understood the problem, but that it was something the team could not control. Eli realized that in every city, at every ballpark, there would be cameras, and reporters, and questions.

And that was something Eli had never thought of.

At least Veeck finished the conversation by saying that he would try to think of something that would keep things like the news photos under control – in Cleveland - but, as far as the rest of the cities they would play... he couldn't promise anything.

His mother. His little brothers and sisters. Had they seen the photo? Were they angry? Probably not as angry as his father. He was hoping there would be no more photographs, but he also realized that a lot of what was happening to him now was not under his control.

As the train sped through the farmland he saw the wildflowers growing near the tracks, just outside the endless fields of corn and soybeans.

Daisies.

Rachael.

Their last conversation before he left with Bill and Hal had been so rushed. Eli remembered holding her hands tightly, and asking if she understood what he had to do, and why.

Rachael nodded, but Eli knew the "why" look in her eyes.

Had she seen the photo...?

Eli smiled.

Rachael probably liked it.

He wished she was sitting next to him at that moment. Rach would never believe this train, he thought. Fancy dinner. Fancy bathroom. Fancy chairs. Fancy... bed.

He wished she was sitting next to him at that moment because she would know what he should do. She always knew the right thing. Buster had been great, but he was an English. The ways of the Amish were not practiced by anyone he had seen in the last four days. Eli knew there were more decisions coming. Decisions that would be bigger than photographs in a newspaper. Rachael would know what to do. What to say. How to say it.

She always did.

She always *would*.

He loosened his tie again.

A lady who said she was Bill's helper had brought English clothes to the ballpark that day. A suit. Shirts. Ties. Pants. Shoes. Socks. Underwear. As he looked down at himself, Eli wondered what Rachael would think of the way he was dressed.

He had a pretty good idea of what his father would think.

A man in a gold-braided cap came through the door at the far end of the railroad car.

"South Bend," he called, "South Bend next!"

He felt the feeling that the train was finally slowing, and as the man in the cap passed him by, Eli turned his head to the window and saw them.

A field. A ballgame. Amish boys playing in the twilight after a long day in the fields or the barn with their fathers.

The sight was in front of him – and gone – within seconds.

Eli craned his neck to look until a slight bend in the tracks turned the train away.

JUNE 28 - 29

"...and the 1-1 to Weaver... swung on, and ooooooooooooh LOOK AT THIS ONE GO!!! OVER THE LEFT FIELD ROOF!!!"

"Jack – Hamner is standing on the mound, and he's tilting his head like he's trying to see what just happened from a different angle – he can't believe it..."

"The fans close to home plate are standing and pointing – they're trying to fathom what they just saw-"

"What do you think, Jack? I know Greenberg cleared that roof, and Gehrig..."

"Maybe Jimmy Foxx...?"

"If Eli Weaver keeps doing things like this, he'll need a nickname like 'Hammerin' Hank', 'The Iron Horse', or 'Double X'..."

"Well – Hamner's day is done. He's headed for the showers, but the horse is outta the barn with the Clevelands now up 6-2!"

"...and Jack, on the Indians' bench, Eli Weaver took a couple hand-shakes, grabbed some water from the cooler, and sat down... like it's another day at the office."

"If this is just another day at the office, I'm sure glad he clocked in today, Bob..."

Sixteen hours later, Eli was at it again:

"...this is Jack Graney with Bob Neal reminding you that nothing goes with Cleveland Indians baseball like a tall, frosty cold P.O.C. – P.O.C. is 'The Pride of Cleveland'."

"Well Jack, the meeting on the mound has concluded, and we're about to find out how the ChiSox are going to handle this."

"...and it's a huge decision, Bob. Somehow, some way, Orval Grove has matched Bobby Feller pitch for pitch today – nothing but goose eggs on the board – we're scoreless in the 8th. Indians on first and second, and here comes Weaver."

"So far today, Eli Weaver is hitless. In the second, he sent Tucker to the right centerfield fence to make an astounding catch against the grandstand. The next two times up, Grove has wanted nothing to do with Weaver – working around him with a walk in the 4th, and a flat-out intentional pass in the 6th-"

"But here in the 8th, first and second are occupied-"

"...and I don't think Grove would walk him again, and load the bases for Boudreau in a scoreless tie."

"Grove to the stretch. His first offering – WAY outside for ball one. Not intentionally wide, just wild. Grove again, ball in hand, gets the sign.

Sets. Delivers. Another wide one! 2-and-0 the count, and the fans here on the South Side are getting nervous."

"That second one was not as wide, Jack – but still not to Eli's liking."

"Orval Grove, not looking ready to do anything at the moment – steps off the rubber to rub up the ball... and Weaver **hasn't** stepped out. He's still in that right-handed batter's box, bat cocked behind his ear, just staring out at the pitcher. Grove, back up top, toes the rubber – and here's the 2-0 – Eli smacks another one to deep right center – Tucker's on the run again, and reachesssss – HE CAN'T GET IT!!! It's bouncing back off the wall toward the infield – Fleming scores! Here comes Edwards! And Eli's standing at third with a triple!"

"...and Bob Feller is leading the cheers from the dugout, Jack!"

"It's 2-nothing Tribe, and that may be all Rapid Robert needs today!"

"Jack, do you think Weaver hit 'ball 3'?"

"It appeared so to me, Bob. It looked a good six inches off the plate, and Weaver just whacked it!"

"What do you have to do to grab a headline, Bob?" a reporter joked – with just the hint of a needle.

"Let's give the kid his due," Feller said, his arm wrapped in ice, "he's come up here and been the spark we've been looking for all season."

"Yeah, but, 13 wins before the All-Star Game, Bob," another reporter chimed in, "that's nothing to sneeze at."

"Fellas," Feller looked serious, "we've been in sixth place all year. The Sox and Yanks look great, but we're one big streak away from putting a little heat on'em. If I keep doing my job, along with everyone else, I'm tellin' ya, we can get back into the mix."

"But, that kid Weaver-" another reporter started –

"Look," the Indians' ace cut him off, "if you want to ask me about my day today, ask. I'll be happy to walk you through it. But, if you want to talk to the rookie, talk to the rookie."

The reporters turned to step toward Eli Weaver's locker, but he was nowhere to be found.

SUNDAY
JUNE **30**

The Hollenden Hotel

Cy Slapnicka had returned to Cleveland to grab a couple changes of clothes and get out on the road again.

So far, his lightning-in-a-bottle find was the only thing any scout had turned up since Bill Veeck's hotel room plea over a week ago. A couple players – World War II vets – had been found, and offered lower-level minor league deals, but they were working, trying to raise a family, and had had enough adventures for a lifetime.

Slap's breakfast, and the morning paper, arrived at his table simultaneously.

"WEAVER'S LATE HEROICS STUN SOX" "Feller Masterful In Chicago Shutout"

The two greatest signings of his scouting career staring up at him from the same sports section.

Amazing.

Comiskey Park – Chicago

Eli had arrived at the ballpark early on this Sunday morning, but had just sat in front of his locker with his head down.

Finally, as his teammates began to arrive, he pulled himself up from his folding chair, and walked toward the small office where his manager was sitting.

The visiting manager's office at Comiskey Park was a glorified closet, into which were shoehorned a desk and a chair. The Indians' manager was jammed inside, working on the lineup cards for both ends of today's doubleheader.

"Lou...?"

Boudreau looked up at Eli in the doorway. Uh-oh...

"Can I talk to you for a minute?"

"Sure, kid," the manager said. He made sure Eli was clear of the door before he tried to nudge it shut with his foot. "What can I do for ya'?"

The silence that followed was more than a bit uncomfortable.

"Eli..."

"I can't play today."

The manager looked him up and down. "Why... are you hurt?"

"No." The young man wasn't making eye contact. Until now. "It's Sunday."

"I know, Eli. We have a doubleheader today. It starts in one hour."

The tall, strong young man looked down at his manager. "Sunday is a day of worship and rest. I can't play today."

Boudreau knew Eli wasn't pulling his leg. "Eli," he said seriously, "you've been our best hitter since you walked in the door six days ago. How am I supposed to replace that bat of yours?"

"I don't know." Eli continued to look Boudreau in the eyes. "I just know that today is the day we are to rest from our labors. And that's what I believe God would have me do."

This kid is serious, Boudreau realized. "Stay here. I'll be right back."

The manager extricated himself from the tiny room. The two minutes he was gone seemed like an hour to Eli.

When Boudreau returned, Bill Veeck was with him. Both of them squeezing back into the small space seemed like a scene from a Marx Brothers movie.

Veeck took a last, long drag off of his cigarette, dropped it, and stepped it out with his good leg. Boudreau was waiting for his boss to explode, but somehow, that didn't happen.

"Eli," the owner stared at him, "Lou tells me you won't play today."

"I can't, Bill," the young man said as he looked back at the owner. "There are six days for a man to work, but we are to rest on the seventh day, just as the Lord rested when He created the heavens and the earth."

Veeck and Boudreau looked at each other, then the owner responded, "Look Eli, I've got no argument with God here, but I do have a contract that you signed last week to play baseball for the Cleveland Indians. We are playing a doubleheader today, and Lou and I have the authority to suspend you without pay. Or cut you and send you home."

Bill let that last phrase hang in the air for a second. He was proud of how scary and final it sounded.

"I can't play today, Bill."

The owner stared down at his manager's lineup cards on his desk.

Veeck looked at Boudreau, "Lou, the kid sits today."

The manager looked like he was ready to spit nails.

"Tell the papers he..." Veeck was searching for the right phrase, "he's been from playing ball on a farm to the majors in less than a week, and he needed a day off. It's been a bit overwhelming."

"Dammit Bill, they aren't gonna *buy that!*" Now Boudreau was ready to explode.

"Lou, unless you can come up with something better in the next hour, that's what we're going to say," Veeck said.

Eli looked down and turned for the door.

"Wait a minute, Eli." This time Veeck's voice had an edge.

Weaver stopped. Then turned slowly in the crowded little room.

Veeck took a deep breath. "Lou is not going to start you today, and he is not going to put you in as a pinch-hitter, or as a substitute out in the field..."

Eli was relieved, but still tense.

"BUT," Veeck continued, "you are a player under contract to the Cleveland Indians. You will put on your uniform, and you will sit on the bench for both games today. Do you understand?"

"Yes."

"BILL," Veeck said sharply.

"Yes, Bill."

Veeck looked at Boudreau. "Make sure Buster sits with him on the bench, and tell him Eli needs to be sitting where the reporters can see him. If he's missing from the bench, then the rumors start... who knows what those guys will come up with."

"And you," Bill pointed at Eli, "...you better not leave the bench this afternoon – even to take a pee. Understood?"

"Yes, Bill."

Bill looked at the rookie. "We're going to talk more about this when we get back to Cleveland. Also understood?"

"Yes, Bill."

"Go suit up," Veeck said. Eli left quickly. The owner looked at the manager.

Veeck shook his head. "I told the scouts to find me a miracle."

Boudreau shook his head. "And they found you St. Francis."

"With power to all fields," Veeck said.

Buster kept Eli glued to the bench that Sunday, with a steady flow of teaching and tips. How to study a pitcher. Watching the catcher's movements behind the plate. Seeing where his teammates positioned themselves on defense, and how he could adjust better in the outfield to help his center-fielder.

The stares from his teammates however, were uncomfortable. And were directed his way often – especially after quiet conversations in the corner of the dugout.

The Indians fell behind early, and tried to rally frequently.

Boudreau was calling for pinch-hitters every time through the line-up: Keltner, Hayes, Meyer, Lollar...

But not Weaver.

The Indians lost 7-3.

In game 2, the rain moved in, and with the score tied 5-5, the game was called, and both teams lit out for the train station. The Sox were headed for Detroit, the Indians were going back home to Cleveland.

And, in the chaos of getting men, luggage, and equipment in motion, the reporters from Cleveland's daily newspapers typed their stories fast, and filed their stories just as quickly. Very little was written about Weaver's absence that day, but some of his teammates took plenty of mental notes.

Most of the grumbling that evening was because the rain delay had caused the Indians to catch a much later train. The 8 o'clock eastbound was not an express. That meant they'd be dragging themselves back in their front doors in Cleveland by sunrise.

Eli ate alone in the dining car as the train rolled east in fits and starts. Behind him were two of his teammates, talking just loud enough for him to hear.

"Nice that our precious rookie got off his ass to come eat."

"Surprised he can lift a fork, when he couldn't lift a bat."

"At least we saved money on laundry. His uniform was so clean, he can wear it again tomorrow."

Eli stared down at what was left of his dinner.

He had lost his appetite.

MONDAY
JULY 1

The John Miller Farm – Mt. Hope

Rachael had once again grabbed the newspaper out of her aunt and uncles wastebin, and tucked it deep into her apron pocket. This time, upon arriving home, she placed the flowers she had brought for her mother in a vase, and ran to the barn. When she reached the hayloft, the noise below and behind her, she reached into her apron pocket, and spread the sports section in front of her.

"TRIBE TUMBLES 7-3 ON SOUTH SIDE"

"Game 2 – A Soggy Stalemate"

Chicago, Illinois (AP)

The Chicago White Sox ended the Cleveland Indians' modest 2-game winning streak yesterday with a 7-3 victory, before a rain-shortened second game was called in front of 19,431 sopping South Siders.

Eddie Smith not only went to 3-5 on the season, but drove in two runs to help his own cause. Taffy Wright also knocked home two markers for the Pale Hose.

The Cleveland offense scored runs, but was never able to deliver the knockout blow to the Sox in either game.

Rookie hitting sensation Eli Weaver was given the day off by Tribe skipper Lou Boudreau. "It's been a long week for the kid," the Indians' player/manager said. "He's gone from being a farm boy to a major league player in a matter of days. He just needed a rest. We have a busy week coming before the All-Star Game."

The lone bright spot at the plate for Cleveland was...

Rachel set the paper beside her and smiled.
He didn't play on Sunday.

Downtown Cleveland

As Eli shoveled down his steak and eggs, his hair kept dangling over his plate every time he leaned forward.
For the first week or so, Buster just let it go. But today...
"That's it." Mills shook his head.
"What?" Eli looked up with a mouthful.
"We gotta fix that."
"What...?"
"That hair's gotta go." Buster waved for the check. "Finish. Hurry up."
Moments later, they were walking to Public Square to see the bar-

ber who took care of most of the Indians' players during the season.

"Buster!" the barbers called. The little bells below the door handle jingled, as he walked inside.

"Al, do I have a project for you!" Mills smiled.

"That's okay," the small Italian man yelled, "you ain't got enough money for me to make you look good anyways."

The room laughed as everyone greeted Buster.

"Whattawe got here?" Al looked at Eli.

"Boys," Buster gestured grandly, "I want you to meet the American League's newest rookie sensation – Eli Weaver!"

Not much could stop the clatter and the chatter in Al's shop. But that announcement did.

Al snapped a towel across his chair. "Awright big shot, have a seat."

"He likes you." Buster winked, as Eli settled into the big chair.

With a flourish, Al ceremoniously spun the cape across Eli, and snapped it at the back of the neck. He grabbed his scissors in right hand, the comb in his left, and spun back toward his newly-famous client.

"What the hell...?" Al flipped the comb at each side of Eli's head.

The noise around the room paused, as the barber walked around the young man in the chair – shaking his head.

"It looks like someone put a *bowl* on your head, and cut around it!"

Al's assistants looked at each other.

Buster lowered his eyes.

Eli turned red. "Well... actually... that's what my mom always did."

There was a second of silence.

Before the shop erupted in laughter.

Even Eli.

WEDNESDAY NIGHT
JULY 3

On the Detroiter – New York Central Railroad

Eli Weaver smiled as the train swayed gently.

After his English haircut, he had just spent three days laying waste to the St. Louis Browns.

Hadn't it worked the other way around for Samson...? Eli wondered.

On Monday night, Eli drove a first-inning fastball into Cleveland Stadium's upper deck in left field to give the Indians an early 3-0 lead in a 6-4 win.

Tuesday afternoon at League Park, Eli smacked two singles and stole his first two bases in a 4-2 victory.

On this sunny Wednesday afternoon, his 2-for-3 day (including two more "unintentional-intentional" walks) with an RBI was helpful to the Cleveland cause. But it was his play in the outfield that drew the oohs and ahhs of the fans in the right field grandstand. Eli began the day by throwing out two runners trying to stretch singles into doubles. In the later innings, Eli gunned down two more Brownies at home plate from the right field wall – the second one on the fly – to preserve Bob Feller's 10-hit shutout.

And... after the game, he had answered a few questions from reporters in the clubhouse for the first time.

"How did you get so strong, Eli?"

"I grew up on a farm. I've learned to blacksmith. I bale hay. I've helped build barns for others in my family. With no modern conveniences such as you have, it's very easy to grow strong, and stay strong."

"Do you think any other teams are going to try to run on your arm?"

"I don't understand your question."

"Will other teams you play try to take extra bases when the ball is hit to you?"

"Oh, I hope so!" (reporters laugh) "That is a fun part of the game. Buster taught me how the balls bounce off the wall here at this small field. Now that I know how far the ball will bounce, all I need to do is turn and throw."

"It's that easy for you?"

"It sure seems like it, doesn't it?" Catcher Jim Hegan laughed from a few lockers away. He nodded at the rookie.

"Is it that easy, Eli?"

"Back home, I chased a ball down that rolled through left field, and into the cornfield. I threw my cousin Joseph out at home from out there. He didn't talk to me for weeks." (reporters laugh again)

The scribes were eating out of the kid's hand, Buster thought.

"Got a girl back home, Eli?"

The kid's face turned crimson.

Eli reached for his chin. Interview over.

"Hey guys," Mills said, "you know rookies are supposed to be seen and not heard. This kid's gotta get a shower, and catch a train." Buster snapped a towel at Eli, "Get a move on, kid. We gotta go."

Eli turned from the sunset over the flat fields outside his window to see Buster sitting across from him.

"Thank you," Eli said.

"For...?" his coach asked.

"Getting me out of talking to the newspaper men." The rookie shook his head, "I was talking too much."

"Not a problem, son," Buster said. Then the Texan looked at Eli with a grin.

"What...?"

Buster laughed, "So... *do you have a girl back home?*"

Eli went just as crimson as he had a few hours ago in the clubhouse. "Yes."

"Is she pretty?"

More crimson. "Yes."

Mills was enjoying himself now. "Does *she know* that she is your girl?"

Eli's face looked confused. "What does that mean?"

Buster said, "Have you ever told her how you feel about her?"

Eli thought a moment. "No. But, it is something we have known for a long time. We don't have to say it."

"Do you miss her?" the coach asked.

"Very much."

"Then ask her – and your family – to come to Cleveland to see a game."

Eli shook his head, "How would they get there?"

"Don't worry about that. Bill can arrange it."

Eli shook his head again, "We could not afford such a trip."

"Bill will take care of it," Buster said. "He likes you, kid."

"I'm not sure of that," the rookie said.

"Trust me," his coach replied, "anyone who can hit, run, and throw the way you can, is gonna be liked by the owner."

Eli looked out the window. "Bill still hasn't talked to me about last Sunday."

"He will," Buster said. "And when he does, just listen to him for a spell. He knows how you feel about playin' ball on Sunday. But, he is your boss. When he does sit you down for a talk, it'd be best to keep your mouth shut."

"I will." Eli nodded.

It was nearly dark outside the train. The last touches of color were vanishing on the western horizon.

The coach saw Eli look at him with a stare and a smile.

"Buster, tell me about the Detroit pitchers."

THURSDAY
JULY 4

Briggs Stadium – Detroit

Eli tossed the ball toward his coach. "I've never seen this many people before."

"In a ballpark?" Buster caught the throw, and sent it back Eli's way.

"In my life," the rookie said.

For Eli and Buster, playing catch every day had become a calming ritual. A way to get the rookie back from the stress of trying to figure out life among the English, to the relative calm of being at the ballpark.

For most, facing a major league fastball was unthinkable.

For Eli, stress was calling a cab.

Briggs Stadium had none of the vastness of the lakefront stadium in Cleveland, it was enclosed on all sides, and that closeness magnified every sound. It was a ballpark that was alive from the moment the first two fans walked in the gates. On this day, there would be over 50,000 of them.

The huge crowd roared their way through the first nine innings of the day.

The Tigers manhandled the Indians.

After the final out of game one, Buster found Eli sitting on the bench, and staring out at centerfield.

"Hey, rookie," the coach yelled, "c'mon back to the clubhouse!"

Eli shook his head. "I didn't get a hit, Buster."

"Yeah. Quite a news flash there, kid."

"It ain't funny."

Mills was not amused. "Look Eli, if you think you're the first guy to get an 0-fer, I got news for ya' – it happens to those of us who never could hit like you do."

"The ball just kept disappearin' on me." Eli shook his head.

"All right." Buster sat down next to the rookie. "We'll make this quick. What did he get you out on in the first inning?"

"Curve ball."

"Where?" the coach asked.

"Outside."

"By a lot?"

"No." Eli was irritated. "Couple inches."

"Why couldn't you hit it?"

"Because everything he threw was a curveball. He had to throw me a fastball at least once. That's what I was waiting for."

"Did he?"

"No."

The rookie's light hadn't come on yet, so Mills kept going, "Second time up – how'd he gitcha?"

"Curve ball."

"Same place?"

"No."

"Where...?"

Eli had to think for a second. "A little further away."

"Third time up."

Eli nodded his head. "Curve ball again." The two spoke in unison this time:

"A little further away."

"And the last time up?" Mills started laughing, "When you swung so hard, you spun yourself around, and fell on top of the plate?"

Eli turned red. "That wasn't funny."

"It was hilarious," Mills couldn't stop smiling, "all of us thought so."

"The whole team was laughing...?" Eli couldn't turn much redder.

"Pretty much." Buster's face softened. "Look kid, the point is that Fred Hutchinson is a good pitcher. He hooked you with that curve in the first, and didn't let you git off the hook all day long. He kept slippin' it a little more outside every time you came up, and you kept followin' him further'n further out there."

Eli nodded.

"Now," Buster said, "if I were pitchin' the second game for Detroit, what would I do to that rookie – Eli Weaver?"

Eli nodded again. "Throw him more curve balls outside."

"I might." Mills looked at Eli. "Son, it's taken these pitchers a week'n a half to figure out that they want nuthin' to do with you. If you don't adjust, you'll be home in time for the next hay cut."

"...and so Case doubles, Conway doubles him home, and Fleming's sharp single makes it 2-to-nothing – there's still nobody out in the first, and here comes Eli Weaver."

"Weaver took his first 0-for-4 in the first game of this doubleheader, Jack – and honestly, he looked a little lost out there."

"And so it must be for every rookie, Bob. Here's Overmire's first pitch – outside with a curve, ball one. The first three Clevelands have greeted him rudely here, and this is no time to give'em a break. Overmire's stretch – he'll toss another – outside again, ball two. The Tiger lefty is digging himself a deep, dark, ditch right now... the 2-0... OH!!! THERE GOES AN-OTHER ONE! It... is... IN THE UPPER DECK!!!"

"OVER HALFWAY UP THE UPPER DECK, JACK!!!"

"Young Mr. Weaver has this Dee-troit ballpark BUZZIN' right now! The Indians now lead 4-to-nothing, there's still no one out in the top of the first, and Eli tips his cap as the flash bulbs pop as he approaches home plate."

"Jack... did Weaver tip his cap, or cover his face...?"

FRIDAY
JULY 5

Briggs Stadium – Detroit | 11am

The bat rep from Hillerich & Bradsby caught up with Eli in Detroit.

"I think you might be around here a while," Boudreau said to the rookie as they walked up the dugout steps, "so I think it would be a good idea for you to get some bats ordered." Boudreau smiled. "So you quit using everybody elses."

"How much do they cost?" Eli asked.

"Team pays for them, kid," the manager said. "Unless you bust a lot, or give 'em all away... Emil, this is Eli Weaver. Fix him up with something that's gonna help him hit 'em a long way."

"You mean farther than 'over the roof' at Comiskey? Yeah kid, I heard what you been doin' up here. Let's see if we can turn great into perfect." The rep reached down to the bats he had fanned out in front of the dugout. "Let's start you off with a K55 – Chuck Klein model."

Eli didn't react as he grabbed the bat.

"He hit 300 homers with that model. Nothing to sneeze at."

Eli still showed no recognition.

The rep looked at Boudreau.

"He's a 'different' kind of rookie," Lou said. Then tried to explain the situation to the veteran bat representative.

After only a couple swings, Eli came back to the bats fanned out by home plate, and grabbed another.

"S2," Emil said, "Vern Stephens."

Still no reaction from the rookie.

"You just played against him in St. Louis."

Eli's teammates standing close by rolled their eyes.

It took only one or two swings with each bat he tried, and even though his swings were producing line drives, they weren't producing satisfaction. On the next trip to Emil's inventory, he reached for a model near the end of the line.

"W215," intoned Emil, "that's made from the Ted Williams pattern – but not from his private stock."

"Is he good?" Eli asked.

"You're kidding," Emil said.

Eli's teammates put their heads down, trying not to laugh, but they were also growing impatient.

"C'mon rook, we gotta get our swings," Ken Keltner said with a bit of an edge.

Emil had an idea. He rolled a few of the bats over in the middle of the ones he had fanned out, looking for one in particular.

"Here it is!" the rep said with a wink at Weaver's teammates. "Try this one."

Eli's first swing produced a drive that arched upwards and was lost to their sight as it sailed over the left field roof.

"Better?" Emil asked.

"Much," Eli said as he sent the next toss into the upper deck to rattle the wooden seats.

After two more swings producing similar results, Eli walked over to Emil.

"I'd like some more of these, sir."

The rep smiled. "Should'a gave ya' this one first. It's the one you've been using."

"What?" Boudreau exclaimed.

"O16," Emil said, "Bob Feller's model."

"No!" said Keltner as he stepped into the box, "He can't use a *pitcher's* bat!"

Feller was grinning from ear to ear. "Told you guys there were a lotta hits in my bats, but you hitters – too damn smart to listen."

"Did I just say something wrong?" Eli reddened a bit.

"No, you most certainly did not, rook," Feller smiled, and slapped Eli on the back. "You picked the best of the best."

Emil held out his notebook and a fountain pen.

"What is this for?" Eli asked.

"Sign your name across the page, son," Emil said. "We want to make sure we engrave your signature correctly on the bat."

"My signature... engraved...?"

"Right there on the bat barrel – if you sign the standard contract with us, of course," the rep assured him as he placed the pen in his hand.

"Will the bats be just for me?" Eli looked at the rep suspiciously.

"On the field, yes. But we'll sell 'em to the public with a cheaper grade of lumber, too. Kids'll buy 'em by the tree the way you're hittin' right now!" Emil lowered his voice, "You'll make a nice bit'a money off 'em – and so will we, of course."

Eli handed the book and pen back to the rep quicky.

"Sorry, sir. Just the bats, please," Eli said quietly, "that's all I need."

Emil looked at the rookie incredulously. "He's turning down free money? Who is this guy... Jesus?"

"Kinda," Boudreau said with a wink.

Eli was embarrassed again. But he looked at the signature on the bat the same way he saw the photographs of himself that were popping up in the St. Louis and Detroit newspapers on this trip. Graven images.

All the attention turned to Feller, as he walked to the dugout, and down the steps, his 'radio commercial' for his bat drew laughter from his fellow pitchers, and hissing from the hitters.

"That's right, kids! The 'Hammer from Holmes County' – Eli Weaver – uses the same 'Bob Feller O16' Louisville Slugger as 'The Heater from Van Meter'! Get yours today by sending 19 Wheaties box tops, and a $3 money order to 'Feller's Fantastic Bat' – Box 19, Cleveland 19, Ohio..."

Cleveland | late afternoon

"Eli!"

The rookie's head turned as he signed one more autograph before walking across the West 3rd Street bridge, and up the hill toward Public Square.

Bill Veeck limped across the square towards him with a smile.

"Hey Millsy," the owner smiled, "can I borrow the kid for a while?"

"Sure, Bill," the coach smiled back. "He's all yours. See you back at the hotel, Eli."

The owner looked at his young hitter. "Do you mind if we give Oscar a ride home? He's our man here at the ballpark who makes sure all the hotdogs and buns go to the concession stands they're supposed to."

Eli had noticed that a tall, lanky negro was walking with his boss.

"Sure." Eli had no idea where he was going with his boss anyway.

Veeck hailed a cab, and the trio squeezed into the back.

"30th and Central, bud."

"30th and Central it is, gentlemen," the cabbie replied. "Heyyy... you're that Veeck fella that bought the team..."

"I am," the owner smiled, "it's Bill."

"Great to meetcha, Bill. Joe Tomsic, here." The cabbie glanced in his rearview again. "Heyyy-hey-hey! You're the kid! Weaver, right?"

"That's me," Eli grinned.

"Whenever I've got the stadium run, I always keep a baseball and a pen in the cab. Would you sign the ball? My boy's name is Tommy. Hey, this is great! The kid'll never believe it! I think we saw your first game – had a day off, took the kid to League Park, and saw you beat up the Yanks! Fun day!"

"Be sure to tell Tommy 'hello' from me." Eli was smiling ear-to-ear now.

He sure learns quick, Veeck thought as he smiled at the young ballplayer.

At a stop light, Veeck turned to Eli. "I want you to know that I've had a talk with all the newspapers in town. There won't be any more photographers waiting for you at home plate, or over by the dugout. They've agreed to respect your beliefs on that."

"Thank you," Eli said.

"A couple of their papers asked if it was okay if their artists did a drawing of you."

"A drawing?"

"A cartoon," Veeck said. "I had a feeling that it would be the same, uhh... rule? Law... as with the pictures."

"You are right, Bill," Eli nodded.

"I figured as much," Bill said. "So... they agreed to draw you without drawing your face."

"Hm." Eli wondered how that was going to work.

Veeck continued, "We can't guarantee what's going to happen when the team is traveling. The photographers will be there – on the field – at every other ballpark in the league. One of our radio broadcasters noticed how you handled it in Detroit a couple days ago. Was that intentional?"

Eli smiled a bit. "I noticed how Mr. Feller tips his cap as he leaves the field when people are clapping. I don't want to be disrespectful, but I also don't want those cameras flashing in my face."

"30th and Central guys," the cabbie said. "This sure was a pleasure. Good luck, kid! Hit one for my boy Tommy tomorrow!"

Veeck reached into the pocket of his sport shirt. "Are you working tomorrow, Joe?"

"Nope. Lookin' forward to the day off."

Bill handed him the fare, and some tickets. "Bring your wife and your kids to the game tomorrow. On me."

"Hey-heyyy!" Joe was one excited man. "What a treat! Thanks, Bill!"

"You and your family have fun tomorrow, Joe." Veeck waved as he stepped to the curb.

The 90-degree heat was radiating off the concrete and asphalt surrounding them. It was a humid July evening in the city, one of those times when you could feel that thunderstorm coming from the southwest before you could see or hear it.

As the three men walked down East 30th, Eli hesitated for a moment, and the other two men sensed it.

The faces that watched them walk down the street were all negro faces.

Eli Weaver had not seen enough negroes in his lifetime to count on one hand.

"Oscar lives in this neighborhood, Eli," Veeck broke into the young man's brain.

"Our family moved here about ten years ago," Oscar said with a hint of a drawl, "came up from Mississippi because of all the steel jobs. Then came the war, and we was all workin' – as much as we wanted. Factories were hummin' 24 hours a day. Making steel. Building tanks. Airplane parts. Weapons. Shells for artillery."

As the three continued walking, the sound of a piano, and singing, were growing a bit louder. Eli could see a number of people outside the building where the sound seemed to be coming from a few hundred feet down the street.

"Thanks for the ride home, Bill." Oscar smiled, as he waved to his friends in the doorway of the building Eli had just noticed. "And thanks for walkin' me to church, too."

Church? Eli thought... it's Saturday.

"If y'all wanta come worship with us for a spell, yer welcome."

Eli said, "Oscar, why do you worship on Saturday when Sunday is the Lord's Day?"

"Well, young man, it's like this," Oscar said, "during the war, the defense plants were working 24 hours a day. Our shifts would change every week. Some weeks we could be in church on Sunday, and some weeks we couldn't. We had to work when we could in order to pay the rent."

Veeck knew where this was going, and kept watching for Eli's reactions.

"Our pastor," Oscar continued, "thought it would be impornant for everyone at our church to be there whenever they could be. So, he decided to try a Saturday evening service. Once the word got out, we had people from all over the neighborhood havin' chuurch on Saturdays 'cause they had to work Sundays. After a few months, we opened a service on Wednesday nights, too. Those people who worked third shift at U.S. Steel were hangin' out the windas."

Eli was lost in thought, but looked up when Oscar and Bill stopped. The sign read "Shiloh Baptist Church".

"C'mon in," Oscar smiled, "you're always welcome in the House of The Lord."

Veeck smiled and limped up the steps. Church was definitely not his favorite thing, but for Eli, he'd make an exception.

Eli followed.

For the next 90 minutes, Eli Weaver spent time in a spiritual world that he had never imagined before.

The music was sung – and sometimes even shouted – with a passion he had never seen. The heat of a July evening was still there, but those in the church brushed it away with their fans. As the piano played, and the choir up front swayed, the melodies he heard gained emotion – and depth. The harmony he heard was not just men he had been used to all his life, but men and women joining together in music that was pointed skyward – not bound to the earth in any way.

Eli was disappointed when the music ended.

But, as the pastor began to speak, his words added to the musical quality of what preceded it.

And then, Eli heard Oscar, his family, and all those worshipping adding their "amens" to the pastor's words.

In Eli's tradition, the word "amen" was the solemn conclusion to a prayer.

But here, at Shiloh Baptist, the "AMEN" was an agreement. The end of a sentence. The "yes" of a worshipping people.

Could these men and women be worshipping the same God that Eli and his family worshipped every Sunday?

His heart sensed the answer to that question.

The service had reached its conclusion.

Families were saying their extended goodbyes.

Eli, Bill, and Oscar sat in the back of the sanctuary. There was just the smallest hint of a breeze breaking up the heat inside the building.

Oscar smiled and looked at the young Amish man. "Eli, Bill told me about your not wanting to play on Sunday. That's why he asked me to bring you here tonight."

Eli stared at his boss.

Veeck shrugged, pulled a cigarette from the pack in his shirt pocket, and moved toward the door. This was his cue to step outside.

"I learned a few years ago – during the war – that if I wanted to worship my Jesus, I was going to have to find a way to do it that didn't only happen on Sunday." Oscar's eyes brightened as they had many times in the last hour, "My Lord is the Lord over Sunday... but, He's the Lord over Monday through Saturday, too. I still love being with Him here on Sunday whenever I can, I'm just thankful He's big enough to cover every day."

Eli looked at Oscar. "Thanks, Oscar. I'm glad I came."

Bill Veeck had already hailed a cab for the ride back to the Hollenden Hotel. It was a short, silent trip, with his young Amish outfielder staring out the window at the city.

A young man with a lot on his mind.

Eli and Bill walked inside the hotel to the elevator. It was a silent elevator ride, too.

Veeck wondered what he had done to the kid this evening.

As the doors opened on Eli's floor, Veeck cleared his throat. "Sunday doubleheader tomorrow," He said softly. "See you there?"

Before he stepped out of the elevator, Eli turned to look his boss in the eyes.

"You will."

Cleveland | late afternoon

It drove Rachael just a bit crazy to wait the entire day before she could reach deep into her apron for the sports section of Monday's paper… which she had once again taken from her aunt and uncle's house.

By the candlelight in her bedroom, she scanned the story quickly and smiled with no mention of Eli to be seen in the story of the two Sunday games.

But, when her eyes ran down the box scores of the doubleheader, the agate type in the column jumped off the page:

"WEAVER, *rf*   3   1   2   1"

And then, a few inches below, in the listing for the second game:

"WEAVER, *rf*   3   0   0   0"

She clipped the story from the newspaper, and tucked it away for safekeeping as always.

But for the first time, she wondered if Eli would come home again.

The Cleveland News

"ALL ABOUT ELI – HAL'S EXCLUSIVE INTERVIEW"
"Should Weaver Have Had An All-Star Slot?"
By Hal Lebovitz
A Cleveland News Exclusive
(Cleveland, Ohio)

His career has spanned a mere 14 games, yet 19-year-old Eli Weaver
of Mt. Hope, Ohio is the talk of the baseball world.

The numbers speak for themselves:

44 at-bats, 21 hits, 4 doubles, 2 triples, 4 homers and 17 runs batted in.
A batting average of .477!

Gaudy as these numbers may be, and as little as they represent,
the Indians' opponents have been quick to offer their opinions. "A
right-handed Gehrig" and "Jimmie Foxx-like" have been common
assessments. One anonymous general manager went so far as to

say, "if Ted Williams were an Amish blacksmith, that's what he'd look like."

But, what of the young man himself?

This reporter was privileged to be there when Weaver signed his contract, and I'm glad that he has consented to this conversation. With no baseball but the All-Star Game in Boston today, let's get to know Eli Weaver a little better.

HL: Where are you from, Eli?

EW: I was born and raised in Holmes County.

HL: How big is your family?

EW: There is my mother, my father, my grandmother, and I am the oldest child. I have 4 younger sisters, and 2 much younger brothers.

HL: That's quite a large family!

EW: Oh, my uncle's families are larger still. We believe a large family is a sign of blessing and favor from God.

HL: Since you have mentioned God, we should talk about that. It's very important to who you are, isn't it?

EW: Yes, sir.

HL: Tell me about your faith.

EW: I and my family are Amish.

HL: What does that mean?

EW: It means everything to us. It is the truth by which we live.

HL: Could you simplify it for us?

EW: Well, it means we believe in Jesus. That He has reconciled us to God. We believe in the Bible, we believe in the Ordnung...

HL: What is the Ordnung?

EW: The Ordnung is... our way of life. How we live out our faith among others.

HL: It's a list of rules?

EW: No. Not that. I don't believe I have ever seen a written list. It is the expectations, the disciplines we live by. It is understood – by all of us in the community. Not a list we memorize. An example we follow.

HL: Such as?

EW: The things you 'English', you 'Yankees' see...

HL: 'English' – 'Yankees'?

EW: All of you. You who are outside the Amish.

HL: You understand that calling someone a 'Yankee' during baseball season might have a little different meaning?

EW: (laughs) Yes. I may have to be more careful with my words.

HL: Let's get back to how the Amish live. What does that mean?

EW: What you... (laughs) not Amish... would notice: Our plain dress. Our children go to school only in our Amish schools. Our horses and buggies. No cars. No tractors. No electricity.

HL: That sounds like hardship to me.

EW: I understand. But to us, it is our way. We are to "be not conformed to this world, but be transformed".

HL: How do you do that?

EW: We try to live separate from the 'non-Amish' around us. We separate ourselves from the 'state' – the country in which we live. We follow God's way. We serve each other – building a house for newlyweds, building a barn for a family, shoeing each other's horses, helping with the hay cuts and baling. And we are committed to peace, always.

HL: Being separate. Committed to peace. That means 'no war', correct?

EW: Yes, sir.

HL: So, you never registered for Selective Service during the war?

EW: I did. We all did. The difference is that we registered as – what you 'English' call 'conscientious objectors'. To engage in war is not the way of God.

HL: So, you registered, but were not drafted? How did that work?

EW: Many of us from Holmes County went on a train to Colorado. We spent a year at the National Park there building shelters and lodges. All of us were Amish, and from Ohio, so it worked out. There were also a few of you English who were there as C.Os., too. They sent us home so we could help our families plant-

HL: That helped the war effort, too.

EW: It did. And, by the time the crop was in, the war in Europe was done, so they never called us back.

HL: So, you did serve our country.

EW: I did. Just not in the ways of war.

HL: With what you have just explained, I must ask how it is that you can be here playing baseball for the Indians at all.

EW: I have not been baptized yet. I am not officially part of the adult community. Before that time comes, we are each allowed a time of 'rumspringa' – a time to be away from our Amish community. For many young men of my age, they use it as a time to – um – 'sow their wild oats'. I have chosen to experience what baseball is like. Bill (Veeck) gave me that chance, and when my time has come to decide which life I will live, I will decide between my Amish life, and the life of you 'English'.

HL: If you choose life among 'us'?

EW: Then I will not be welcomed by my family, or my Amish community.

HL: I cannot imagine such a choice.

EW: God will direct my choice, I'm sure.

HL: Let's talk about your two weeks of baseball. How have you been welcomed?

EW: I am learning what the word 'rookie' means. It is almost as hard as learning the Ordnung. (laughs)

HL: Have your teammates helped you at all?

EW: Yes. My plain dress from home was not very plain here in the city. My team has taken me to the store for pants and shirts... and, now I have an English haircut. They now say I am quite sharp, but I am not sure about that.

HL: Have there been any problems?

EW: I miss my family.

HL: I understand.

EW: It is also very noisy at night here in the city. I do not understand how people can sleep.

HL: Have you had any difficulty on the baseball field?

EW: Oh, yes.

HL: What sort of difficulty?

EW: Hutchinson of Detroit, and Lopat of Chicago make it very hard to hit the ball. (laughs) The curve they place on the ball is not like anything I've seen in our games at the farm.

HL: I would think not. Otherwise, I'd say you're hitting the ball very well. The speed of the fastballs doesn't seem to bother you at all.

EW: Not really. There are many men I play against on the farm who are as strong as the pitchers here, and throw just as hard.

HL: Really?

EW: Oh, yes. (pauses) They don't know where the ball is going when they throw it, but they throw just as hard.

HL: Not the same amount of "control" as the pitchers in the big leagues?

EW: "Control". That's a good word for it.

HL: What else?

EW: It is strange that so many can come to watch the baseball games during the daytime. Do people in the city not have important work that must be done in the daylight?

HL: Well, we do have lights.

EW: Baseball at night. That has also been very different. It doesn't seem quite right.

HL: Anything else that gives you difficulty?

EW: I do not understand the need of all the photographs being taken. But, I am thankful to Bill for helping the newspapers understand how the Amish feel about such things.

HL: Those photos are offensive to you?

EW: It is part of the Ordnung. When Moses was told to not have 'graven images', we believe that applies to photographs of us. I want to thank you and your newspaper for promising not to photograph me.

HL: How about the fans? How have they treated you?

EW: They have been very kind to me. At the small ballpark (League Park), the fans who sit close to me in right field are very funny. I also notice they seem to like to drink during the games.

HL: (laughs) I think you will be finding that to be true in most ballparks. Eli, your life has changed so much in the last two weeks. Everything in your life has been so new. Is there something you really enjoy right now, that you don't miss from home?

EW: Yes, sir. Playing baseball. Every player here can hit, and run, and throw. The most fun I have every day is to see if I can be better than they are when I bat, or throw, or make a catch. To be around the other men, this is a kind of – ohh – the word –

HL: Competition?

EW: Yes. But we Amish would say it is about how we are measured. We have a saying, "A tree is best measured when it is cut down." Every day in baseball, you are measured. Some days you stand. Some days you are cut down. So far, I hope the people who come to the games feel I have "measured well".

HL: If you keep hitting .477 Eli, I think you will measure very well.

EW: Thank you, Hal.

Eli Weaver is a very quiet young man. A rookie who "knows his place". A rookie who has been separated from every part of everything his life was just a few weeks ago. He's also a surprisingly engaging young man, speaking at length for the first time in this conversation.

On Friday night, Eli makes his first trip to New York City. The Indians and The Bronx Bombers begin a 3-game weekend series at The House That Ruth Built.

Yes, Cleveland is a big city – America's 6th largest – nearly a million inside her borders, but NYC is something else again.

As "unbiased" as a reporter like me is supposed to be, I have to admit, it's hard not to root for a kid like this.

TUESDAY
JULY 9

Schlabach's Store – Mt. Hope

At the Miller farm, Rachael learned of the newspaper article from a passerby who didn't have a copy, but told Rachael that all of Mt. Hope was carrying newspapers an hour ago when she was passing through town.

Rachael rushed to finish the morning yard work, hitched Old Joe to the spring wagon, and hurried off toward Mt. Hope. She was worried that she would arrive too late to buy a newspaper, anxious over what this article contained (the passerby said it was a long article, but offered no other details), petrified that she would have to beg someone for their used copy, and guilty that she was pushing the old fieldworn workhorse to move so fast.

As she rounded the corner toward the town square, she slowed Old Joe's pace immediately.

No one seemed to be driving their buggies in a straight line. Passengers were holding newspapers in front of the faces of the buggy drivers.

No one was paying any attention to where they were walking.

Everyone on the street or the sidewalk was reading a newspaper. Almost as if in a mass Amish trance.

With urgent nonchalance, Rachael got the wagon to a shady spot at the rail, and tied Old Joe off (not that he needed it – he'd have stayed right where she left him anyway), and moved quickly toward the open door at Schlabach's.

In the last few weeks, she'd become used to being pointed at in public – a small penalty to pay for being the girl Eli was courting, but also carrying a growing annoyance that accompanied the immediate thought: "What did he do now?"

Today, Rachael entered the crowded store unnoticed.

Everyone's heads were buried in the newspaper.

One person did notice her entry into the store. Erna Schlabach was behind the counter, and looked like she was going to acknowledge Rachael's presence, but was shaking her head sadly at every customer who approached her. What was she saying?

"I'm sorry, we're out of newspapers today."

Oh, no.

Erna finally met Rachael's gaze as the crowd in front of the counter cleared, smiled, and made a small "wait" gesture with the hand at her side.

It took a few minutes for the counter to clear, then the older woman smiled broadly as Rachael approached.

"Dear Rachael, I knew you'd be by," Erna said, "I set your order aside." She reached below the counter, and produced a long bag with asparagus poking out the top.

Rachael took the bag with a curious look on her face.

"Your mother was needing these for dinner," Erna smiled again, "and there's something you needed in there, too." Leaning closer, Erna whispered, "Eli spoke well. I believe the baseballers would say he 'hit a home run'."

Rachael reached for the small purse inside her apron.

"No need dear," Erna said with a wink, "all paid for. Hurry home!"

There was no time that summer that Rachael had slipped into and out of Mt. Hope so easily. She pulled off the road at the creek crossing just out of town, to give Old Joe a long, cool drink.

Rachael sat cross-legged underneath the sugar maple on the bank as she read:

"One of the most exciting rookies to reach the majors since Ted Williams." ("Who...?" She wondered.)

"Our newspaper syndicate feels baseball fans across America will enjoy the story of this dashing young star of the diamond." ("...across America..."? Rachael gulped. "...dashing..."? Rachael gulped again.)

Old Joe was in no hurry to head home, and neither was Rachael. As she read, she felt a quiet satisfaction. For the first time in almost a month, she heard Eli's calm, measured voice in the words of the interview.

Her mind quickly flashed back to just moments before as she passed through town. She remembered the heads buried in their newspapers, but now, she realized those heads had been nodding in agreement, pointing to Eli's words.

Eli had her love. They were confident of their future together. But today, she saw the beginnings of something else in town: a nascent respect for what he was doing among the English.

Despite her worries at his departure, for the first time since Eli left Mt. Hope, Rachael had the feeling that – maybe – everything was going to be all right.

Hotel Pennsylvania – New York City

The crowd had been growing in size, and in anger all morning as they paraded in front of the Hotel Pennsylvania on 7th Avenue.

Veeck and Boudreau were the first from the ballclub to make it downstairs, and caught the sound of the mounting protest out the front windows of the hotel's restaurant as they ate a late breakfast.

"Welcome to New York," Boudreau said as he shook his head.

The waiter scowled, "You gotta be pretty mad about something to be out screaming before noon."

"What does that sign say?" Lou asked.

"'Won't fight – shouldn't play!'" Veeck said. "Waiter?"

"More coffee, sir?"

"In a second." Veeck gestured at the window. "Can you tell me what the hell's going on out here?"

"Oh, that-" the waiter said, "-just a bunch'a people all wound up about the guy who wouldn't fight in the war."

"What guy?" Boudreau asked.

"He's on the Cleveland Indians – he's staying at this hotel," the waiter said.

Veeck and Boudreau swallowed and stared at each other simultaneously.

The waiter continued, "Big article about him in the papers yesterday. The *Journal-American* got pretty mad about this guy using his religion as a dodge from going to fight. Coupla' guys on the radio start chirpin' about a protest last night. This morning, there was more stuff in the papers, and on the radio, and now the crazies are out here today, and headin' to the ballpark."

"There's going to be protesters at Yankee Stadium?" Veeck asked.

"Sure sounds like it," the waiter said. "Me? I think some people aren't happy unless they're angry. Live and let live, I say. Still need that coffee, pal?"

"Later," Veeck said.

The waiter moved quickly to another table.

"Dear God in heaven," Boudreau said.

Hal Lebovitz entered the restaurant with a few of the team's beat reporters.

"Hal, come here!" Veeck called too loudly.

"Good morning to you, too," Lebovitz snapped back.

Veeck gestured at the crowd outside. "It looks like your interview with Eli has had some unintended consequences."

"What are you talking about?" Hal replied.

The owner filled the reporter in on what he'd just learned.

"That's ridiculous," Lebovitz said, "that's two completely misquoted and out of context sentences out of a 1,500-word interview!"

"Well, those are the two sentences the *Journal-American's* editorial board bent the hell out of shape!" Veeck snapped back.

Hal spread his hands, "I can't go get all the newspapers and bring'em back!"

"No," the owner said, "but you can go find Eli. I don't want him walking out the front door into this mess. Lou?"

"Yeah, Bill?"

"Spread the word to the players: their only comment is 'no comment'. You can bet there are reporters out there with those people, and they're just waiting to see a juicy 'ballplayers fight with fans' headline drop right in their laps." Veeck found the waiter, "HEY!"

"Finally ready for that coffee?"

"No," Veeck said, "I need a phone to make a call out."

"In the lobby, sir. White phone by the concierge. The waiter gestured with the coffee sloshing around in the pot.

Veeck speed hopped to the phone in the lobby.

"Number please?" the hotel operator crackled onto the line.

"New York Yankees at Yankee Stadium."

A few clumps and a trill on the line later –

"New York Yankees."

"This is Bill Veeck with the Cleveland Indians, young lady. I need to speak with Larry MacPhail."

"One moment please."

More thumps. "Mr. MacPhail's office."

"Doris, this is Bill Veeck with the Indians. Can I speak to Larry please?"

"He's not in the mood for one of your crazy ideas today, Bill."

"Nothing crazy today," Veeck said quickly. "I need five minutes."

"Hold on, Bill."

Thunk. Click.

"NO. You're not getting Keller for ANY combination of your out-fielders, Bill!"

"Hi, Larry." Veeck smiled. He was starting to get under Larry's skin. It hadn't taken long. "No trades today. I need to ask you something."

"What's up?"

"Have you had people showing up with signs for a protest at the Stadium tonight?"

"Yeah. Some of the ticket staff called up here about it. Worried these people are going to block the windows and turnstiles," MacPhail said.

Veeck said, "You know the reason, right?"

"Yeah," the Yanks GM replied, "they're pretty angry with your kid who refused to even go to the Selective Service center, I hear..."

"What the-" Veeck just about popped, "that's not true! Weaver registered! He's Amish! They don't fight! He served as a C.O. C'mon Larry, your radio stations and newspapers twisted this thing way outta shape! Just send some cops out there and tell the crowd to go home."

"That's not my problem, Bill."

"Jesus, Mary, and Joseph! C'mon Larry, he's a kid. He's 19!"

Now it was MacPhail's turn, "Sure, Bill. And he's also hitting .477, and my pitchers have about six hours to figure out how to stop him. If he's mature enough to put that uniform on, then he's mature enough to handle some fans who might be giving him a hard time outside AND inside the ballpark tonight!"

"Inside...?"

"Yes, Bill," MacPhail was starting to enjoy himself now, "they're buying tickets while they're waiting to protest your 'kid'. And it sounds like they all want to sit in the right field grandstand."

"Thanks for the help, Larry," Veeck exhaled.

"See you later, Bill." Click.

Lebovitz came running back through the lobby. "He's gone, Bill."

"Where is he?"

"Buster was telling Eli all about the subway, so they're taking the "B" to the Stadium."

"So," Veeck breathed deeply again, "Eli's going for his first subway ride to The Bronx with a bunch of people who want him in front of a firing squad."

"What?" the reporter looked at the owner wide-eyed.

Veeck told Hal about his conversation with Larry MacPhail, and the situation developing in front of the ballpark.

"Good God," Lebovitz said.

"We'd better hope so," Veeck replied.

On the "B" Train – Northbound

His arrival in New York City the night before included the approaching skyline as the train swept down the Hudson, the sheer size of Penn Station, and the massiveness of the Hotel Pennsylvania.

Now, on a sweltering Thursday afternoon, his Manhattan baptism continued: the sheer number of people on the subway platform, the rush of wind as the train approached, and the synchronized squeeze of entering the car.

As Buster told him on the platform, now he was with real New Yorkers.

The train rattled and swayed its way northward as the coach gave the rookie the lowdown on the hows and whys of the subways in a city of seven million people.

As they rolled toward The Bronx however, they began to notice the tourists, the shoppers, and the businessmen skipping out on afternoon meetings exiting the train, and being replaced by...

The angry.

Eli looked at them with curiosity.

Buster looked at them with concern.

Trying to figure out what they were in the middle of was not necessarily easy. Buster tried to read the signs some of the people were carrying, but he didn't want to tilt his head sideways and appear too curious – too much like a tourist.

As the train approached Harlem, Mills finally got a clear view of one of the signs:

"IF HE DIDN'T SERVE – HE SHOULDN'T PLAY"

"Didn't serve...?" Buster wondered...

A few seconds later, any questions the pair had were answered by the young men who squeezed into a space in the middle of the car directly behind where Eli and Buster were standing with their arms in the straps above them.

"What's the punk's name?"

"Weaver. Eli Weaver."

"Yeah. Said he wouldn't fight because of his religion."

"My older brothers killed Krauts all across Europe, an' the priests said the Mass with them twice a week."

"DiMag, Williams, Spahn – they all served."

"Feller – his teammate – fought the Japs!"

"Wonder how that'll go over in the locker room?"

The train climbed, and transitioned from subway to elevated. Sunlight flooded the car. Eli stared at Buster. Neither of them moved a muscle.

"He'll take his buggy home cryin' to mommy after tonight."

The speaker on the subway car crackled to life.

"161ST – YANKEE STADIUM"

The train began to decrease in speed, and the protestors began to huddle towards the doors.

As they were jostled, Buster grabbed Eli's arm, and pretended to steady himself against the sway of the subway car.

Mills leaned in toward Eli, trying to whisper over the noise as quietly as he could. "When the train stops, let them out. We go last."

Eli nodded his head once.

The train lurched to a stop. The doors flew open, and the sweaty group of protestors on the train joined the sweaty group of protestors already on the platform.

"WON'T FIGHT!"

"CAN'T PLAY!"

As the last of the mob cleared the doors, they began to close.

"Now," Buster said quietly.

"But, the doors-" Eli blurted.

"GO." Buster stuck out his arm, and held the door as they stumbled out on the platform. "Follow them."

"BAN WEAVER NOW! BAN WEAVER NOW!"

"Go ahead," the coach leaned into Eli again, "let's join the protest."

Eli completely missed the great sight of the historic stadium rising up before him as he and Mills shuffled slowly behind the angry fans.

His mind was swimming. Who were these people? Why did they hate him? What had he done? What would they do if they knew who he was? His father, his uncles, the older men playing checkers outside Schlabach's in Mt. Hope, they'd all told him about the anger inside the English, and how irrational that anger could become. He looked at the people around him as Buster encouraged him to chant against himself.

Would they rid themselves of this anger by showering it upon him? Or, would they take it home with them, and pass it on to others? "The tongue is a fire, a world of iniquity," the Bible said. Was this what the world outside of Holmes County was truly like? Baseball was fun. It was easy for him. But, if this was what he faced outside his own people, was it worth it?

Buster tugged at his sleeve.

"They're headed for the players' entrance," he pointed.

"What do we do?" Eli felt slightly panicked.

"To the left, look-" Buster nodded, "see where those vendors are going?"

Mills guided the rookie away from the mob.

The vendor's door was guarded by a man who may not have moved since the day the park opened. Buster fast-talked his way through and pointed toward the visitors' clubhouse as he and Eli raced past.

In the darkened concourse, the just hosed-down concrete added a damp cool to the heat outside, and there was the smell of hot dogs beginning to cook.

"Do they hate me, Buster – or what I believe?" Eli asked with confusion.

"You're different, kid." Buster shook his head. "We-uh, English don't like different."

The two began walking through the shadows toward the clubhouse.

"They don't even *know* me, Buster." Eli had never shown frustration on the field, but this was different. "They certainly don't know what I said to Hal – because I didn't say anything like *this*!"

"I know you didn't, kid. I read Hal's story, and it was just right." Buster shook his head. "Some people aren't satisfied with right, I guess."

The most famous rookie in the major leagues laughed. "They were standing right next to me, and they had no idea who I was!

Buster put his hand on the doorknob to the visitors' clubhouse and smiled. "Nope. They didn't know you from Adam."

Eli shook his head sadly.

They walked down the ramp toward the clubhouse. Eli looked up at his coach as Buster patted Eli on the chest.

"Because they don't have a picture of you."

THURSDAY NIGHT
JULY

Yankee Stadium – Indians vs. New York

"He's gotta' play, Bill. I need that bat," Boudreau said as he looked at his boss.

"I know, Lou," Veeck replied. "I hate to admit it, but MacPhail's right. We put a uniform on the kid, he needs to be out there... and take whatever's coming his way. It's not right to hide him. By the way, where is he?"

"Out playing catch with Buster," the manager replied.

"Good Lord," Bill muttered.

Over 50,000 people were entering the ballpark, and most of those already inside were showering boos down upon two of the men playing catch in the outfield.

"You sure know how to make friends, rookie," Mills almost yelled, as he threw to Eli.

"Do the fans always throw food onto the field?" Eli said, trying to conceal his concern. "It seems like quite a waste."

"If I throw one over your head, and it rolls toward the grandstand –

leave it lie," the coach yelled as the boos reached their peak every time Eli caught one of his throws.

An empty beer bottle landed six feet from Eli's feet. "I think I'm warmed up."

"Me too," Buster said quickly, "let's get outta' here."

Inside the clubhouse, the booing was more felt than heard.

The Cleveland Indians, dressing for the game at their locker stalls, had been confronted with the New York newspaper and radio opinions of the lack of Eli's military service from the revolving doors of the Roosevelt, to the clubhouse door of Yankee Stadium.

Eli's teammates were in a foul mood. Regardless of how they felt about their quiet, young Amish teammate (they definitely thought he was a bit weird), they were unanimous in their thoughts that some of the New York media had crossed the line on an issue that they didn't even try to understand.

Player/manager Boudreau stepped to the center of the room. "All right, we know what Chandler's done to us already this season. We're going to have to be *patient*. Do not go fishing out there. You see a ball headed for the outside corner, *let it go*. It's gonna fade on ya' – you know that. If we scratch out 2 or 3 runs, Bob'll take us home. Let's go."

Short and sweet. Not a word about what was happening off the field.

The tone of the evening quickly became apparent with the announcement of the Indians' starting lineup.

"Batting fourth – the right fielder – numbah 17..."

The booing roared to life from the right field grandstand.

The protest signs began to wave.

The noise caught a large number of the fans in the box seats by surprise. A mainly white-collar suburban or Manhattanite group, their media choices were not the same as the anti-Weaver blue-collar crowd in the cheaper seats. The box seat fans could be seen leaning back or forward to ask their fellow Yankee fans what was up with number 17... and a large number of shrugging shoulders could be seen.

Spud Chandler surrendered a bloop single to Cleveland's leadoff hitter, George Case. After quickly dispatching Conway and Wasdell, it was time for the opening act of the evening's drama.

"For Cleveland – numbah 17 – Eli Weav-"

The boos and catcalls again rolled out of the right field corner.

This time however, the fans in the boxes joined in – convinced, no matter what shred of evidence they had heard from each other or the hot dog vendor – that this young man had insulted or besmirched God, America, or the New York Yankees in some way.

Chandler's first pitch – a fastball – buzzed past Eli on the inside corner.

"STRIIIII-" was the umpire's energetic call.

The fans in The Bronx ate it up.

On 0-and-1, Chandler's curve was (as Boudreau had said in the clubhouse) dipping away from the outside corner from almost the moment the ball left his hand.

Eli waved at it as it passed him. He wasn't even close.

"TWO!!!"

The roar around Eli was louder now.

He thought about home for a split second.

An evening breeze and lemonade on a summer night in Holmes County.

Taking Rachael home as the sky darkened colorfully around them as they crested the last hill near her parent's farmhouse-

Chandler had the sign, and began his stretch – snapping the rookie back to reality.

Fastball. High and-

Eli's head snapped back as the ball passed his chin.

He completely lost his balance, and landed in an uncoordinated, un-athletic sprawl outside the batter's box.

A small cloud of powdery dirt surrounded him like a halo.

The Yankee fans went wild.

"How doya' like New York so far, rook?" Robinson – the Yanks' catch-er was smiling from ear to ear inside his mask.

Eli dusted himself off as best he could, stepped immediately back into the batter's box, and cocked the bat behind his head as he stared out at the pitcher... waiting.

It's going to be a curveball – Eli said to himself.

It was.

Eli timed it perfectly.

Eli missed it almost completely.

He felt the slightest contact as his wrists whipped the bat around – his swing so hard he felt he was losing his balance again.

Eli stumbled out of the box as the baseball floated toward the Yankee pitcher on one soft, high hop.

Chandler waited for the ball to fall into his mitt, took a couple steps toward the bag, and ended the inning with a soft flip of the ball to his first baseman.

In a ballpark that had been shaken by so many great moments, great games, and great players, rarely had The House That Ruth Built heard a roar that filled so many with such satisfaction.

Boudreau pulled up twenty feet from Eli, and flipped the right field-er his glove.

"Get'im next time," his manager said as he jogged to his shortstop position.

In the bottom half of the innings, the fans in the right field grandstand unleashed their media-infused anger upon Eli.

"GO BACK WHERE YOU CAME FROM!"

"SCREW YOU, BUGGY BOY!"

As the game continued – and Eli tried to remain focused on it – the fans' attempts to rattle him became a wall of noise where individual sounds were swallowed up within the group's own chaos.

After Eli's weak pop-up in the 4th, the fans got organized.

"WON'T FIGHT. CAN'T PLAY! WON'T FIGHT! CAN'T PLAY!"

In the bottom of the 5th, already up 4-1, the Yanks exploded for 5 more to put the game away.

The capper came with the bases loaded when the Yankees' catcher Aaron Robinson lined a ball over the first base bag, and down the right field line.

Because the right field corner in The Bronx was closer to home plate than in almost any ballpark in the major leagues, Eli was at a full sprint to cut the ball off before it reached the corner. He slid to a stop at the spot where he felt the ball would ricochet to his glove when it kicked off the stands.

It didn't.

"-and OHH it's under Weaver's mitt-the ball hugging the grandstand wall, and still rolling! Weaver runs it down, and OHHMY – Weaver's been hit in the back by two full cups of beer!

Three runs are home!

Robinson has a triple!

Weaver is soaked!

...the Bombers now lead 9-to-1, and Bobby Feller's night is done, as

Boudreau takes the baseball from his ace's hand. Krakauskas is coming on to pitch, and I'll be back to sort out the damage after Bob gives you this word from Erin Brew – Cleveland's beer for baseball."

A BEER CHASER FROM THE FANS IN THE BRONX

"The Yanks – especially Robinson – had my number tonight." Bob Feller was sitting in his undershirt in front of his locker. He stood and shook his head. "That's just baseball, boys. I've had their number before, and I'll have it again soon."

The reporter from the *Journal-American* nudged his way to the front of the group in front of Feller's locker. "So what do you think of this guy on your team who wouldn't fight for his country?"

Feller had gathered his toiletry bag, and was ready to hit the showers, but he spun around immediately to face the reporter.

"Look," Feller said as he pointed at the scribe, "he's entitled to believe-"

"You fought for your country."

"Shut up while I answer your question," Feller snapped. "Yes, I did. Enlisted on December 8th, and served proudly. But when I served on the Alabama, I served for every American. I'm not a big religious guy, but I served for everyone's freedom of religion, including Weaver's – and for your freedom of speech. Where did you serve, by the way?"

The reported slipped out of the semicircle around Feller and headed for Eli's locker stall.

"Dear God-" Boudreau said, as he stepped to stop him.

Veeck's arm stopped the manager.

Buster Mills saw him coming as well, and looked at the owner.

Veeck motioned "let him talk" in Eli's direction.

"What happened out there tonight, Eli?" the reporter from *The Plain Dealer* asked.

"I was too jumpy," Eli said softly. "Mr. Boudreau gave some pointers on that pitcher before the game, but I guess I couldn't help myself."

The reporter from the *New York Post* jumped in, "Were you rattled by the size of the crowd?"

"I don't think so," Eli said, "I guess my results say something different."

The reporter from the *Journal-American* moved in front of Hal Lebovitz, who glared at him.

"What gives you the right to play in America's pastime if you won't fight for your fellow Americans?" It was more an accusation than a question.

"Hey!" Feller was walking across the room to intercept the reporter.

"Bob-" Veeck shook his head.

Eli turned and took a step toward the reporter. The reporter flinched as Eli stood, and looked down at him. Weaver outweighed the man by at least 40 pounds.

"My people – the Amish – have always believed in non-violence, that God is King, that His Kingdom is above every nation, and that He will always preserve His people," Eli began softly. "We were persecuted for this throughout our history in Europe. Here in America, we have been looked on as strange, but not persecuted. We are thankful for where we live, and how we're allowed to live. We simply believe that God is the ultimate King, not any king of this earth."

The room was quiet.

Eli stared at the reporter.

"You didn't write that down," Eli said quietly. "Isn't it your job to write down the things we say?"

Veeck laughed loudly.

So did Eli's teammates.

Feller winked at Eli and walked back to his locker smiling.

FRIDAY JULY 12

The Hotel Roosevelt – New York City

DEAR RACHAEL,

It is a rainy day here in New York, and there will be no ball game tonight.

I'm sorry it has been so long between letters. It seems we are always moving, and I never know rightly where I am. But that is no excuse for not writing.

I'm sure you heard about my talk with the newspaper man from Cleveland. It seems that many people outside of Cleveland read it. I'm not sure how that works, but my talk about our Amish ways made many people angry in this city. I can't tell you some of the awful things they yelled at me last night for it is not proper. I was not angry at them in return. I did feel sorry for them. If they are so angry at someone they have never met, I think I understand how the English can get so violent so fast.

There is not much about this life I think you would like. Here in

New York I have seen almost no grass at all. There are too many people, too much noise, and no cows or horses – I have realized they are much more easy to reason with than city English.

One thing I know you would like very much are the trains. To travel by train is like nothing I have known. After playing baseball, the train is my favorite thing now. I eat meals brought to me on fancy dishes as we travel. We sleep in a special railroad car with beds in it. And to sit and watch the country go by my window is amazing. America is a much bigger place than we were taught at our school, Rachael. Some of the farms I see make ours look humble and small. I think all the English farms must have tractors. I can not think how they could farm without them. Oh what I could do if the Bishop would let me have a tractor or two! Please forgive me for that.

Rachel, here is exciting news!

Bill Veeck is the man who is my boss. He would like you, your parents, my parents, and my brothers and sisters to come to the baseball games in Cleveland on Friday, August 2 and Saturday, August 3. Mr. Veeck will send someone to get you. He will give you a place to stay. You will see 2 baseball games. One game will have fireworks! On Saturday after the game, Mr. Veeck will have you home in time to sleep well before rising for Sunday service. <u>Do not worry it will not cost a dime. Veeck will pay for all of it.</u> I know my father did not like him when they first met. But he is a very nice English. He cares for those who work for him very much. I think everyone will like him better this time you meet. Before I left I gave you the number of the lady in the ball club office. Her name is Ada. The next time you go into town, use the phone outside Schlabach's to call her and tell her you will all come. Please do.

I miss you terrible. Our walks and rides together after Sunday dinner were most special. I have a calendar in my room in Cleveland,

and I "X" every day at the end before I go to sleep. It reminds me that it is one less day until I am home.

Baseball is just as fun as I thought it would be. The people yelling and cheering for me at the games makes it hard to be modest, though. It is giving me a swelled head I think. Don't tell my father that. He always said I had one anyway. Do you think that too? Hope not. I will always love baseball. God made me good at it. I think he also made me good at smithing and planting, but baseball is more fun. I hope God is happy when he watches me play. Do you think he cares about that, Rach?

But I never thought I would miss home and you so much. I always wondered what it would be like to live away from my home and now I know. I miss Mt. Hope. I miss quiet at night, and quiet in the day time. I also know that if I keep going with life in baseball, I could make a lot of money. That money would buy us a farm so big you and I can't imagine it.

There are hard decisions to make and I will have to make them after harvest. For now, I hope you will come to Cleveland on August 2. To see you will be so good.

Tell my brothers and sisters I will send a special package next week for them to share with all at the ball field.

I miss you and think of you so much.

YOURS,

ELI

Yankee Stadium

"Case on first, and Conway on second – we've got a 1-1 nail-biter here in the sixth. Now here comes Weaver again, this time with 2 out. The crowd in right field hasn't let up on him one bit. At least tonight, Eli has remained unsoaked by beer out there. Weaver scorched a single to right and stole two bases in the first. First pitch from Bevens – inside, ball 1.

Weaver died at third on Boudreau's drive that DiMaggio pulled down over 400 feet from home-out by the monuments in left-center.

The 1-0 – LINED to right and FOUL! Weaver has shown no trouble connecting against Bevens-in this game, or when he saw him in Cleveland."

"Solid contact every time, Jack. Bevens hasn't fooled him once."

The stretch, and the 1-1 – Weaver swings and drives it DEEP to left-center – DiMaggio's not gonna get this one! It's rolling toward the monuments – here comes Conway, with Case flying around third right *behind him! DiMaggio ran it down, and fires it – a slide – a cloud at third annnnnnnnnd SAFE! Weaver is safe with a TRIPLE, and the Tribe leads 3-1!"*

"Pretty quiet in the right field grandstand at Yankee Stadium now, Jack. Weaver's been a one-man wrecking crew tonight!"

Third base umpire Bill Summers called time, kicked the third base bag, and smoothed the powdery dirt a bit. As he walked back to his position behind the sack, he brushed by Eli, giving him a quick tap on the rear.

"That's the way to shut'em up, kid," he said softly with his head down. "Good job."

SUNDAY
JULY 14

Fenway Park

The first game of the doubleheader was done. The Indians had scored 10 runs – and lost.

In the Indians' clubhouse between games, Boudreau smacked the chalk on the blackboard so hard as he copied off the lineup, that Eli thought he'd bust the board – or his hand. The player/manager threw the chalk in the tray, turned, and faced his team.

"Have you had enough of Ted Williams? I sure as hell have!" Boudreau looked at the stat sheet in his hand. "4-for-5, *three* home runs, *eight* RBI. If we'd got him out one more time, we would have won the game!"

"All right," Boudreau turned, and erased a section of the blackboard, replacing what was there with a hand-drawn baseball diamond, "I've been thinking about this for a long time, so here's what we're gonna do when Williams comes up in game two:"

Lou drew three large dots between first and second base. "Jimmy, I want you to play first base at the cut of the grass and on the line. Jack, you're going to play second by moving to your left – halfway between the bags, but 15-20 feet out on the outfield grass. I'm playing shortstop right here – almost in Jack's normal spot near second."

Boudreau drew another large dot at the shortstop's usual position.

"Kenny, you're playing third from my usual shortstop spot."

Keltner nodded.

Most of the players were trying not to look at their manager as if he were nuts.

"In left," Boudreau plowed ahead. "George, you need to play halfway between Kenny and that wall. Tight enough to swallow up a blooper, deep enough to scramble back to track one down. Pat, you gotta lotta room out there in center – if we play deep enough in the infield, you just need to make sure Teddy doesn't blast one over your head."

Okay, Eli," the manager turned to his young right fielder. "You've got to cut balls off at the line, before they wrap around that low wall, and – if the ball makes it to the wall, you have to keep balls away from rolling toward that cutout that goes to 420 feet. Can you do that?"

"Yes, sir," the rookie said confidently.

"All right. I want to try this shift every time Ted comes up," Lou said, as he took a breath and calmed down a bit. "We'll stop that Williams."

There was a pause. "Or, at least slow him down a bit."

Boudreau's team looked back at him doubtfully.

Lou smiled. "Or, we'll give the writers plenty to write about. Let's go."

Hal Lebovitz scribbled in his reporter's notebook:

7/14 game 2 – Sox 6 Clev 4

Eli 2/5 single HR RBI

Interesting shift pulled by Tribe every time Williams at bat. Ted went 1-for-2 with 2BB. Kept looking out at the alignment after almost every pitch. Still tried to pull everything, though. Admitted after the game that it bugged him a little.

Eli still pull-happy as all get-out. Single was hit so hard off the wall that Williams short-hopped the ricochet, and flipped it to 2nd – he was laughing as he did it. Everything else Eli hit was popped up into Williams' glove. Overswinging like crazy. Zuber finally messed up in the 7th – Eli hit it onto Landsdowne Street. Saw Lou and Buster in clubhouse. They tried to get Eli to use the whole field like he always does, but left field wall is in his head.

Big difference between Splendid Splinter and Eli being pull-happy: Ted's a star – Weaver's a rook.

7/16 – Indians 6 Bos 4

Williams 2/5 1RBI for Sox – still pulling into the shift. Lou sez "At least we got him out 3 times." Ha.

Eli 0/4 3 Ks – Nice to slow Sox down a little, but they're headed for the World Series (unless there's a <u>complete</u> collapse) Back here in 6 weeks. Maybe blinders would be a good idea for Eli.

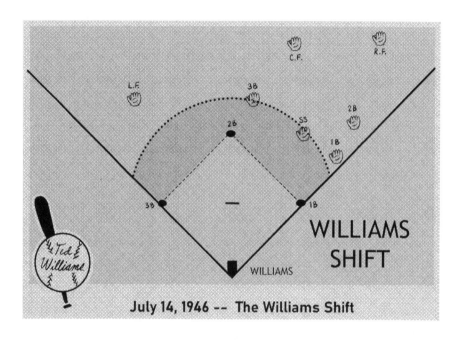

July 14, 1946 -- The Williams Shift

FRIDAY
JULY **19**

Shibe Park – Philadelphia

Eli knew what Buster and Boudreau had told him in Boston was true. He saw that big green wall the first time he stepped on the field for batting practice, and yes, he wanted to hit every ball pitched to him clean over it.

His manager had told him to keep his eyes on Boston's left fielder. Williams.

Williams hit every ball hard. And, he seemed to hit every ball he wanted to hit, whenever he wanted to hit it.

"Just the same way you do back home," Buster said when Eli came back in the dugout after chasing one of Williams' drives into the right-center field alley a few moments before.

Eli knew Mills was right.

But that wall was so **close**.

"So, when did the light finally come on for you in Boston?" Buster said, as he tossed the ball to Eli.

"What?" the rookie replied.

"Oh yeah," Mills laughed, "you don't have lights back home. When did you finally realize we were tellin' ya the truth?"

"That last time up," Eli admitted, as he zipped the ball back to his coach. "Remember how I kinda spun around in the box?"

"Just like a ballerina." Buster shook his head as he caught Eli's throw. "Didn't think it was possible for you to strike out three times in a game."

"Me either," the rookie shrugged. "But… it was just like you and Lou said… they kept pitching me more and more outside every time."

"And…?" Buster spread his arms, then threw the ball back to Eli.

"And, I kept chasing everything they threw."

"Because…?"

Eli frowned, and tried to be angry with his coach, but he knew that he was the one wearing the goat horns. "I was trying to hit the darn ball over that wall."

"Did you just say 'darn'?" Buster winked after he winced while catching Eli's sizzler.

"Yes," Eli laughed.

"We English really are corrupting you," the coach flipped the ball back to the rookie. "Clubhouse meeting… let's go."

Now, after two games in Philadelphia, Eli was as hot as he could be.

He bounded up the dugout steps after the team meeting, and couldn't wait for the top of the first.

Eli stepped on the field, and felt another big day coming his way.

"Hey Eli," Jim Hegan yelled from the batting cage, "I think your fans are out there in the right field corner."

The rookie looked up, and his heart jumped.

The Amish stood out from the crowd wherever you saw them, but nowhere more than amidst the bright colors of a ballpark.

In the right field lower deck were a few dozen of Eli's Pennsylvania "cousins", and Eli Weaver was sprinting to the corner almost as soon as he saw them.

The rookie heard the young boys first.

"Eli!" "Eli Weaver!"

For the next 10 minutes, Eli was "home". The firmest of handshakes. Backslaps. The conversation in the language of his people. For just that short period of time, the smiles were genuine, and the homesickness vanished. Familiar surnames, horse talk, barn raisings, hay cuts, and talk about the progress of the crops were in the air. The city sights and sounds that surrounded them faded for just a while. The only annoyance was the Philadelphia newspaper photographers who kept appearing from every corner of the park, snapping away at the scene, while the Amish turned away, or ducked their heads from each spying lens with perfect timing based on years of experience.

Mills stood at the top step of the dugout with Boudreau, watching the "homecoming" scene in the right field corner.

"Ya' think he knows he needs to take batting practice?" the Texan drawled.

"Ah, let's let it go. This is doing him a world of good," the manager replied. "Besides, the way he's hitting right now..."

As Eli looked at the field, and realized he needed to get back to work, the Amish ladies sensed that this was their moment. They produced three large baskets and presented them to Eli.

"For you and your team," they said in Pennsylvania Deutsche.

The young Amishman knew what he would smell before he even lifted the lid.

The Indians' pitchers in right field shagging flies picked up the scent quickly.

"Hey, rook! Whattya have there?"

Arriving on the scene, the mood of an entire team on a long road trip brightened considerably.

"Look at this postgame meal, boys!"

By this point, the entire ballclub was jogging toward the right field corner.

"Okay, guys – batting practice is over," Boudreau said to the empty batting cage.

For the rest of the night, between innings, or as pitchers made their way to the bullpen, Boudreau smiled to himself as he noticed all of his players detouring to the Amish fans in the right field corner. They thought what they were doing was going undetected, but the number of balls in the ball bag, and the number of bats in the bat rack kept shrinking. And, as the game wore on, the number of smiling Amish children with a baseball, a bat, or both... kept rising.

Meanwhile, the Indians were playing the game at a record clip (No doubt anticipating the postgame feast to come). The ancient Mel Harder, and the A's Bob Savage breezed through four scoreless innings.

Then, in the 5th:

"So, Hegan – not fleet of foot – has to hold at third. Case is still behind the Tribe catcher at second, and Conway's now on first, after that sharp single up the middle. They're loaded for Weaver."

"A rough night for the rookie, Jack. Weaver has struck out, and grounded into a double play."

"He has quite a group of Amish fans – clad in their traditional garb – gathered in the right field corner watching his every move. Savage now works carefully – SWING and a miss! The right-hander jammed him up-

and-in right there. Eli settles back in. Savage with the sign, and the lon-nng stretch... here it comes... called strike two! Outside corner – Weaver flinched, but didn't offer, and now he's in a real hole."

"Oh, those Amish kids in right field are jumping up and down, waving their bats, imploring a hit out of Weaver right now...... hey... where'd they get those baseball bats...?"

Weaver is ready. And here's the right-hander's delivery:

High... fly... ball to left. Stainback is cruising over... it's hooking... and... it's... GONE!"

"Just inside the pole!"

"A grand slam for Weaver, a 4-nothing lead for the Tribe, and delirium – or at least the Amish equivalent – across the way in the lower deck in right field!

"And Eli turns as he crosses home plate, and tips his cap to his admirers in the right field corner."

"I'll tell ya', that ball may have grazed the '340' sign as it dropped into the front row of that pavilion out there, but it sure does count! 4-nothing Cleveland in the 5th!"

As Eli scooped his glove up from short right field, and ran to his position, he came out to a tremendous a roar as three dozen Amish have ever mustered. Small hands were reaching out for his. Old, gnarled hands that had worked the soil for 50 years slapped him on the back. Some of the fans weren't exactly comfortable with hearing the excited calls to the rookie ballplayer yelled in German, but they couldn't help their own smiles at the scene.

"Hey! HEY!!! '17'!!! First base umpire Art Passarella stood with his hands on his hips, 30 feet out on the outfield grass.

Eli turned and saw the little man in the coat and tie with the small-billed cap staring at him with hands now stretched out toward him.

"Ump?" Eli said.

"May we continue our little game here?"

"Yeah…" the rookie replied. "Sorry!"

The Amish fans waved at Passarella, the only man on the field dressed remotely close to how they were. Plainly. In dark colors.

The umpire paused – smiled just a bit – and waved back… as inconspicuously as he could.

The players on both sides saw it and were ribbing the veteran ump the rest of the night.

Three innings later, Eli got one more swing.

"Weaver snuck a grand slam just over the fence in the left field corner in the fifth, and now, the left-hander Griffeth will take his measure of this hard-hitting rookie.

Griffeth loves that curve ball-"

"And Jack, I'm sure I saw Mills pull Eli aside in the dugout before this inning started. Buster may have been telling the rookie exactly that."

"From the full windup, Griffeth delivers-

SWUNG ON AND BLASTED TO DEEP CENTER! HOW FAR? HOW FAR??? That one cleared the right centerfield wall in the deepest part of the park! A tremendous drive onto 20th Street that might have bounced into one of the row houses across the way!"

"Jack, I don't know if Jimmie Foxx himself ever sent one out there!"

"The Amish fans in right field are as stunned as everyone else! They're standing and pointing to where that ball left the park!"

"Weaver's teammates – and Connie Mack's A's – are doing the same

from the top step of their dugouts! Jack, I can't imagine where this young man will hit one next!"

"Two home runs tonight for the rookie from Mt. Hope! And now, this ballpark has to calm down so the game can continue!"

"Oh, and by the way friends, the Indians lead is now 5-1, Eli Weaver has knocked in all 5... and the way Old Mel has been slingin'em tonight, I'd say this one's out of reach!"

After the game in the clubhouse, Eli sat and smiled as his teammates gorged themselves on homemade Amish chicken and biscuits, bragging about how many bats and balls they snuck to the Amish kids... "and Lou never knew!"

Eli looked at his manager.

Boudreau smiled back at his phenom, rolled his eyes, and shook his head.

Kenny Keltner stood in the center of the room.

"Eli... none of us knew what to expect when you came here. Some of us thought you were a stunt... something to distract the fans. Because..." the big third baseman paused, "we were playing so stinkin' lousy. And because we all know that our new boss is famous for pulling stunts. But now, we're playing well, we passed the Browns, and we're closing in on Washington – and we're headed the Senators' way for our next three. A lot of that success we've had is due to you."

Boudreau watched the room. All smiles.

Keltner raised his beer. "Thanks for dinner tonight, rook. And thanks for bustin' your ass every day, and reminding us what a privilege it is to play here."

The room went silent.

Keltner smiled. "Okay, guys… GET HIM."

Within seconds, the rookie was covered in beer and foam. Although he'd never really tasted it before, Eli wondered how good it might taste on a hot night like tonight coming from a bottle, and not running down his nose.

SATURDAY
JULY **20**

Washington, DC

Eli had spent the morning walking the National Mall with Buster and Bob Feller.

From the Capitol, to the Washington Monument, to the White House, and along the Reflecting Pool approaching the Lincoln Monument, Feller talked at length about the greatness of the United States.

The rookie had little to say.

America was great, and powerful. Eli certainly couldn't deny that.

He noticed immediately the pride that swelled in his teammate as he looked at the flags encircling the Monument. He saw the respect when sailors in uniform walking The Mall recognized Feller, and wanted to talk with him about his wartime experiences.

At the same time, Eli felt the conflict of who he was, and where he was.

What was he to make of who he was?

He was a citizen of the United States, and yet his faith told him he was a citizen of the Kingdom of Heaven.

What did that mean?

One was a kingdom that could only exist on this earth.

One was a kingdom he could only know after he left this earth.

Eli thought about the walk from the hotel to The Mall. All along the way, he saw them again. The negroes living in the rundown houses just off the main streets. What did that mean? How could all this beauty before him exist just steps away from the poverty he just passed? Eli saw it in Cleveland. And in Boston. And here in the Capital. Couldn't anyone see it? Did they choose not to see it?

As he climbed the steps of the Lincoln Memorial, he turned to look at the awe-inspiring sight, knowing what lay just a few streets beyond. His upbringing was pushing him to ask why everyone couldn't join together to bring every member of the community to livable housing. He knew it would take months... years, even. But, at home, to allow any member of their community to live in such conditions was unthinkable. Everything in his upbringing told him:

To work. To respect. To share the need.

Eli walked into the opening, and looked up at the massive figure of Abraham Lincoln. His eyes looked to the words carved near him... and he read:

"With malice toward none, with charity for all, with firmness in the right as God gives us to see the right, let us strive on to finish the work we are in, to bind up the nation's wounds, to care for him who shall have borne the battle and for his widow and his orphan, to do all which may achieve and cherish a just and lasting peace among ourselves and with all nations."

Eli turned and stared back at Lincoln.

The words rang very true to him.

Abraham Lincoln seemed to have some Amish in his background.

SUNDAY
JULY 21

Mt. Hope

DEAR ELI,

I'm very excited to tell you that our visit to Cleveland is all set.

Miss Ireland has been so nice. We call her every Friday at 11am from Schlabach's when we are in town. She said that Mr. Veeck has made all the arrangements.

As you might guess, your little brothers cannot stop talking about the trip to come. They cannot seem to decide what excites them the most: riding in the bus Mr. Veeck is sending, seeing you play baseball, or the fireworks after the game. (I think it is the fireworks haha)

I believe your father is quite excited, too. Although he will not admit to it.

The community is talking about you. Every time I'm in town, every-one seems a bit more tired than usual, but everyone wants to talk. And you are almost always the favorite topic. People seem to be keeping up very well with what you do every day. I am glad everyone wants to give

167

me their newspapers with the stories telling of what you have done. Do that many newspapers write about every game you play? I have been keeping a scrapbook of the clippings. I think it will be fun to look back on when you return home.

Please return home when this is over, Eli.

I know your father needs you in the fields. We all need you back reshoeing the horses.

And, I need you back, too.

See you soon. But not soon enough.

EVER YOURS,
RACHAEL.

JULY

The State Theater – Euclid Avenue – Cleveland

(music fanfare | on-screen graphic: SPORTS with Mel Allen)

(MEL) **Hello again, everybody! This is Mel Allen – it's time for Fox Newsreel Sports! Shibe Park in Philadelphia was the most recent scene for the heroics of 19-year-old rookie Eli Weaver of the Cleveland Indians.**

(EDIT CLIP: Weaver triples in Phila add bat&ball sound fx)

He's been smackin' the horsehide at a .400 clip. Here, you see him turning Connie Mack's A's every which way but loose as he streaks around the bags for a triple!

(EDIT CLIP: Weaver greeting Amish fans – cut before they turn away from camera)

This young man's literally 'fresh off the farm' – an Amish farm to be exact – and some of his Pennsylvania sisters and brethren came to the City of Brotherly Love to see him play.

(EDIT CLIP: Weaver home run add bat&ball sound fx)

Then came this prodigious blast!

(EDIT CLIP: Smiling boy on rowhouse stoop holding ball)

This young fella didn't have a ticket, but he snagged Weaver's wallop on his front steps – over 500 feet from home plate! HOW A-BOUT THAT?!

(EDIT CLIP: Young ladies wave to Weaver as he approaches dugout)

Sorry, girls – no closeups of this young man. His Amish faith makes him a bit camera shy.

(EDIT CLIP: Boudreau facing camera looks at Weaver's bat / Weaver shown from behind nods as Lou talks)

Player-Manager Lou Boudreau is going be seeing a lot of that big bat in his wigwam's future.

(EDIT CLIP: Weaver home run add ball&bat sound fx)

From shoeing horses on the farm to shooing pitchers from the mound, keep your eyes peeled for this big fella all summer long!

(music fanfare | Fox Movietone News – "It Speaks for Itself")

FIGHTING FOR FOURTH

Lou's Crew Hasn't Solved The Nats Just Yet

Big 6-Game Tilt This Weekend

By Hal Lebovitz

These Indians have me talking to myself.

What's going on with your hometown team?

Well, the ballclub Bill Veeck bought a month ago seems to keep bumping into things.

Are they clumsy?

I don't think it's clumsiness. They just can't climb over the Senators in the standings.

So, Washington's not 'first in war, first in peace, and last in the American League' anymore?

No, they're 4th in the American League, and Our Tribe can't seem to figure out how to get past them.

It's the hitting isn't it?

There are hits. But the timeliest one seems to elude them.

The pitching has been terrific.

There have been fine pitching performances. But nothing seems to be happening at the moment it really needs to.

You certainly can't ask any more from Feller.

He's been magnificent. But, we only get to see him once every four days. Even Rapid Robert has fallen victim to the team's ability to capitalize on opportunities.

What would have happened to this team without Eli Weaver?

Do you really want to keep me awake tonight thinking about that?

He's been terrific, but how long can he realistically keep this up?

Normally, I would give you the standard answer that he can keep hitting like this until his second time around the league-

And the second time the Red Sox saw him, he went 3-for-15...

And the second time he saw the A's pitching, he went 6-for-11 with 2 homers!

Different teams with different talent.

And all major leaguers.

Point taken. So, what about Veeck? What's he doing since he found a needle in a haystack (literally) with Weaver?

What can he do?

A trade or two would be nice.

The problem is 'who' and 'what' does he have to trade?

Weaver.

What?

Who knows if Weaver will ever do again what he's doing now?

Who knows that he won't?

Think about what a 2-for-1 or 3-for-1 trade would bring. Fourth place? Maybe even third. That could set up a bigger deal down the road.

The ladies love Boudreau. The bobby-soxers adore Weaver. Veeck is drawing more fans down to the lakefront than this team ever has before. Do you think he would give away his box office this year, for success next year?

I'm asking the questions here. And Veeck could have success in '47, and for a lot of years after that, if he plays his cards right – you bet he'd make that deal.

You're giving me a headache.

I love big trades. They shake things up.

I'd just love to win 4 out of 6 this weekend, and make the Senators' manager Ossie Bluege blue.

What?

The series with Washington this weekend? Big fireworks show tonight? Getting into 4th place? Getting a big winning streak going into August?

Let's hope Eli has a great weekend. Then, we can talk trade again on Monday.

(sigh)

—30—

MONDAY
JULY 29

League Park – Cleveland

Six games in four days.

Back-to-back afternoon doubleheaders in the late July heat and humidity that is Northeast Ohio, took its toll on the rookie. Eli went 2-for-9 in the Monday twinbill, and overall, the Indians' plans to jump into the first division faded fast – losing the first two. The Indians rallied to sweep the Sunday doubleheader at the lakefront, but then got swept right back again by the Nats in the Monday doubleheader at League Park.

Even Eli's tremendous blast into the left field bleachers over 400 feet away didn't lighten his mood in the locker room afterward. He tilted the back of his head against the cool, concrete wall at the back of his locker.

"Buster, how could I be so tired from playing a *game*?"

Mills sucked on a popsicle. "Six games in four days, kid. It's a lot."

"Yeah, but it isn't keeping a horse still to fit it with shoes while the flies are landing on your nose. Or lifting beams for a barn," Eli said quietly.

"The work is different," Buster said, "but, it's still work."

It was just a game.

Eli detected something different in the clubhouse as well.

In almost a whisper, Eli leaned toward Buster. "These guys giving up...?"

"Not giving up," Buster whispered back, "just facing reality."

The reality that strikes the vast majority of ballplayers as July folds into August.

It's over.

The pursuit of the World Series, the apple of every players' eye in April, slams headlong into some cold realities on some of the hottest days of the year... only two of the 16 major league teams advance to October. This season, the Boston Red Sox ran away early, with the Yankees giving chase as best they could. But as spring turned to summer, Boston's hitting machine shifted into full gear, and even the mighty Bronx Bombers couldn't keep pace... especially after DiMaggio's injury.

For teams like Cleveland, a first division finish meant a little extra money at the end of the season, but to lose 4-of-6 at home – to the team you're pursuing – sends a harder dose of reality through a major league locker room.

And of course, the 69-28 Red Sox were due into Cleveland in less than 24 hours – with the Indians already 23 games behind.

Eli looked across the room at Bob Feller. Rapid Robert hadn't removed his uniform yet. He stared into his locker without looking at anything in particular. Across the room, his manager answered the reporter's questions with a mechanical, monotone voice.

Baseball on the farm had always been fun for Eli. Laughter and bragging rights.

Here it was fun too... but, it was also serious business.

The livelihood the Weaver family extracted from the land year by year – these men extracted from a child's game.

The farm's growing season, and baseball's season roughly mirrored each other in length, but looking around the locker room, Eli now realized that whenever he returned home, there would be another growing season. Another baseball season? Never guaranteed for these men.

Returning home...

Would he?

What a life this was! Hotels. Trains. Fans cheering. Money.

What a life he had. Peace. Quiet. Satisfaction. Family.

Rachael.

She could never walk away from that life.

He did.

For now.

Forever?

Eli sat in front of his locker now.

Not looking at anything in particular.

THURSDAY
AUGUST 1

Cleveland Stadium

The series opener on July 30th was another depressing effort in front of over 56,000 on a Tuesday night at the lakefront. Veeck's promotions were bringing fans to Cleveland Stadium in droves, and attendance was way up. But the sag in the Indians' fortunes sent them to their fifth loss in 7 games.

On the next day, the last day of July, Bob Feller won his 20th game, ended his slump, and got his team pointed back in the right direction with a 4-1, 1-hitter. Feller worked in and out of danger all day walking 9 (and striking out 9), surrendering the lone Boston run on a double play.

"Don't forget, folks: big crowd expected here at Municipal Stadium tomorrow night as the Yankees come to town. It's 'Ohio Dairy Night', with a huge fireworks show after the game – and we hope to see you here... so, the Indians need a run here in the 8th to give Mel Harder a

possible win. Mel's pitched a wonderful ballgame today. The Red Sox have banged out 7 hits, but have only one run to show for their toil. Harder has kept the ball in the park, and kept Moses, Pesky, and Williams at the top of that Boston order from making too much noise. One out, and nobody on for Eli Weaver."

"Eli is in the middle of the first slump of his young career, Jack."

"Weaver has only 3 hits in his last 22 at bats, and his batting average has dropped to .368."

"Honestly Jack, that sounds rather strange – 'dropped to .368'."

"That it does, Bob. So, here's Klinger after setting down the first two in the 8th in relief of Dobson. Righty-righty matchup, and that first one's outside for ball one."

"Weaver didn't reach for that outside curve that time-"

"Klinger works quickly – and another wide one, on another curve, and it's 2-and-0."

"Weaver's been trying to pull that pitch in this 3-for-22 stretch, but he's showing a little more patience late in the game."

"A fastball leans Weaver back – but it's called a strike! No reaction from the rookie, but over 14,000 veteran umpires in the stands are letting home plate umpire Bill Grieve know that he's 100 percent wrong on that one. Klinger's ready again – and the 2-1 – ball 3! Again the slow stuff – again outside. The righthander's ready to go again – the Sox have a train to catch, after all – and that's ball four low. Weaver takes his base."

"How about a steal, Jack?"

"That sounds good to me, Bob – Weaver hasn't been caught picking the pitcher's pocket yet. Klinger toes the slab, and takes the big stretch. He delivers to Becker-and there goes Weaver! Ball one-and the throw to seconnnnnd-NOT IN TIME! A steal for Weaver!"

"The lead run standing at second, and still just one out, with two tries to bring him home."

"Klinger gave Weaver a good look on that first pitch, but Eli just pure-and-simple outran that throw to second... Now, Klinger needs to attend not only to Weaver behind him, but the dangerous Heinz Becker in front of him. The first baseman digs in. The righthander's stretch. And Klinger steps off as Weaver dances away from second. Fans here at the Stadium hooting a bit at the Sox slinger. Becker's hitting from the left side this time, so Pesky is sliding over just a bit more toward the bag. Can't keep Weaver close, though–he's just bouncing out to that big lead again... the 1-0-THERE HE GOES AGAIN! A swing and a miss-throw down to third, NOT EVEN CLOSE! A cloud of dust and Eli Weaver has stolen bases on consecutive pitches!"

"He's stolen 5 bases in 5 attempts we're being told, Jack."

"Well now... a 1-1 count on Becker, and Weaver's 90 feet away with the go-ahead run in the 8th... Boudreau went pale when Eli lit out for third, but now Lou's leading the cheers from the on-deck circle. Weaver keeps edging out as Klinger stretches – and stares right at the rookie... the 1-1... in the dirt! Blocked by the catcher Partee, who pounces on it as Weaver took some bold steps down that third base line."

"These Indian fans have been waiting all afternoon to make some noise, and they've finally a reason!"

"The young rookie in a 3-for-22 slump has walked, and stolen two bases in a tie game here in the 8th-"

"And the crowd is yelling 'GO-GO-GO', Jack – they want Eli Weaver to steal home, too!"

"If he tries Bob, I think Boudreau's going to run out there and tackle him. Lou wants Becker to get a swing... Klinger with the sign. The stretch. The 2-1 pitch-chopped HIGH in the air off the plate! HERE COMES WEAV-

ER TO THE PLATE! Pitcher grabs and flips-the sliiiide-SAFE! SAFE at the plate! 2-1 for the Clevelands!

"Weaver never hesitated, Jack-and the play wasn't even that close!"

"So, the Indians have conjured up a run out of thin air on a walk, two stolen bases, and a fielder's choice chopper back to the mound! There's still only one out, a runner at first, and here comes Boudreau to hit in a game where his boys now have an unlikely 2-1 lead!"

Harder and Joe Berry danced around trouble in the ninth to preserve the win. And, after winning 2-out-of-3 from a team looking to go to the World Series, Eli noticed the renewed spring in his teammates steps in the clubhouse right away.

The reporters had left to file their stories, and Eli sat in front of his locker accepting a handshake from one of his teammates, when the owner limped across the room to his locker.

"All set for tomorrow, Eli. Cy's going down with the bus to pick up your family," Veeck winked, "and the Millers."

The rookie blushed.

Happiness. Hopefulness. And a little twinge of fear.

A fear that he didn't feel on the bases a half hour ago.

FRIDAY AUGUST 2

Cleveland Stadium

Bill Veeck concealed the limp well as he strode down the shallow steps past the box seats to the public address microphone beside the Indians' dugout.

"Good evening, everyone!" Veeck waved as he surveyed the vast ballpark. Full almost all the way to the end of the upper deck in left and right field... more than 60,000, he thought to himself.

"It's Ohio Dairy Night tonight," Bill said, hearing the echo coming back at him. "And, we want you to be sure to stop at the milk trucks stationed all throughout the lower concourse, and grab your FREE ice cream sandwich!" The kids in the crowd let loose with a high-pitched cheer at Veeck's announcement.

"Hey... did everyone get their free cowbell?" Veeck barely got the words out of his mouth before the deafening clatter of 60,000 cowbells rang out in unison. "All RIGHT! That's what we want to hear every time the Yankees are batting!" The Indians fans rang their approval back at their young owner almost immediately.

The crowd began to murmur starting in the left field corner as two cows were led toward home plate along the track.

"Okay," Veeck continued, "there's no way this can be 'Ohio Dairy Night' if we didn't have a good old-fashioned cow milking contest…"

The fans applauded a bit.

"…between the Indians and the Yankees!"

Now the fans were climbing into the palm of Veeck's hand, but he wasn't done setting things up just yet.

"Tonight: a battle of two rookies."

The buzz from the crowd told Veeck they had a good idea who Cleveland's rookie cow-milker would be, and he smiled in anticipation.

"For the Yankees," Bill waited just the right amount for the boos and catcalls before jumping back into ringmaster persona, "a rookie catcher from the The Hill neighborhood in St. Louis, Missouri – Larry Berra!"

Berra had to literally be pushed out of the dugout – which of course, added to the fun of the moment for the crowd.

Veeck couldn't help himself. "You've never seen cows before, am I right, Larry?"

The crowd laughed and applauded.

"Now, for the Indians," the crowd leaned toward the Cleveland dugout to look, and Veeck paused just long enough to hear the cheer start, "our rookie right fielder from Mt. Hope, Ohio-"

Veeck could have said anything after that. He never needed to finish the sentence as the roar went up for Eli. Standing next to the dugout were the Weaver and Miller families.

A few hours before, Eli's reunion with his family (and quite likely his future in-laws) at the Hollenden Hotel took on a number of different temperatures.

His six siblings, four sisters at 9, 12, 14 and 15, were outraced to Eli by his little brothers, age 5 and 6, and the boys quickly caught the fascination of the water fountain in the lobby.

Eli's mom embraced him with a smile. His father – a nod and a firm handshake.

The Millers – still a little more befuddled than proud of their possible future son-in-law, greeted him with smiles and handshakes.

For Rachael, a fast embrace and holding on to Eli's hand was as close as they would be in the next few hours. But, their eyes were meeting at every opportunity – in the lobby, on the bus to the ballpark, and at the clubhouse door.

But now, both families looked around them, mouths open, not able to comprehend the roar of 60,000 baseball fans who had fully embraced the young man who had left them just six weeks before.

As Eli bounded up the dugout steps, the fans stood and roared even louder. The rookie's siblings covered their ears. The Weavers and Millers were dumbstruck.

Rachael looked directly at Eli.

It was a look of amazement, being startled at the cacophony of color and noise, and immense pride.

Eli smiled sheepishly, and with a small shrug in Rachael's direction, ran to his 'position' next to his appointed cow.

"You know the rules, gentlemen," Veeck was sounding as official as he could, "the first to fill his milk pail is the winner. On your marks, get set – GO!"

Berra looked about as lost as a city boy could look in a situation like this.

As expected, the spray was hitting the bottom of Eli's pail with strong regularity, and it was filling quickly.

A few of Berra's more 'countryfied' teammates emerged from the dugout to assist him. The Cleveland fans hollered in protest.

"No, no-" Veeck assured the crowd, "I think the Yankees always play by their own rules!"

The fans booed and laughed simultaneously.

The owner smiled and waved to the Cleveland dugout. The youngest of the Weaver children – the two boys – came to their big brother's side as the crowd's anticipation grew again.

"Now batting for Eli Weaver," Veeck intoned as the crowd hushed to see what twist he had in mind, "also from Mt. Hope, Ohio, Eli's 6-year-old brother, Lukas Weaver!"

The crowd erupted again as Lukas ran to take his brother's place.

Again, the crowd cried foul as an Indians assistant switched the pails underneath Eli's cow, but Veeck waved his hand and lifted the microphone again.

"Wait, wait... let's see how little Lukas can do!"

Immediately, the crowd responded by cheering him on.

And, within seconds it seemed – Lukas' pail was two-thirds full, and a group of Yankees kept squeezing, but delivered little more than a trickle into their first pail.

Veeck wasn't done yet.

"And now," Bill intoned again, "batting for Lukas Weaver, his 5-year-old brother, Isaiah!"

Isaiah sprinted toward his brothers as only a 5-year-old can, leaping into Eli's arms as the ladies in the crowd cried "Ohhhhhhhh!" almost as loud as the rest of the fans cheered.

The Yankee veterans had moved Berra aside, and were straining to complete one full milk pail. Meanwhile, the tiny Amish boy had tuned out the cheers of the crowd and was totally focused and something he had known how to do since he could walk.

When the third pail filled and Veeck declared a victory for the Weaver boys, the Indians players emptied onto the field, and ran straight toward Eli and his little brothers. Brushing past their rookie teammate, they lifted Lukas to their shoulders, while Eli grabbed Isaiah. Both boys got a champion's ride back to the dugout.

The ballpark went wild.

Rachael looked at Eli with a broad smile.

The Weavers and Millers were smiling, too.

And the biggest smile was Veeck's.

He had won the night, and the first pitch was still 15 minutes away.

THE WEAVERS WIN
THE MILKING CONTEST

Veeck had provided the Amish families with field box tickets right next to the Indians' dugout, but Rachael had asked if they could sit in the front row in the right field lower grandstand. She wanted to watch Eli. The idea of the best seats in the house, and seeing some of the finest major league players alive, held no interest for her at all.

As the top of the 1st began, and Eli ran out to his position, the crowd in the right field seats began chanting:

"E-lye, E-lye, EEE-LYE!!!"

Weaver tipped his cap to a big reaction. Eli knew right where his family was sitting, and caught Rachael's eye again. She raised her eyebrows and smiled. Her beau shrugged again and turned to have a catch with the batboy before the start of the inning.

After a leadoff single in the top of the first, Allie Reynolds set the Yankees down quickly.

"So, Seerey gets a free pass, pushing Case down to second, and here comes the 'Ohio Dairy Night' cow milking champion, Eli Weaver!"

"He had a terrific assist in that milking contest from his 5 and 6 year-old brothers, Jack. And those kids may have drawn the biggest applause from this huge crowd so far tonight."

"A fun start to the evening, no doubt. And now, a beautiful sight indeed, Bob. The sight of over 60,000 Indians fans are gathered on the lakefront on a beautiful summer night. Two on, one out. Bonham stretches, and looks toward second. The first pitch to Weaver – there's that breaking ball outside for ball one."

"It's been a while since Eli has went fishing for that low outside curve, Jack. I think he has adjusted to the Yankee pitchers' adjustment."

The 1-0, is IN-side with a fastball. 2-and-0, and Bonham is in trouble at the ballgame's onset. The runners lead again. And here she comes… WEAVER SWINGS, and sends one to deep, DEEP left center! This one's going to bounce and roll… this will clear the bases! Weaver's flying past second, and ROUNDING THIRD – and the relay to the plate has Weaver DIVING back to the bag! Weaver has ANOTHER triple! This huge crowd is going WILD, and the Indians have an early 2-nothing lead on the Yanks!

"His 6th triple in his six-week career, Jack! Remarkable!"

"I'd say young Eli Weaver is faster than a jackrabbit, but that's giving the jackrabbit too much credit!"

In the right field seats, Rachael recognized the daring she knew from back home in Holmes County. But here, a lot of players looked like they had some of Eli's profile and stride. The bagginess of Eli's uniform seemed to conceal the strength and speed she knew was underneath. She looked around her at the fan's response to Eli's hit, and began to understand what Mr. Veeck had tried to explain to her six weeks ago.

Was this the world where Eli truly belonged?

How could any one of her people who played baseball like Eli ever hope to keep their humility as God required?

As Eli came out for the top of the second, the number of fans calling his name continued to multiply.

"Mother, how do all these English know Eli?" 5-year-old Isaiah asked. "Are they all his friends?"

"Isaiah," his mother considered her words carefully, "because Eli is such a good baseball player, he has become very popular among the English, and-"

"Well I want to be such a good baseball player!" Isaiah proclaimed.

His mother reached out her hand to the child, as she turned to reply – and then, pulled back. This theological conversation could wait until she was somewhere other than a giant stadium filled with cheering people, and vendors hawking everything from hotdogs to cotton candy.

The Indians added another run in the 4th, and Reynolds – who had been inconsistent for much of the season – was at the very top of his form tonight.

In the New York 7th, third baseman Billy Johnson led off with a double, and for the first time all night, the Yanks had a runner in scoring position… and with nobody out in the inning.

"BATTING FOR RIZZUTO – NUMBER 5 – JOE DIMAGGIO. DIMAGGIO PINCH-HITTING FOR RIZZUTO."

"So, The Yankee Clipper – injured on and off this season – will be called upon to bat for Rizzuto."

"This is the first opportunity for the Yankees tonight, Jack. You can't blame player/manager Bill Dickey for rolling the dice right here."

"Well, this crowd of 60,000-plus certainly knows that this ballgame could completely change in the next two minutes. Reynolds – working carefully for the first time tonight – checks Johnson at second, and delivers – SLASHED FOUL into the seats down the left field line! Watch out below!

"Oh boy Jack, if that pitch had been a little more out over the plate..."

"Reynolds dodged the proverbial bullet right there. The stretch, and the 0-1 – a ball WELL outside."

"Reynolds is not fooling around there, Jack. He was playing 'keep away'.

"And now the 1-1 – DRIVEN to deepest right center, this is ALL KINDS OF TROUBLE!"

The fans around her were cursing the line drive rocketing between the outfielders as Rachael stood and said in a loud voice that surprised even her –

"He's going to catch the ball."

Her parents looked at her, but Eli's father was on his feet as well.

"He's got it," Elijiah Weaver said calmly – but loudly.

A second later, parallel to the ground, and fully extended, the ball landed in Eli's glove. Another split second, and he crashed to the track, and rolled over once on the grassy incline – then back down to the track – extending his left arm to show the ball inside his mitt.

The roar literally shook the ballpark.

But, the play wasn't over.

Johnson had already rounded third and taken his first steps toward home.

Eli sprang to his feet, and fired the ball toward second, where Boudreau was waiting for it. Even though it arrived on one hop, it arrived in plenty of time for the shortstop to cradle it, step on second base, and show the ball to the umpire, who raised his right arm dramatically.

"A DOUBLE PLAY!!! Bedlam in the ballpark!!! I do not believe The Gray Eagle – Tris Speaker himself could have made that play!

"Johnson is standing to the left of second, and DiMaggio is standing to the right of the bag. They both have their hands on their hips staring out at Eli Weaver!"

"The fans in right field are throwing their hats in the air, and it looks like some hot dog wrappers have been turned into confetti in the

DIMAG DENIED!

upper deck! Goodness GRACIOUS – I hope the newsreel cameras were running for that play!!!"

Fans in the seats surrounding the family were pounding Elijiah Weaver on the back.

"Ohh, I've seen him make many catches better than that one," Elijiah explained to the fans behind him paying rapt attention. "Once I saw that boy disappear into a cornfield to pull one in – farther away than that, too," the now-proud father's memory growing more selective by the minute.

His wife turned to him and gently squeezed his leg. Usually that slowed her husband down a bit. But not tonight.

You, too? She thought, as the crowd continued to buzz.

Rachael's eyes had remained locked on Eli. She watched him look up and tip his cap to the fans. Then, his eyes sought out hers.

He tipped his cap again. Directly at Rachael.

There was no embarrassed shrug this time. Just a nod. And a very obvious wink.

Oh my, Rachael thought as she turned red in an instant.

Reynolds cruised through the final seven batters, and his two-hitter got the Tribe a 3-0 win, and another great roar.

Within moments of the game's end, Bill Veeck and an assistant escorted the families through a gate down the right field line, to the Indians' dugout, to watch the fireworks with Eli.

As the great banks of lights extending upward from the upper deck were extinguished, and the fireworks began to rise from behind the center field bleachers, the young Amish girls and boys – and their parents were captivated by the color and the sound.

Eli's hand found Rachael's hand.

And for the first time in over six weeks, they were alone.

In a sea of 60,000 people.

But, as alone as they could possibly be.

SATURDAY
AUGUST 3

"So. When are you coming home?"

Elijiah Weaver was as direct as ever, his son thought.

It was a beautiful summer day and the sight of Amish families enjoying a picnic by Wade Lagoon, surrounded by the city's museums and cultural center, was not one that Clevelanders were used to. Bill Veeck's secretary Ada organized the excursion before the bus would take the Weavers and Millers back to Holmes County.

"Hey, Eli! Great game last night!"

Of course, the other thing about a large Amish family picnicking in the middle of a bustling city of nearly a million, was the fact that if one of the members of that family was a star rookie major league baseball player, he was certain to be noticed. Often.

"Hey Eli, would you sign an autograph for me?"

As the fans crowded around, Eli's father was crowded out. Eli could feel his agitation from ten feet away.

When the well-wishers had moved on, Eli and his father continued their walk around the lagoon.

"I didn't want to interrupt your being famous," Elijiah Weaver said flatly.

"They care, father. They just want to say so."

"So, you are not coming home."

Eli knew he would have to choose his words carefully. "When I signed that contract in June, I committed to play baseball here in Cleveland until the end of the season."

"October. After much of the harvesting is done," Elijiah said. "Not much point in you ever coming home then, is there?"

"Hey, you're Eli Weaver! Wow! Can my kids have your autograph? C'mere kids, look – it's Eli Weaver!"

After another round of signing for that family, and the others who were attracted by the commotion, the walk resumed. Elijiah was fuming.

"Your mother is worried sick that you will not return. The Millers think you are going to turn their daughter to the English life. Your sisters haven't spoken to you much, have they? They don't know what to make of you in English clothes. And your brothers. Their heads are full of English baseball. They want to be just like you! To leave their family, their faith, their way of life..."

Eli placed his hand on his father's shoulder and turned him so their eyes met. "*When* have I *ever* said I'm not coming home? *When*?"

"You don't have to say it." Elijiah waved his hand derisively at his son. "How will you turn your back on all of this being famous – the same way you turned your back on us?

"Eli! Hey, Eli! Can we have your autograph?"

As the next group of autograph seekers surrounded him, Eli watched his father shake his head and climb back up the path to the picnic.

Eli signed every autograph for every fan who surrounded him. When he looked back up the small hill, he saw Rachael looking down at him.

First with a smile.

Then with concern.

Saturday Evening

The goodbyes were sad, but not prolonged, as Eli stood at the steps of the bus.

His family was beginning a 3-hour journey home to Mt. Hope.

With all eyes watching, his goodbye with Rachael was short, but sweet.

"Don't change, Eli," she whispered in his ear before she climbed the steps.

With all eyes watching, his goodbye with his father was short, and definitely not sweet.

"Be home for harvest," he said curtly before turning and climbing the steps.

The first, whispered words, were a request.

The last were more of a direct order.

As he watched the bus round the corner and turn south, Eli started walking.

The humidity soaked his shirt through within the first few blocks but Eli kept moving. He turned east on Carnegie, head down, trying to force thoughts through his head that would help him sort out his situation.

His father was right.

He was the oldest son, Eli knew. The farm would pass to him. His responsibility lay there. His family, his place in his community, his standing before God – it was all tied to God's will for his life – his farm. His people. His home.

But... what about God's will?

It hadn't taken him six weeks to notice that there was no one with the Indians who could hit the ball, who could throw, or who could run... like he could.

If he continued to play, Eli thought – as he walked the city blocks – he could make enough money from the English that he could do anything he wanted. Live anywhere he wanted. Be anything he wanted – when those days after baseball inevitably came.

His father – and the elders at home – would call that *pride*.

But, what if that was *reality*? At least among the English...

Eli looked up mid-thought as he heard the music reach his ears. He turned right down the side street and walked toward it. He convinced himself 30 minutes ago that he just needed to walk awhile to clear his head. But now, in his heart, Eli knew where he had intended to wind up the entire time on this Saturday evening.

Shiloh Baptist Church.

Oscar saw him right away, and this time, pulled Eli up to sit in the fourth row with his family. If the young Amish man had been sprinkled in his first worship experience at Shiloh, this visit was a full-immersion baptism.

Seated about fifteen feet from the choir, Eli let the hymns and spirituals, the melodies and the goose-pimple producing harmonies, wash him clean.

He listened intently and let the prayers of these worshipers – so distant from his own tradition – become his own.

Thirty minutes later, the pastor spoke. Directly to Eli. Or so he thought.

"...and Jeeeesus said, to 'let our light so shiiiiiine before men, that they might SEE our good works, AND GLORRR-ify our Father in heaven'! You get that?

When y'all shinin', it's not so people can see YOU! Y'all are shinin' so that you DISAPPEAR, and people can only see the Jeeeesus IN you!

They need to see HIM where you work!

They need to see HIM in your home!

*They neeeeed to see Jeeeeesus in YOU in the days of change that are comin' – and comin' **SOON!!!**"*

The congregation – and Eli – were on their feet.

SUNDAY AUGUST 4

Cleveland Stadium

"What's the matter with you?" Buster snapped as he fired the ball at Eli's head.

"Nothin'." Eli caught the throw with a flick of his glove and lazily tossed the ball back toward his coach.

"Nothin'?" Mills said as returned the ball hard in Eli's direction. "That's not nothin'. That's whinin' like a little boy 'cause yer girlfriend went home."

"Shut up, Buster." Now Eli sizzled one back at his coach's chest. "It's not her. It's my father. He started in yesterday as soon as I saw him about coming home."

"I see." Buster returned the ball to the rookie on a soft, smooth arc. "When are you leaving?"

"I'M NOT LEAVING."

"Damm'boy," Mills snorted. "Take it easy. Just pullin' yer chain."

"I don't want my chain pulled." Eli eased up on his toss, too. "I just want to figure out what the hel- heck I'm supposed to do."

"You can say the word," Buster smiled. "Lou won't bench ya'."

"This isn't funny."

"I know." The coach sent one back belt high and hard. "You have a decision to make. You also have a ballgame to play. Go get some swings and get all this stuff outta' yer head... you got 45 minutes."

As Eli stood in right field, it was hard to keep his mind on the game at hand. There were over 74,000 filing into Cleveland Stadium, and his name was on every child's lips in the ballpark. The kids were ripping open Veeck's latest promotion as soon as they walked through the gates – giant 'autographed' baseball cards.

"I've got an 'Eli'!" a child would squeal.

"Me, too!!!" a little girl would reply.

Of course, no matter which players were in each pack, Veeck made sure there was an 'Eli' in every one.

The fans – especially the kids – kept calling to him all afternoon, but other than a few tips of his cap to the fans in the right field grand-stand, Eli was stewing over the pastor's words from the night before.

Eli sprinted to right center to cut off a gap shot by Rizzuto. As he gunned the ball to Boudreau holding The Scooter at first, and robbing him of a double, Eli thought about 'being Jesus' to his father. Would he see it, no matter what form it took?

As he hustled down the line on a topper to short, he thought 'Is this what being Jesus looks like?' as Rizzuto returned the favor, and threw Eli out by a step.

On this day, New York's Bill Bevens had the measure of the rookie, and sent him to an 0-for-4 day.

Eli's teammates fared little better, scrounging up three singles and a double in a 2-0 loss. The Indians had scrambled back to within two games of Washington, but once again felt like they had bumped into that invisible wall as they boarded the train for a bumpy 8-hour journey to Chicago.

For Eli, the baseball was still coming as naturally as it ever had.

It was the 'life' part – the future – that wouldn't leave him alone.

Comiskey Park

"We've been trying to catch up with everyone who has been called up to the majors in the last few weeks," the representative from the Playball Baseball Card Company said as he sat down in front of Eli's locker stall. "We issued our first set of cards in April. Now, it's time for Series 2, guys like you who've been called up mid-season.

The rookie stared back at the rep as he opened his briefcase.

Veeck entered the clubhouse and walked toward them.

"Your boss," the rep gestured toward Veeck, "told me you're a bit of a special case. We don't usually change our layout, you see... every card should basically look the same – face in profile, with your glove on, or your bat in hand. But, in your case, I guess we're going to make a – ummm – *religious* exemption?"

The rookie looked at the Indians' owner, who nodded back at him.

The rep pulled a small stack of baseball cards bound with a rubber band from his briefcase, pulled off the rubber band, and spread them out before Eli like a deck of playing cards.

"As you can see, we like to go with full-face closeups." The rep wasn't used to defending his job. "Every player, every team, every card. We do black-and-white photographs and then colorize them at our studio. But, we understand that your face can't be on the card."

"That's right," Eli said politely but firmly.

"So, here's what we're gonna do..." The baseball card man reached dramatically back into his briefcase.

He slid a piece of card stock in front of Eli. The photo was of him, batting at League Park. He had swung at, and connected with the ball, and was finishing his backswing as his momentum had begun to shift toward first base.

"It's *still* a photograph-" Eli began-

"Eli," Veeck put his hand on Eli's shoulder. "Look closely. How do you know that's you?"

"I'm a right-handed batter," Eli said.

"We have plenty of those," Veeck replied.

"Blond hair." Eli pointed.

"You're not the only blond-haired player we have." Veeck shook his head.

"I'm number 17." The number on his back was clear as could be – Eli thought – they can't argue that.

Veeck nodded. "That you are. But, look at your face, Eli."

The rookie stared closely at the image in front of him.

He didn't see his face.

There was an ear on the side of his head. Perhaps the very tip of his nose was just barely visible, but...

"That *is* still me," Eli said, "in this photograph."

The man from Playball spread his hands and looked at Veeck.

"Yes Eli," Veeck said calmly, "but there is nothing in that photo that actually shows your face, or any feature that clearly identifies you."

"Other than my number."

"That's correct." Veeck nodded.

"Guys, I gotta get over to the White Sox clubhouse," the baseball card man said.

"Eli, we went through a lot of photographs to find this one," Veeck said. "We're not looking for a way for you to betray your beliefs, we're just trying to find a way to keep our contract with the baseball card company, while keeping your face off of the card. Playball has come halfway on this. I'd appreciate you coming through for us as well."

"Bill..." Eli shook his head. He looked up at both of the men in front of him. "Who are these baseball cards for...?"

"Kids." The man from Playball smiled. "Usually between the ages of 6 and 12. Heck, I learned how to read and do my 'rythmatic from the stories and stats on the back of the cards."

Eli shook his head again.

"Every team has a contract with Playball, Eli," Veeck said. "You get a little money out of this too. We could put it towards baseball equipment for all the Amish kids back home. We could even send a little to Shiloh Baptist Church if you like."

Eli stared at Veeck.

"Oscar told me you came back on Saturday night," Veeck smiled.

"Is there anything going on with your players that you don't know?" Eli asked.

Veeck winked.

"Okay guys," the man from Playball said as he started to pack up, "is this gonna happen, or what?"

Eli exhaled. "All right. Do I have to sign something...?"

The Playball rep walked out of the clubhouse with Veeck a few moments later.

"I have never in my life met any young ballplayer who wasn't jumping out of his chair to have his own baseball card." The rep shook his head. "That is one odd duck you've got there, Bill."

"It's just the way we like him, Tommy." Veeck was shaking his head, too. "Just the way we like him."

SUNDAY
AUGUST 11

Sportsman's Park – St. Louis

"Weaver swings, and sends one way up, and WAY OUT! GONE to the back of the left field pavilion! Here comes Mackiewicz trotting home in front of Weaver, and the Indians have doubled their pleasure! The Clevelands now lead St. Louis 4-to-nothing."

"And fans, you can double your pleasure, and double your fun, with Doublemint, Doublemint... Doublemint Gum!"

"Well Bob, whatever was ailing Eli Weaver back that last week in Cleveland, he has certainly shed that slump on this trip!"

"And how, Jack! Let me look here... in these eight games (flipping scorebook pages) Weaver has...... (more flipping) banged out 11 hits, 2 homers, knocked home... 5 runs, and stole a few bases, too!"

"While we have a conference on the mound, we just want to remind you about the makeup game tomorrow at League Park at 3pm, and then on Tuesday night at Municipal Stadium, it's Ladies' Night!"

"*Bill Veeck was the master of these nights in the minor leagues –
flowers, perfume, and special giveaways for the ladies – all night long. It
should be a lot of fun!*"

"*I'm just wondering how many fans of the female persuasion we'll
have in the right field grandstand Tuesday night...*"

"*Whaddya' mean, Bob?*"

"*Well, I'm just saying that over the last few weeks, there have been
more and more young women choosing to sit in the right field lower deck
when there are usually a lot seats available in the shade at home plate
under the upper deck.*"

"*Now Bob, are you suggesting that the young ladies of Cleveland are
sitting in the right field seats because of the Indians' young right fielder...*"

Bill Veeck jumped off the couch in his office and grabbed the
phone off his desk.

"Ada!"

"Yes, darlin'...?"

"Get me the box office."

TUESDAY AUGUST 13

Cleveland Stadium

It was "Ladies' Night" at Cleveland Municipal Stadium.

The players were stationed in the concourses adjoining each of the five ballpark gates. Alongside them was a quickly moving line of volunteers getting the truckloads of carnations into their hands as fast as they could.

Just behind them, the Indians' owner had hired the ladies of the Halle Company department store's fragrance department. Right beside them were boxes containing thousands of sample-sized bottles of a "reasonably" elegant perfume... which the store had been having trouble selling.

Behind those two groups, Veeck had another group of women from the Indians offices, ready to hand out official Cleveland Indians compacts.

At Gate D – the closest to the right field stands – and the ability to be as close to Eli Weaver as they possibly could be, the crowds of excited young women gathered early.

With the rising of the metal gate, the surge of young women pushed toward the turnstiles. The older gentlemen in their uniforms – who were used to a steady, methodical flow of fans into their ballpark – were totally unprepared for what happened next.

Eli Weaver was spotted in the concourse walking toward the gate with a large armful of carnations.

At this point, Bill Veeck's master plan for his first Ladies' Night as the Indians' owner collapsed.

First came the scream.

It was intense, it was high-pitched, and it was in unison.

At the sight of the Indians' handsome 19-year-old outfielder, the young women outside of the turnstiles then attempted to get inside the turnstiles as fast as possible.

The bravest of the ticket-takers bravely held their ground, attempting to use the turnstile itself as a shield.

The wisest of the ticket-takers... just ran for their lives.

As Eli saw the young women leaping the turnstiles and heading straight for him, he froze for a split-second. The gate was wide, the young women were many, and he was in his baseball spikes on a concrete walkway. There was only one way of escape.

Eli took two quick shuffle steps and jumped onto the back of the truck filled with carnations.

With three quick pounds on the roof of the cab, he yelled, "GO, GO, GO!!!"

The driver, who had scored an early hot dog from a nearby concession stand, saw the danger surging toward him. He started the small truck, ground every tooth on every gear in the gearbox, and jerked it to life, heading down the concourse toward the sections by home plate.

"Where am I going???" the driver yelled.

"The clubhouse is another 300 feet on your right! Blue door!" the rookie replied.

Eli tried to throw bundles of flowers to the female fans sprinting after him, but all it resulted in were crushed carnations.

The vendors, who were walking with their wares from the commissary toward the right field grandstand and upper deck ramps were cursing a blue streak upon the truck as its driver tried to thread his way through them. Once done yelling at the truck, the vendors quickly realized that the flower truck wasn't their biggest problem. Vendors jumped quickly into concession stands, and dove into any available bathroom to avoid the female tidal wave sweeping toward the east end of the ballpark.

Fortunately, the driver was able to get a slight lead on the surging crowd of young Ladies' Day fans which was building by the minute behind the first wave.

Eli yelled, "HERE!!! STOP!!!"

As the truck reached the clubhouse door, the driver jammed on the brakes, sending Eli into the stacks of carnations in the back of the truck.

"OH!!!"

On top of Eli landed the young lady from the flower shop who had been neatly stacking the flowers by the opening of the truck in order to hand them out.

"Hi. I'm Jane."

"Eli Weaver."

Although one can't be sure what 17-year-old Jane McCarthy had been expecting when she left her parents' flower shop in Lakewood to work at the ballpark that night (handing out the biggest order for carnations her parents had ever received), one can be reasonably sure that laying in the back of a truck on a bed of flowers with the best-looking young ballplayer in America was not a part of those expectations.

"Sorry, gotta go!" were the last words she heard Eli say during their all too brief encounter.

Eli wrenched open the steel clubhouse door and slammed it shut behind him.

Outside – there were more footsteps, there was door pounding, and there was screaming.

A lot of screaming.

Eli took a deep breath and turned toward the clubhouse-

"Eli!"

Bill Veeck was hobbling toward him.

"You're supposed to be at Gate D making nice with our female fans!"

"Bill, I can't-"

"You have to. It's part of your contract!"

"Bill there's too many-"

"Don't give me that Amish nonsense, you can't plead 'bashful' to get out of this." Veeck knew he couldn't control the ballgames – but you'd better not mess with his promotions. "If I have to walk back out there with you, I suppose I will."

"Bill, don't-" Eli stammered.

Veeck opened the clubhouse door.

A mistake.

The surge came quickly, along with the renewed screams once the young women saw Eli again. Veeck yelled for the cops he'd hired to guard that very door, and along with some fatherly pushes of arms and legs, they were able to get the door shut, and order restored. At least in the hallway they were occupying.

"Damn!" Veeck exclaimed, "that's nuts!"

His prize rookie outfielder looked a bit shaken.

"You okay, kid?" the owner asked.

"I think so," Eli exhaled.

The screams and ruckus continued outside the door.

Veeck nodded with concern toward his young rookie.

Then the owner looked away and smiled.

Tonight might exceed the dreams he hadn't even had yet.

"Hey, Rosebud!"

That was about the kindest thing Eli's teammates called him in the moments before the game. The ribbing and roasting was unrelenting – and because the guys in his locker room now knew that he could take it, they laid it on thick and fast.

To that point, the other players on the Indians had only heard about the scene at Gate D and the clubhouse door. When the players took the field for a quick game of catch in front of their dugout before the game, the magnitude of Veeck's promotion became readily apparent.

Two by two, the Indians left the field because trying to carry on a conversation while tossing a baseball back and forth was useless.

All of a sudden, Buster noticed that he and the handsome rookie were the only two still attempting to warm up.

"You feel loose, Eli?" Mills said as he sent the ball toward Weaver.

The ball's arrival at Eli's glove brought a high-pitched cheer.

"Let's get out of here!" the rookie yelled back.

Another shriek of delight as Eli sent the ball back toward his coach.

Buster caught the throw head-high. "Dugout steps!"

"Millsy – look at the dugout!" Eli said nervously.

As the young women cheered Eli's catch of his last toss, Buster saw the problem.

The police had given up the battle of keeping the aisles clear in the field box sections by the dugout. In fact, the ushers and off-duty cops had now also surrendered the top of the dugout to female fans.

"We're going to have to make a run for it, kid!" Buster yelled.

Eli froze with the baseball in his hand. "You first."

"Nope." Mills had never faced combat during his recent service in the military, but…

Eli looked down at the baseball in his right hand.

"Buster – get ready to run for it!"

Eli looked at the ladies in the aisles and on top of the dugout – directly – for the first time… and smiled – as big as he could.

The ladies, to put it mildly, were thrilled.

Eli waved.

Rapture.

"Have a great time tonight, ladies!" Eli yelled – as he underhand flipped the baseball as high as he could toward the seats behind the dugout.

That set off a stampede for the ball that turned the ladies' attention and cleared the top of the dugout – just long enough.

"GO!" Eli yelled.

Weaver and Mills bolted down the dugout steps and up the adjoining concrete walkway to the clubhouse as quickly as they could, as the sounds of the scramble for the baseball disappeared behind them.

In the top of the first, the Cleveland Indians took the field.

The sound from the right field grandstand as Eli jogged out to his position was other-worldly.

"Dear God in heaven," first base umpire Eddie Rommel yelled to Indians first sacker Heinz Becker, "what the hell has Veeck done now?"

Eli kept his focus completely on the pitcher, the catcher, and the flight of the ball. To allow anything else in his mind at that point would be foolish.

To turn around and look behind him would be disastrous.

As the top of the first played out, the Tigers were unsuccessful at reaching Bob Feller.

So were the women in the lower deck in right field who were trying to reach Eli Weaver.

By the third inning in this scoreless game, the Tigers were getting frustrated.

So were the women in the lower deck in right field.

With both pitchers working quickly, and the game moving rapidly, the young women began getting bolder.

Scorecard pages were being torn out, love notes were being written in lipstick, folded into paper airplanes, and sailed out toward Eli's defensive position.

At the end of the top of the inning, the grounds crew dutifully jogged out to the right field track and spread out across deep right field to gather up the notes to the screaming disapproval of thousands of young women.

Before the top of the fourth, the umpiring crew ordered Veeck to the stadium public address microphone to order the women to cease and desist. The Indians' owner tried to appear as cooperative as possible, but he was enjoying every moment of the proceedings, and his feeble attempt at stopping the young women from exercising their First Amendment rights slowed the flight of the love notes not one bit.

The game was still scoreless in the fifth, when a lovely brunette in the right field upper deck hit upon the perfect note, with the perfect folds, under the perfect breeze off Lake Erie.

The paper airplane drifted down from above in a graceful arc. At one point, a brief gust stalled the tiny aircraft.

The crowd gasped.

But the north breeze gathered the love note again, and sent it swirling downward.

As the crowd saw where it was headed, the roar began building from the right field corner...

For fifteen of the sixteen major league owners, the interruption of a scoreless pitcher's duel in the fifth inning by a paper airplane would be insulting. Disruptive fan behavior that distracted from America's Pastime.

Bill Veeck was in the aisle by the right field wall... cheering on the paper plane.

The crowd's anticipation paid off.

The aerial love note fell to the ground.

In front of Eli's left foot.

65,000 fans went absolutely wild.

Veeck wished he could shoot off all the fireworks loaded in the scoreboard.

GO. GO. GO.

The crowd had begun a rhythmic chant.

They made it clear they wanted Eli to pick up the note in the grass at his feet.

C'mon, kid... thought Veeck – I'll give you a $1,000 bonus...

Boudreau snagged the final out of the top of the fifth (the game, for some reason, had continued) on a popup. Eli trotted in toward the dugout, leaving the note in the outfield grass as the crowd – and his boss – groaned.

"It's Ladies' Night here at the Stadium, and so far Bob, the only excitement of the night has happened out in right field where Eli Weaver has been catching flyballs, and swatting away marriage proposals!"

"And the bottom of the sixth is brought to you by Ladies' Furnishings department at Sterling-Lindner on Euclid Avenue near East 9th... Hoping for a little rally here, Jack! It may not take more than a run or two tonight."

"We're scoreless in the last of the sixth as Mackiewicz leads off... he's 0-for-2 so far. Trout delivers a fast one for a strike-"

"Oh boy, Jack the ladies in the right field seats are already on their feet as Weaver comes on deck..."

"Trout's 0-1... and Macky nubs one right back to the mound. Dizzy Trout snaps it over to Greenberg, and there's one away... well, friends... if you're just joining us, that sound you're hearing is not the sound track to a Boris Karloff movie, those are the young women who have come out to the ol' ballyard on Bill Veeck's first Ladies' Night! And have they ever found a favorite in young Eli Weaver (crowd noise)... Trout stares back out at the right field stands – shakes his head – now turns for the sign. Here's the wind and pitch – outside, ball one."

"Just two hits for the Indians, and two hits for the Tiges tonight, Jack."

"Trout's next offering – outside corner, and a strike. Weaver looks back – but says not a word... he felt that was wide. But it's 1-and-1."

"Disagreement among the ladies in right..."

"They must have had a better angle than the plate umpire... Dizzy

Trout is winding it up again, and lets it fly – SMASHED to right-center – no one's going to catch that one! It splits the outfielders – Weaver's got his head down sprinting for second – the slide – and the throw is way late, it's a DOUBLE for Weaver, and with one out in the sixth, the Clevelands have a man in scoring position for the first time tonight!"

"And for the first time tonight, 65,000 fans have something to roar about!"

"Well Bob, I'd say 30,000 are roaring. The other 35,000 are... shreiking? Becker's the batter now. The big first baseman is hitless tonight. Trout stretches – and fires... Inside for ball one. Outfield playing Becks straightaway. The 1-0... SWING and a miss! Becker trying to tattoo that one to Ashtabula. Trout finds his sign... and takes his stretch... the pit- THERE GOES WEAVER – it's outside, and the throwww not NEARLY in time!!! Weaver's stolen third!"

"Eli Weaver has stolen eight bases in his young career, and has yet to be caught!"

"And if you think the ladies in right field cheering on Weaver are loud on your radio speaker, you should be here at the lakefront... the walleye and perch in the lake are headed for Canada! Now, it's 2-and-1 on Becker-"

"...and the Detroit infield has pulled in to the cut of the grass."

"Becker's hitting from the left side against the righty Trout – here's the 2-1... RIPPED to Greenberg! Knocks it down – looks at Weaver, and jogs to Becker to tag him for the second out... that leaves Boudreau with one out left in the Indians' sixth."

"Lou solved Trout for a single in the second."

"Trout – big windup – and a STRIKE on the inside corner. Lou steps back and runs his hand up and down the bat barrel. Trout with a glance at Weaver, he's edging away from third – the 0-1... strike TWO on the outside corner – and just like Weaver, Lou's not buying what *the ump is selling. Either way, Lou's in a pickle right now. Trout with a long look – shakes his head once – nods. Here's the pitch – SWING and a MISS, strike three! Lou thought the last one was outside, so Trout threw the next one even FARTHER outside, and Boudreau went fishin'. A promising double for Weaver, but nothing for the Tribe, and we're still scoreless going to the seventh."*

The young ladies of the right field grandstand were not necessarily upset by Boudreau's strikeout. It got Eli back to his defensive position that much quicker. Once again, the tidal wave of adulation swept toward Eli as he approached, head lowered.

"ELI, ELI, ELI..."

Once again, it was a fast-moving inning, with Feller working the top half of the innings as rapidly as his Detroit counterpart worked the bottom half.

Every owner, every baseball P.R. man, wants every promotion to be the best one they've ever done. Giveaways are planned for the anticipated crowd, fireworks shows are built for the biggest booms for the buck. It's all about making the fan want to come back again. Leaving them with that 'want' to come back for another evening with their family where the giveaway will be treasured, and where – especially in the game itself – anything might happen:

"One out in the seventh. Feller and Trout in a scoreless duel. Here's Skeeter Webb... he blooped one over Keltner's head for a single in the third... Fastball from Robert – right down Euclid Avenue for a called strike. Bob's got the ball back, and he's all business – windmills and kicks – another BLAZER for strike two."

"I don't think Webb's blooping another one out there tonight, Jack."

"The 0-2 is swung on and lifted high to right, and headed for the corner – but Weaver is there on the track by the foul pole waiting... and Eli's got it for out number two-"

(CROWD ROARS)

"Well, here we go again... someone has thrown something on the field, right by Weaver's feet... and... it's... a... Bob...? What is that?"

"Uhhhhh, Jack... I think that might be a-"

Eli looked down – eyes wide – frantically gestured to the ground crew to come to his aid.

One of the young men obliged, ran out to Eli on the track, reached down, and picked up the item. Then he froze, as the realization broke in the right field corner as to what he was holding, and the crowd nearby was roaring.

With his crewmates cheering him on, the young man lifted a bra into the air.

A very... nice... bra.

The stadium went wild.

This time, the roars of the men in attendance found a volume level much louder than the young women had achieved.

The young man from the ground crew kept the undergarment lifted high as he walked slowly off the field to the increasing cheers of the crowd.

Bill Veeck had settled in to visit with some advertising sponsors in the box seats by the Indians dugout.

The owner of a local men's store looked around the ballpark at the 65,000 fans cheering wildly at something that had absolutely nothing to do with baseball. "Bill, did this ever happen on Ladies' Day in Milwaukee?"

Veeck smiled. "No. Dammit."

"What are you going to do about that kid on the ground crew?" asked the frowning gentleman from Standard Oil.

"Give him a raise." Veeck slapped the Sohio rep on the shoulder before limping up the steps to the concourse with Ada in tow.

Because the young man from the ground crew took his time returning to his bench by the bullpen, it gave the Indians infield plenty of time to congregate at the mound. No Cleveland infielder made eye contact with any other. They didn't dare laugh.

Bob Feller was pawing at the dirt on the mound... frustrated and chomping at the bit to get going.

"I've got a 2-hitter going here, Lou," Feller snarled.

"Nobody cares, Bob." Boudreau whacked his ace on the butt with his glove and jogged back to short.

As Eli walked back toward his position in straightaway right field, in the midst of a cauldron of sound beyond anything he'd experienced in his very short career, he let his mind drift to where he would be, and what he would be doing if he were home in Mt. Hope. He thought of the cows lowing in the barn, and getting some equipment oiled for a hay cut in the morning. A last look in at the draft horse team tucked away in their stalls. A glass of cool lemonade from down in the cellar. The sound of a distant train off to the west as he began to fall-

"Hey, rook!"

First base umpire Eddie Rommel was staring at him.

"Yeah, ump?"

Rommel jerked his thumb toward the Cleveland dugout. "You wanna go in now? You got three outs..."

As Eli ran past him, the veteran umpire slowed him down, and winked. "You shoulda took it back up to her."

Eli stared at the ump.

"The bra..." Rommel shrugged. "Rookie mistake."

An hour later, 65,000 fans snaked their way out of the giant stadium toward the giant parking lots that surrounded it.

Bill Veeck stood by the Gate D exit as the tired river of humanity passed him by.

Boys and girls imitating the booming fireworks, or Eli's steal of third.

Women of all ages who had been out with their friends for a night downtown.

Men who were already practicing their stories for their fellow workers at the water cooler the next morning. ("Yeah, I was *there!*")

Young mothers and fathers trying to explain the top of the seventh – gently – to their little ones.

And one anonymous young woman passing him by, Veeck mused, who was headed home with one less article of clothing than she arrived with.

On a warm August night, everyone in this crowd would head home with a story. Of a ballpark. A crowd. A hot dog with spicy brown mustard. Great plays. Big fireworks.

And the completely unexpected.

The newspapers would record that in front of 65,765 fans, in a game that was played in two hours and fourteen minutes, the Cleveland Indians had lost to the Detroit Tigers 1-0.

But Bill Veeck knew that he had won.

Because Bill Veeck knew those fans would be back.

Anything can happen at the ballpark.

AUGUST 14

DEAREST ELI,

I have just read the story of the ball game on August 13.

I see you have many female admirers in Cleveland.

It must be quite exciting to have so many to choose from.

If any of them should prove to be less than you expect, I suppose I will still be here in Mt. Hope. If you return, of course.

My father and mother send their concern.

They saw the newspaper before I did.

Although I continue to hope for your return, now might not be a good time for you to do so.

YOURS,

RACHAEL

SATURDAY
AUGUST **17**

Cleveland Stadium

As he arrived at his locker for a Saturday night game with the White Sox, Eli saw the familiar angled cursive, and the Mt. Hope return address on the envelope on top of his fan mail stack, and opened it immediately.

DEAREST ELI,

I have just read the story of the ball game on August 13.

I see you have many female admirers in Cleveland...

"MEIN GOTT."

Indians vs. White Sox | later that evening

"...so, there's two out in the eighth, and here's Weaver again. Eli is 1-for-3 tonight – a single in the 4th the only damage he's been able to do. Haynes delivers – and DOWN goes Weaver AGAIN!"

"Every time up tonight, he's sent Weaver to the dirt, Jack!"

"I guess the Pale Hose have had just about enough of Weaver's

229

heroics. This is the fourth time the Clevelands and Chicagos have bumped into each other since Weaver's arrival-"

"...and honestly Jack, Eli's been wearin'em out!"

"The wind and the 1-0... AGAIN AT WEAVER'S HEAD! Weaver's somewhere in that cloud of dirt at home – and now he straightens himself, and dusts himself off a bit."

"Jack, the fans have had enough! That's the fifth time Haynes has sent Weaver to the canvas! The Indians bench is now jawing with umpire Joe Rue at home plate."

"Not gonna do much good, I suspect. So, 2-and-0 to Weaver – hitter's count – IF he gets something to hit. The windup - and here it comes – NAILED HIM IN THE BACK!"

"RIGHT BETWEEN THE SHOULDER BLADES!"

"Weaver's up, and trotting to first."

"...and Haynes is following Eli – right down the first base line!"

"C'mon, farm boy!" Haynes screamed over the 40,000 in the crowd. "Take a swing at me!"

"Shut up, Haynes!" Boudreau was headed to the on-deck circle, but now was advancing toward the mound. Bat in hand.

"He's a big baby, Lou!" Half a wad of chew flew out of Haynes mouth as he screamed. "He wouldn't fight the Japs or the Krauts, and he won't fight me!"

"Get your ass back on the mound, busher!" Boudreau was ready to go.

"Haynes! On the mound!" The umpire pointed, then pivoted to Boudreau, "Lou, get back in that circle! And if you cross that white line with a bat again, you'll be sittin' for a MONTH!"

With order restored, Rue pulled his clicker back out of his right pocket and yelled out to Eli, "Ready to go, kid?"

Weaver nodded, but did not turn his eyes away from Haynes.

The White Sox pitcher spit the rest of his chew toward first, and blew Eli a kiss.

Eli, keeping his hands by his hips, subtly – but unmistakably – pointed toward second base.

Haynes took a step toward first.

"HAYNES!" Rue bellowed from behind his mask, "you step off that damn mound again, and you're GONE!"

From shortstop, Luke Appling yelled, "Get back in the game, and get the last out. Let's GO!"

Heinz Becker stepped in for the Indians.

Haynes finally looked at his catcher and got the sign. As he went into his stretch, he thought he saw motion out of the corner of his left eye-

"JOE!" Appling screamed.

Haynes had the presence of mind to step off the rubber, and saw Weaver three steps toward second. He raised his arm to throw to first, then thought – NO – and wheeled toward second.

Luke Appling, the Sox shortstop, was already headed for second with his glove extended, waiting for the ball to lead him into the bag.

40,000 fans jumped to their feet, as Haynes snapped a throw across his body.

Appling gloved the throw as he approached the bag, then dove for second as Eli slid hard for the front corner of the bag. With no second base umpire that day, first base ump Ed Rommel trailed the play getting an angle from the infield grass as he peered into the dust cloud from Eli's slide.

"OUT!!!" Rommel's right arm shot skyward.

Haynes let loose a string of happy expletives on the mound.

The Indians' bench let loose some unhappy expletives at their impulsive rookie.

But Eli – his foot not moving from the bag – pointed at the ground behind Appling.

The baseball. Rolling free.

"SAFE!!! SAFE!!!" Rommel immediately pointed at the ball, and spread his arms wide.

Eli stood – without celebration – and dusted himself off.

Haynes' fury returned.

Upon placing both feet on the bag, Eli turned with his hands on his hips, and stared once again at Haynes on the mound. Then smiled. Then pointed – a little more obviously – toward third base.

Both dugouts saw it.

"Dammit Lou," Jack Conway yelled from the dugout, "he proved his point, and we're still down four!"

"Let him go," the manager said to his second baseman. Eli's going to win this little battle his way. And if he doesn't, he can sit for a while and think about it, Boudreau thought as he knelt on deck.

Weaver bounced out to a big lead, and Appling kept juking – and cutting behind him – keeping Eli as close as he could.

Finally, Haynes delivered a pitch. A curve in the dirt, low and in.

"Ball one!"

The Sox catcher dug the ball out of the dirt, and immediately had it cocked in his throwing hand, but Weaver had turned back to second. A split-second before the moment the catcher looked back out to the mound, and brought his arm forward, Eli pivoted, and was on his way to third.

The crowd noise told Haynes everything he needed to know as the toss from his catcher seemed to hang in the air between home and the mound. He caught the ball, and spun toward third, but there was no hope.

Eli didn't slide. He eased into the bag, and now stood on 3rd, hands on hips, staring at Haynes.

Bill Veeck stood behind Lebovitz in the press box with his arms crossed, surveying almost 40,000 people in his ballpark, who, up to about two minutes ago, were enjoying a 4-0 summertime snoozer along the shore of Lake Erie. Now, for the first time that day, they were on their feet. Clapping. Stomping. Yelling. Their team was three batters away from getting the *tying* run to the plate, but at the moment, that didn't matter a bit.

Now, every eye in the stands, the pressbox, the field, and both benches, was on a tall, muscular, 19-year-old farmboy, who two months ago had never put on a proper uniform.

Veeck shook his head, smiled, and thanked God for Cy Slapnicka's choice of parking places on that drive through Holmes County.

On the field, Eli and Haynes locked eyes again.

This time, when the rookie pointed, he wasn't smiling.

But, Eli didn't point at home plate.

He pointed at *Haynes*.

Haynes, who had been rubbing up the baseball at the back of the mound, wheeled and took two steps toward Weaver before he caught sight of the home plate umpire – mask off – moving in the same direction.

Haynes stopped. Umpire Rue did as well.

Joe Haynes took a breath as Rue turned, dusted off home plate even though it didn't need it, then turned again toward the field to stare out at Haynes and Weaver before settling back in behind home plate.

For just a moment, Haynes mind flashed to the fact that he was 3-8 for the season, his ERA was climbing, he hadn't completed a game in a month, and there was absolutely no guarantee he'd have a job when he got to camp next March. He needed this shutout, dammit... especially against Feller. Anything that could help him at contract time, he had to hang on to. He needed one out to get out of the 8th with a 4-nothing lead, and only had Boudreau to deal with in the 9th, before the cupcakes at the bottom of the order.

Haynes climbed on top of the mound.

Eli stayed on top of the bag.

Haynes placed his right foot atop the pitching rubber. He would go from the windup.

Eli stayed on top of the bag.

As Haynes began his windup, he noticed – still distracted in spite of his attempt to calm himself down – movement from the corner of his right eye.

Eli had sprinted off the third base bag.

Haynes speded up his delivery, and fired the ball toward home plate as fast as he could.

White Sox catcher Frankie Hayes saved the situation, leaping from his crouch, and snaring the ball when it was almost past him.

Eli Weaver shuffled back atop 3rd and surveyed the situation.

The count was now 2-and-0 on Becker, and Haynes was on the verge of losing it again. He exchanged stares with Eli again as he climbed the mound.

This time, Haynes placed his right foot into the canyon in front of the rubber that had been created by Feller over the course of eight innings. He would go from the stretch.

He *needed* this shutout.

"EE-LIE! EE-LIE!! EE-LIE!!!" the kids started the chant. The adults in the ballpark brought it to a crescendo.

As Haynes took his stretch position, Eli stepped off third.

As Haynes held his pose, Eli took another step... slid his right foot out, and dipped into a slight crouch.

Haynes stepped off.

Eli didn't move... he held on to his lead.

The Sox third baseman moved to the bag.

Haynes placed his foot back into Feller's trench in front of the rubber, looked at Eli, looked in for the sign, and looked back at Eli.

As Haynes raised his arms and began to lower them into his stretch position, Eli dug in with his left foot, and his right foot turned slightly towards home.

Haynes saw it out of the corner of his eye.

But, as he tried to lift his right foot, his spikes got caught trying to get up and over the rubber. Haynes' hands came apart-his left foot shuffled for balance-

...and the third base and home plate umpires raised their hands in unison.

"BALK!!!"

Eli Weaver trotted slowly home, and stepped unceremoniously on home plate.

40,000 fans went wild.

Eli shook Becker's hand, turned to the pitcher's mound-

...and blew a kiss at Joe Haynes.

The shutout was gone, and so was Haynes' mind. He took off straight for Weaver, and was on him before anyone on the field could react.

Except Eli.

The rookie ducked the pitcher's punch while getting his left arm underneath Haynes' right, and rode him to the ground.

All of a sudden, Eli was on top of him. Haynes realized that Weaver was not only straddling him, but that he couldn't move. Both of the pitchers' arms were pinned by a young blacksmith's strong left hand... and that Eli's right hand was free, and directly above his face.

However... Eli's right hand wasn't in a fist.

The rookie now had Haynes' full attention as he stared him down – faces just a foot apart.

Both men realized that if Weaver so chose, he could put Haynes' lights out – with one punch.

At that point, both benches had emptied, and swarmed the plate – grabbing and pulling arms separating Weaver and Haynes.

The melee continued.

The crowd roared.

The score was 4-1.

Thirty minutes later, the game was over.

The Indians had lost.

4-1.

Once again, Bill Veeck stood at the gates, greeting fans, and watching them depart after another fireworks spectacular into a humid summer night. As they had earlier in the week, the children were imitating the booming fireworks, and their hero Eli – this time, his daring base-running.

Once again, though his team had lost, Veeck had won.

He was confident these fans would return in 1946, and if he could find some help for Lou, for Feller, and yes – for his phenom Eli Weaver... they would return in 1947, too. His team was headed upward. He could feel it. He could see it – even though some of the newspaper writers in town couldn't.

In the locker room, the reporters surrounded Eli's locker.

Buster had his eyes on the rookie, and kept watching for the "stroke the chin" signal to get him out of there... but, on this night, it never came. Eli seemed at ease. Confident. In a way Mills hadn't seen before.

"What were you thinking with your team down four in the eighth?" Lebovitz asked directly.

Eli looked sheepishly at the reporter. "Yeah. That wasn't very smart. Mr. Boudreau told me it wasn't very good baseball."

"Was that all he said?" Lebovitz asked quickly.

"Uhhh… no." Eli lowered his head. "He said some other things before he said 'Good job.'"

The reporters laughed.

"Eli," Whitey Lewis of *The Cleveland Press* piped up, "I grew up on a farm. When Haynes came at you after you scored, were you trying to 'rope a calf'?"

Weaver smiled. "Well Mr. Lewis, every now and then a calf just doesn't want to go where you want it to go, and you got to calm him down a bit."

The reporters were eating it up.

AUGUST 18

Cleveland Stadium

Max Patkin couldn't figure this Weaver kid out.

After arm troubles ended his pitching career early, some clowning while playing baseball in the service during the war had caught the attention of Bill Veeck.

Now, Patkin was a 26-year-old "coach" with the Cleveland Indians, and whenever he stuck his nose out of the dugout, the fans started laughing.

Most of the time, before he had actually done anything.

Because his joints were so loose and limber, his exaggerated imitations of batting stances, pitching motions, and umpires' calls were cracking up everyone in the American League.

Everyone except Eli Weaver.

And that became a personal challenge for Patkin.

He had mirrored Eli's throwing motion and posture to perfection when warming him up in the outfield between innings. Max had fallen over "dead" when Weaver was called out on strikes a month before (and had almost been ejected for his trouble). The clown had even allowed a hard-hit foul ball of Eli's to drill him in the back.

Patkin had collapsed in the coaching box – drawing everyone's immediate concern... and attention.

Eli jogged down the first base line, bat in hand, as concerned as everyone else. But, as Weaver leaned over his "stricken coach", the fake, comic spasms started, and Veeck braced himself.

As soon as Eli patted Patkin on the shoulder, Max sprang to his feet, and leapt into Weaver's arms, wrapping his legs around the rookie, and planting a huge kiss on his forehead.

The crowd ate it up.

Eli was not amused, and shook off the comic coach, pointing his bat at him as he walked away.

The fans at Municipal Stadium, thinking it was part of the act, laughed even after the game restarted.

Everyone except Eli, of course.

What do I have to do? Patkin thought.

In game one of the doubleheader, Eli winced after drawing a walk as he saw Patkin waiting for him again "coaching" at first base.

Patkin clapped his hands vigorously as the rookie approached. "One down, one down. Get a good lead, but watch the line drive to the right side!"

Finally, Eli thought, he's quit the screwing around.

Weaver got off to a good lead, and two pitches later, he drew a throw over to first that sent him diving back toward first in a cloud of dust.

As Eli rose, Patkin helped him dust himself off and slapped him on the back.

Almost immediately, the rookie heard the laughter from the box seats.

Seconds later, Joe Haynes, Eli's nemisis, was on the top step of the White Sox dugout letting loose with a flow of profanity that was as creative as it was vulgar.

The first base umpire called for time and walked up behind Eli. Yanking at the back of his jersey, Weaver felt something come loose.

When the umpire handed Eli the "target" Patkin had taped to his back, the other side of the ballpark saw what the fuss was about, and started laughing, too.

"For cryin' out loud, Max," Umpire Ed Rommel yelled at Patkin, "we just got the ballpark calmed down after last night, and now you've got everyone riled up again."

The Indians' first base "coach" made a buffoonish 'who me?' gesture, as he backed himself into his coaching box again to the cheers of the crowd.

Rommel pointed at Max. "You step out of that box again tonight, and you're **gone!**"

Max Patkin made his rubbery face appear as angelic as he could, as he slunk away from the umpire. The fans, who never really knew what was part of the act, and what wasn't, were still enjoying every moment.

But the comic coach wasn't done yet.

"UH-OHH! THERE GOES ANOTHER ONE! Weaver hits it DEEP to center, and the outfielders are off and running! Case will jog home with the 12th run, and Eli's about to turn second and looking for more! The

ball rolls to the grass berm in front of the bleachers! There's going to be no chance at the plate! Weaver won't even have to slide! A 450-foot, inside-the-park home run for Weaver, and it's **13-TO-1, CLEVELAND!!!**

"*Jack, the Sox only hope was that an outfielder could have got in the way of that liner, and knocked it down!*"

"*I know Veeck wants a fence out there, but that one might have hit a fence, and bounced back in!*"

"*Well, I've been keeping track… and since Eli Weaver got drilled in the back by Haynes last night, he has stolen two bases, singled, walked, stole another base, homered, drove in two runs, singled, tripled, homered again, and driven in three more!*"

"*Thank you, Joe Haynes!*"

In the 8th inning of the doubleheader's second game, Eli drew another walk. He trotted down to first base, and Patkin caught his eye in the coach's box. They nodded to each other as Eli stepped on the bag.

"One out. Stay close. 10-run lead. You steal a base now, they'll be drilling you in the back until you're forty," Patkin said.

For some reason, Eli looked at Max's back pocket, which was bulging outward.

Then the rookie looked up at Patkin, and saw the gleam in his eye.

Oh, no. Eli thought.

He couldn't look.

He mustn't look.

Weaver led off the bag – just two steps as a courtesy. After the pitch, he skipped back to touch first before leading off again. That's when the laughter started behind him.

Don't. Look. Eli repeated to himself.

As the rookie led off first, the laughter grew.

Eli tried backing into first after the next pitch so that he wouldn't have to look at Patkin, but he missed the bag. Startled, he spun to make sure his foot touched the bag before the Sox' pitcher threw over and picked him off.

"VAHHHT ARE YOU DO-INK, DUMKOPF!!!"

Eli looked up.

Patkin had produced a full, fake gray beard from his back pocket. A fan in the front row of the field boxes had thrown Max a broad-brimmed straw hat.

Eli was now being coached by a bearded Amish elder in a Cleveland Indians uniform, who was imitating the pitcher's stretch, imitating Eli's leadoff, indicating to Ed Rommel that he wasn't leaving the coaching box, and yelling instructions to the Amish rookie in fake German.

The crowd was enjoying every moment.

Bill Veeck's last sip of club soda nearly came out his nose.

And... at first base... Eli Weaver's shoulders were shaking with laughter.

At the close of the inning, Max Patkin bowed low to the crowd, and with his thumb to his nose, wiggled his fingers at Eli as he ran out to right field for the ninth inning.

Max Patkin *always* got his man.

Cleveland Union Terminal – Terminal Tower

The suitcases, equipment bags, and steamer trunks on the train platform were many. This was a "meatgrinder" – a 21-day, 19-game trip that separated husbands from wives, fathers from small children, boyfriends from girlfriends...

And Eli...?

It shrank his small world in Cleveland to the size of a series of hotels and ballparks on the road.

"Eli!"

Bill Veeck limped across the platform with Boudreau.

"Eli," Veeck looked him in the eye, "you've been *suspended*."

"Suspended...?"

"It means the commissioner of the American League has decided you can't play for six games," Boudreau said.

"Why?"

"Because you and Haynes were fighting on Saturday night," Veeck said.

Eli was confused. "Bill, I *stopped the fight*. I ducked his punch and wrapped him up so he couldn't punch anymore!"

"I know that Eli," Veeck said, "and I know that because you're Amish you would never have hit him anyway-"

"So, I'm not going on the trip?"

Veeck reassured the rookie. "Oh yes, Eli. You're going! And you're playing!"

Eli shook his head. "How?"

"We are allowed to file what is called an 'appeal'," Veeck explained. "That will give me time to get all the facts of what happened a couple days ago to the Commissioner's Office. Then, there will be a hearing to determine if the penalty is enforced, reduced, or dismissed."

"But, I get to play?" Eli asked.

"Yes," Veeck assured him, "you let me handle this. The reporters will know about this when they board the train, and they're going to want to talk to you about it. When they ask you about being suspended, or the appeal we're going to file, your answer to them is 'No comment.' Okay?"

"'No comment'?" the rookie asked.

"'No comment,'" his manager replied.

Eli lowered his voice, and furrowed his brow. "No comment."

Veeck shook his head, and looked at Boudreau. "Now, he's Jack Benny. A real comedian."

Western Union Telegrams | August 19

1600HRS-CLEVOH
MR.A.B.CHANDLER
COMMISSIONER OF BASEBALL
MICH AVE-CHICAGO

HAP-
APPEALING WEAVER DECISION
NO FIGHT IN OUR BOY
WILL PRESENT FACTS IN YOUR OFFICE
REGARDS-BILL

As the train rolled eastward through the Allegheny Mountains that evening, Veeck got the answer he was hoping for from Commissioner Albert Benjamin "Happy" Chandler at the Pennsylvania Railroad depot, when the train stopped so that the engineer could take on more water and coal.

1655HRS-CHICAGO
BILL VEECK
CLEV INDIANS
STATESMAN-PENNARR

BILL-
WEAVER APPEAL APPROVED
MY OFFICE-NOON FRIDAY AUG 30
BRING WEAVER
WANT TO MEET HIM
HAP

AUGUST 22

The ball snapped back and forth as Eli and Buster had a catch in left field.

"Y'allright?"

Eli was still amazed at how many syllables Buster could drawl into one word.

"All right, I guess," Eli replied.

"Uh-huh." Buster shook his head. "A guy hitting .360 has problems?"

Eli shrugged. "You never told me baseball could get boring."

"Every night ain't 'Ladies' Night', son." Mills smirked back.

"Not funny." Eli blushed.

"Hellitain't!" Buster came back at him, "Y'know how many ball-players are playin' like you right now? None. Zero. Not Williams. Not DiMag. Not even your manager!"

251

Eli shrugged, and zipped the ball back to Buster.

"Eli," Mills flipped the ball up with his mitt, and caught it with his bare hand, "you see any'a those guys getting' bras thrown at'em?"

"Buster-"

"Eli, when you're at the plate, every guy on our bench is staring at you. They're trying to figger out what you're doin' up there." Buster fired the ball back. "Hell, kid – every player on the *other* bench is starin'atcha, too! Everybody up here is always lookin' for an edge – and you got it! You honestly ain't seen the guys imitatin' your stance an'swing at batting practice?"

Honestly... Eli thought – it had never occurred to him to look.

Buster winced as Eli burned the return toss in. "You got another letter, didn't ya'?"

Eli lowered his head.

"What did it say?"

The rookie sighed, "It's not what the letter said, Buster. It's what it didn't say."

"Yeah...?"

"Rachael was pleasant. She's happy I'm playing well. She's also happy women aren't chasing me across the field every night."

Buster snorted and slapped his thigh.

"But there was a note from my mother tucked inside." Eli shook his head. "Mother said how tired and sore my father is when he comes inside 'after dark' every evening-"

"Did she underline 'after dark'?" Buster asked.

"She didn't have to." Eli shook his head again. "She just mentioned that he will need all his strength in a few weeks, and that she's worried about him."

"Harvest." Mills nodded.

"Yep." Eli flipped the ball into the air from his glove. "He's had the pains in his joints for the last few years now. Nothin' no one can do about it – he's just gettin' old."

"All right," Mills stared at the rookie, "what's on yer mind?"

Eli drew a big breath, exhaled, and said nothing.

"I can see where Lou could probably let you go for a few days. This team ain't goin' nowhere right now-"

Eli said, "you've been on a farm, Buster. Harvest isn't 'a few days'. You and I both know that if I go, I'm gone."

"Just get that cash crop in-"

"Harvest is more than cash, Buster – it's a gift from God," Eli said firmly. "It's also about family. My father would be shamed to see a family other than ours do the reaping."

"Eli, that sounds like pride."

"Family," the rookie said, even more firmly. "It's all our people start with, and it's all we end with."

"All right." Mills flipped the ball at Eli and hit him in the chest. The rookie snatched it with his bare hand. "You're gonna have'ta talk with Lou about this. Soon."

"I'll need your help," Eli said. "You understand."

Buster shook his head. "Nope. This one's up to you, son. Just look Lou in the eye and talk to him. He ain't gonna bite'cha."

The two stood in the outfield for a moment. The sounds of a ball-park coming to life surrounded them.

"Lemme ask ya' somethin'," Buster spit some tobacco juice. "You still love playin', right?"

"Oh yeah, Buster," Eli answered immediately. "It's just that this game has always been 'play'. It was a break from work. Now... there's work to be done."

Mills smiled. "Well son, you're right. There is work to be done – in about 30 minutes – and you best be gettin' your mind on it."

"Yep."

"...Weaver was straightened up by that fast one. He may have been leaning out over the plate a bit, right there – and the count goes to 2-and-2. Keltner leads off second, representing the tying run. Fowler checks him, and delivers - Weaver wallops a SCREAMER down the right field line annnnnnnnnnnnd GONE! And just like that – Eli Weaver turns this one around, and it's the Clevelands who have the lead back!"

"Jack, it seems like every time we visit Philly, Eli sends his Pennsylvania Dutch fans a souvenir out there in the right field seats!"

"He does make a habit of it, doesn't he? Weaver's 15th round-tripper of the year gives the Indians a 6-5 advantage!"

THE CLEVELAND NEWS

Best Sports In Town

PEN GETS F's VS. A's

Late Lead Vanishes As Tribe Falls 8-6 To Lowly Phila

3rd Straight Loss To Start 19-Game Trip

MONDAY AUGUST 26

"Hey, kid!" The voice from over Eli's shoulder was sharp and direct.

The Boston ballplayer strode confidently out toward the Indians players taking batting practice like he owned the place.

He basically did.

"Ted Williams." He extended his strong, calloused hand to Eli.

"Eli Weaver."

"Just call me 'Ted'." Williams smiled. "So, you know who I am? I hear you don't know a lot of folks you're playin' against."

"That's true, but I know you." Eli tried not to blush.

"I know you're up soon," Williams said, "mind if I stand back here and watch you hit?"

"Watch me?" the rookie stammered.

"One thing I've learned, is that you never stop learnin'," Williams said sharply.

Eli started cranking out line drives – the sharp crack of the bat echoing through the ballpark, followed a few seconds later by a sharp metallic bang or hollow wooden thud – depending on which part of the left field wall the rookie's liners collided with.

The consistency of it might have been boring to those who arrived early, but Williams was smiling and nodding. A few of his Boston teammates would sidle up to him and whisper a question, and The Splendid Splinter would step back from the mesh, point at Eli's hands, shoulders, or hips, and then demonstrate for his teammate – replicating Weaver's moves precisely.

After about a dozen swings, Williams motioned to the batting practice pitcher, and began pointing to where he wanted the next pitch delivered.

Soon, Eli was sending rockets to every corner of the park.

Ted Williams behind the screen, was directing the rookie's batting practice, increasing the pace at which the pitches were delivered, and moving his bat around directing location like a conductor of an orchestra.

And the rookie, Eli Weaver, was so locked in that he didn't perceive what was happening.

Both teams saw what Williams was doing, and turned to watch the show.

After hitting four in a row deep into right field, Eli lunged at a pitch that was well outside, and sent a spinner down the right field line. It curled perfectly around the foul pole and rattled around in the wooden seats.

Eli heard laughter behind the plate and spun around to see Williams comically directing the next pitch to be ridiculously outside. The rookie realized the veteran had been pulling his strings.

Both teams started laughing.

Eli dropped his bat, bent over, shook his head, and started laughing, too.

"C'mon, rook!" Boudreau smiled. "I need Ted's 'help', too!"

Williams threw an arm around Weaver's shoulder as he stepped away from the screen.

Of course, there was a standing rule in major league baseball against players on opposing clubs fraternizing.

But who was going to reprimand Ted Williams?

Ted put one of his forearms next to the rookie's.

"See? Look at that!" Williams exclaimed to no one in particular. "My arm's like that from hitting a few hundred balls a day. His arms are like that from pitchin' hay and hammering horseshoes! Good swings, kid!"

"Thanks," Eli paused... and looked at a man who was identifying himself as his peer, "I appreciate it... Ted."

"Let's go, Eli!" Buster Mills yelled. "Back in the clubhouse!"

Williams ignored him and draped his arm around the rookie again.

"Hey Eli," the veteran leaned in toward the rookie, "have you ever smelled smoke from the wood of your bat?"

Eli stared at Williams. He was thinking.

"Five or six times," Williams said. "Hitting against a guy with good stuff, I swung hard and just fouled it back. Really hit it hard. And I smelled the wood of the bat burning a little."

And then the light came on.

"Yes," the rookie smiled, "the first day. At my tryout. When Feller was pitching to me. I do remember that."

Williams punched the young man in the chest and laughed. "Yeah – batting off Feller! Me too!"

"Let's go, Eli," Mills called again.

Ted nodded toward the Indians' dugout. "Have a good trip, kid. We'll talk more in Cleveland."

"...and it's a lazy pop into short left... Pesky is drifting back – and he makes the catch, right in front of Ted Williams. The two shake hands, and this one's over. The Sox polish off the Indians 5-to-1, and sweep the 3-game series."

"A very discouraging series on a very discouraging road trip, Jack. Cleveland has now lost 7 out of 8, and 9 of their last 11. The only bright spot of the trip continues to be Eli Weaver. The 19-year-old rookie doubled, tripled, and knocked home the only run Boudreau's men could muster today. The young man from Mt. Hope has his batting average back up to a sizzling .348, but if there's no one on base, and no one can knock you in, the Tribe's prized rookie might as well be playing 'one against nine'..."

THE CLEVELAND NEWS
Best Sports In Town
POWER OUTAGE
Tribe Swept in Beantown – Yanks Next
Weaver Lone Bright Spot in Listless Wigwam

AUGUST 2 9

"Weaver swings, and it's a harmless, little roller to Rizzuto. The Scooter flips to Gordon at second, and Cleveland takes another beating – this time 9-to-1 at the hands of the Yankees."

"For a Yankee club that's going nowhere but 2nd place behind Boston, the Bombers certainly took it out on the Indians in this 2-game set, outscoring the Clevelands 13-to-1 in the series."

"...and Bob, the Indians have now lost nine out of ten-"

"...with Chicago, St. Louis, and Detroit yet to go on this 21-day cross-country jouney."

"Speaking of Chicago, Bob, with their win this afternoon, the White Sox are now tied for 5th place with the fading Indians, and could send them straight to 6th place when we arrive in the Windy City for the weekend."

"Three hits apiece in the two games here at Yankee Stadium for Weaver, Keltner, and Hegan – but only one precious run in 18 innings."

1600HRS-NYCPENNHTL
MR.A.B.CHANDLER
COMMISSIONER OF BASEBALL
MICH AVE-CHICAGO

HAP-
TRAIN DELAY IN NY
SCHED ARRIVAL NOON IN CHI
IS MEETING STILL ON
VEECK

1630HRS-CHI
MR.B.VEECK
CLEVINDIANS – PENNAHOTEL NYC

BILL-
I WILL BE HERE
DO YOUR BEST
SAFE TRAVELS
CHANDLER

The losing was certainly bad enough.

Now, after rushing through a game in just over an hour-and-a-half to beat the approaching thunderstorms, then fighting their way through Manhattan traffic, the team disembarked and the porters unloaded the contents of the bus and carted them to the platform... only to find an engine with a busted front axle that had to be dragged to the roundhouse and replaced.

With the thunderstorms unleashing on Midtown Manhattan, the group of angry players discovered their only good fortune of the day at the curb of Penn Station.

Their bus was still pinned to the spot at the curb by the gridlock that had surrounded them when it had dropped them off 20 minutes before.

The Cleveland Indians reboarded the bus... and sat. For another 20 minutes.

At least they were dry.

After another 15 minutes where they traveled a grand total of two blocks back to the Hotel Pennsylvania, the team fanned out into the lobby to await the call to return to their train – which might be hours away.

Eli watched the storm sitting in a bay window looking out at the pedestrians trying to keep their umbrellas from turning inside out as they scurried along 7th Avenue.

"Hey, rook. Wanna'git some dinner?" Buster called.

"No, Buster. Thanks."

"You sure?" his coach persisted. "Could be hours 'till they call us back to the train."

"I'm sure," Eli said quietly.

"You allright?" Mills asked with a frown.

"Okay. Just thinkin'."

"That's dangerous." Buster winked.

"C'mon, Mills!" a group of players yelled from the revolving doors.

The coach disappeared out the door, and into a waiting cab.

As the storm intensified again, Eli got up, and walked over to the big radio console a few feet away and turned it on.

Before venturing into the world of the English, the only place Eli had seen a radio was in the hardware store in Mt. Hope. A couple of times, his father had caught him listening to it near the store's display window. That got Eli dragged out of the store by the ear. And a lecture. All the way home.

Now, the radio was the one thing he looked forward to in the hotels where the team stayed. Although the music was strange at first, he gradually began to enjoy it. There was the brassy music that the chambermaids were dancing to in the hallways if he left the volume turned up. Every now and then he saw them as they spun each other around – laughing in the corridor.

One night in St. Louis, two negro chambermaids called him into the hallway, and asked Eli if he wanted to dance. After protesting that he didn't dance, the ladies decided they could teach anyone.

And they tried.

For five minutes.

At that point, they decided that they had too many rooms yet to do – and that this young farm boy was hopelessly lacking in rhythm.

Actually, Eli was hoping he would have another chance to learn. After the next two games in Chicago, there were four games coming up in St. Louis.

Plenty of opportunities to leave the hotel room door open.

And wouldn't Rachael be surprised if he came home and taught her to dance down by the creek!

Of course, he wouldn't have music from the radio… but then Rachael wouldn't really know that he couldn't really dance.

Rachael.

His mind drifted away from the program on the radio, and back out the window to the thunderstorm.

Every day, his time of decision got closer.

And every day of this road trip, Eli did his best to push it out of his mind.

As long as he was on the road, he knew he was out of reach of Rachael's letters, the distant possibility of a family phone call to the hotel where he stayed, and... making a decision.

The lightning outside picked up again. The buzzing and static on the radio from the electrical storm jolted him back from Mt. Hope.

Eli didn't like the "funny programs", like the one that was on now.

He didn't understand the joking that was going on, but he knew it had to be funny because the people who were there sounded like they were having the time of their lives.

Eli smiled as he thought of his favorite show on the radio: *The Shadow.*

He liked the feeling the mysteries made in his stomach, and The Shadow's laugh when he caught the bad guy.

He *was* becoming *English*, he thought.

Dancing?

Radio shows?

Had he changed that much in ten weeks?

A pretty young woman stepped from the revolving door, and at the next quarter-turn, a young man was closing his umbrella as he stepped into the lobby after her.

She offered her arm to him, and as they walked toward the elevators, she laid her head on his shoulder.

Eli drew a long breath, and let out an even longer sigh as he turned his attention back to the radio. The "funny program" was still on, and the audience laughed and applauded as the band played a series of happy notes.

Eli stared out the window. The storm was moving east.

"All right friends, this is 'Bob-for Pepsodent-Hope'. Remember: 4 out of 5 dentists in a recent survey recommend Pepsodent. So, if you don't wanna get drilled anytime soon, choose minty-fresh Pepsodent! Well, I wanna tell'ya, we have a real treat for you right now. The last time this young lady was with us, you loved her so much that you let us know how much you wanted her back. But this time, she returns to our show with a song that took her to the top of the charts just a few weeks ago. Will you please welcome back, Miss Dinah Shore!"

(audience applauds – orchestra swells)

"I'm laughing on the outside
Crying on the inside
'Cause I'm so in love with you

They see me night and daytime
Having such a gay time
They don't know what I go through
I'm laughing on the outside
Crying on the inside
'Cause I'm so in love with you

No one knows it's just a pose
Pretending I'm glad we're apart
But when I cry, my eyes are dry
The tears are in my heart

My darling, can't we make up?
Ever since our breakup

Make believe is all I do
I'm laughing on the outside
Crying on the inside
'Cause I'm so in love with you

Yes, I'm laughing on the outside
Crying on the inside
'Cause I'm so in love with you

As the applause rose, so did Eli.

He turned the radio off and sat back down on the wide window sill, as the drizzle leftover from the storm ran slowly down the window.

AUGUST  30

The Office of The Commissioner of Baseball – Chicago

"C'mon in Bill, Eli, have a seat!"

Albert Benjamin (Happy) Chandler was the former Governor and Senator from Kentucky. With the passing of Judge Kennesaw Mountain Landis just one year before, baseball needed a Commissioner for the first time in over a generation. The owners of the 16 major league teams quickly realized that with change coming to their sport, and their nation, it would be in their best interest to have a leader who understood the political workings of Washington DC.

Landis had saved the game from itself 25 years before. Chandler's job was to move baseball forward – racially, geographically, but most importantly – economically.

"Eli Weaver... well, well. Hello, son. Happy Chandler. You sit here. Right across from me."

After the handshakes, the Commissioner circled the desk to his chair. While he did, Veeck mouthed the words 'let me do the talking' to his young rookie, who willingly nodded.

"Thanks for being flexible with your time, Hap," Veeck said. "Our train didn't pull in until 4 a.m."

"I'm sorry about your road trip, Bill." Chandler shook his head. "Between the train schedules, and the road trip schedule, your guys haven't caught many breaks."

"Happy, I just want to thank you for not making this a formal hearing," Veeck smiled. "It's good to just be able to speak my mind."

"Uh-oh!" the Commissioner laughed.

"...and it also means I didn't have to wear a tie." Veeck smiled more broadly.

Chandler's laugh was long, loud, and rich.

He had softened him up, now Bill thought – to turn on the charm. "Hap, I think this whole thing has been a big misund-"

"It may interest you to know," Chandler interrupted, "that I have watched the newsreel footage of this altercation in Cleveland, and also the previous dust-up you two had at Comiskey not too long before. From what I've seen, Bill – I do think we've got a little mountain from a molehill here... and you, Eli – were obviously good at handling livestock."

Veeck relaxed. "Thanks, Happy. I knew that if could jus-"

The Commissioner turned directly to Eli. "It may also interest you to know, young man, that although I do not know you or your family personally, I know your people quite well."

Eli glanced nervously at his boss.

Veeck's eyes widened into the 'I have no idea where he's going with this' look.

It appeared his rookie would have to face these next few pitches on his own.

"The Amish were a big part of the population in my part of Kentucky. Fine, upstanding, honest as the day is long. If they'd been more dependable at the polls, I mighta' won a few more elections than I did." Chandler laughed at his joke.

As did his guests.

"Because of that," Chandler continued, "I have taken a particular interest in the first ten weeks of your career, young man."

Veeck liked where this might be going.

Eli remained as petrified as when he entered the room.

The Commissioner looked straight at the rookie. "I saw the modesty in your fast start at the plate, I saw how you handled those protestors in New York, and I noticed your handling of your boss' 'ladies night' a couple of weeks ago. Honestly son, you coulda' had quite a night if you so desired!"

Chandler laughed again.

The rookie blushed.

"Mmm-hmm," the Commissioner nodded, "but I know that's not who you are, or what you're made of. That's why I specifically told Bill that I wanted to meet you."

Eli's eyes met Chandler's.

"I know that living the life you've lived for all your 19 years, you probably know little of what's been happening outside your county... hell, your town."

The Commissioner leaned forward in his chair and folded his hands in front of him. "The world you were born into is not the world you live in now. A depression. World War Two. The speed of news spreading by way of the radio. It's a different world, Eli. Baseball is changing, too. I'm sure you've heard talk of the negro player – Jackie Robinson – who is playing in Montreal this season."

"Yes, sir," the rookie said.

"Robinson will be in Brooklyn next summer. He will represent his race well. And after him, there will be many more great negro players coming – unless I miss my guess, your boss over there will be the next owner to sign one. Won't you, Bill?"

"The thought never crossed my mind, Mr. Commissioner," Veeck said with a smile.

"Eli," Chandler returned his attention to the rookie, "as I have watched you, I have seen in you the type of player for this new era that is coming."

"Me?" Eli barely got the word out.

"A player who is strong, yet meek. A player who rarely speaks, but always speaks wisely – at the right moment. A player who appeals to the parents – the one they can point to on the field and say 'be like him'. And yes, as I think Bill has proven with his right field grandstand full of young women, a player who the ladies find... umm... let's say – interesting."

Veeck felt like he was being issued a license to print money.

"However," Chandler's look turned serious, "as I said, I understand you – your people. I also realize what continuing to play baseball beyond this season might mean for you."

Oh – don't wreck this, Hap – Veeck thought.

"This is about rum... rumma..." Chandler stumbled on the word.

"'Room-spring-uh'." The rookie pronounced it slowly, and phonetically.

"That's the word," the Commissioner said. "If you stay among us – we're the... English, I believe?"

"Yes, sir."

"That will come at a great personal – family – cost for you, I know."

"It will."

"I believe the word is-" Chandler paused, "*shunned...?*"

"Yes, sir." Eli looked at the floor. "That is one of the words."

"Son, I can't take your swings at the plate for you," the Commissioner said, "but I know a lot of people who can help you. In the next few years, we can make baseball on the field look a lot more like life looks for Americans every day. You've been thinking about going home, haven't you?"

Eli froze.

Veeck stared at his rookie.

After the slightest nod, Eli said quietly, "Yes, sir. I have."

The Commissioner nodded. "Like I said before Eli, I've spent some time around your people, and I understand what 'family' means to you... not to the depth you feel it – but I feel it nonetheless."

Chandler looked at Eli. "There aren't many young men with the talent for the game – *and* your disposition, Eli. Damn, I wish I had a little finger full of your talent. I'd'a chucked the Kentucky State House, and the Capitol Dome to play ball like you."

The Commissioner laughed again.

There was silence for a moment – but for the sounds of traffic on the street below.

"Think about this, son: I can help you. So can Bill. Promise me you'll seriously think about baseball and your future."

"I will, sir."

Chandler stood, looked at his watch, reached across his desk, and shook the rookie's hand. "Great to meet you, son-"

"Hap?" Veeck was still seated.

"Yeah, Bill?"

"The *suspension...?*" The owner spread his hands apart.

"Aww hell's bells," the Commissioner shook his head. "Haynes is gone for six games. I can't have pitchers throwing at players about stuff that didn't even happen on the ball field. If a kid objects to war, and doesn't go get his leg blown off, that's not a reason to drill'em with a baseball."

Chandler stopped. His face fell.

"Aw, dammit Bill, I'm sorry. You know I didn't mean that!"

"No offense taken," Veeck said, "but what about my boy?"

"The Commissioner looked out the window. "Bill, I can't just drop the whole suspension."

"Why not?" Veeck decided he could push a little since Chandler felt guilty.

"Aww, the White Sox will raise holy hell if I did."

"But you said Eli was innocent!" Veeck pushed again.

"I most certainly did not!" the Commissioner replied.

"You just as well could have!" Veeck was having fun now.

"Three games-" Chandler said.

"Oh, come on-"

"Shut up, Bill," the Commissioner said, "I wasn't finished."

Veeck folded his arms, and sank back in his chair, trying to look penitent.

"Three game suspension." Chandler pointed at Veeck. "You choose the games. You're out of the race. You're going to need all the box office you can get down the stretch."

It still stunk. It still wasn't justice. But the Indians' owner stretched out his hand. "Sounds okay, Hap."

"Just let me know a few days in advance so we can get the press release out," Chandler said. "Now gentlemen, I need to meet with the gentlemen of the press... in the bar downstairs."

The Commissioner beat them out the door of his own office.

Eli walked slowly beside his boss, whose limp had become more pronounced as the season progressed.

"Bill," the rookie shook his head, "why did I still get suspended if I really didn't do anything wrong?"

"Son," Veeck imitated Chandler's drawl, "you got a lot to learn about major league baseball. Sometimes, even when you're not guilty, you tend to wind up a little bit guilty anyway."

The owner stopped before the elevator and looked at the rookie.

"Eli, have you honestly thought about going home?"

The rookie looked down at his English suit, English tie, and English shoes.

"Yeah, Bill. I have."

Veeck put his hand on Eli's shoulder. "Will you please come and talk to me when you need to?"

"There's always a crowd in your office."

"I'll make the time," Bill said. "Have I treated you fairly? Is what I'm paying you okay?"

"I don't have time to spend it."

"Are your teammates treating you well? Are the reporters backing off when Buster asks them to?"

"Yes, Bill."

"If there's ever any reason I'm not available, just ask Ada – she's there for you, too."

"Okay."

"Do you know what the Commissioner meant by what he said?" Veeck realized that Eli may not have truly 'seen' his surroundings at the ballpark. "Have you ever noticed all that advertising all over the ballpark?"

Eli thought for a moment. "I spose' not."

Veeck nodded. "Every business that buys space in the ballpark, puts up those signs because they want the fans to buy their products. Do you realize that you can be a part of that?"

The young Amishman shrugged.

"Eli, besides the money you make for playing the game, the people at Ford will pay you to drive one of their cars. The people at Sohio will pay you to use their gasoline. The people at Richman's will *pay you* to wear their clothes."

The elevator doors opened and the pair stepped inside.

"Ground floor," Veeck said to the elevator operator. Then, he turned back toward his phenom. "If you endorse products, and you keep playing well in the future, your life will change in ways you can't imagine," Bill said.

"It already has, Bill," Eli replied as the elevator doors closed.

SEPTEMBER 1

SUNDAY | **1**

Comiskey Park – Chicago

The sound of the snap of the baseball hitting their gloves echoed in the upper deck above them. Buster and Eli were quieter than normal as they played catch before their Sunday game.

"C'mon rook!" Mills teased, "you're quiet as a mouse! I need to know what the Commissioner talked to you about..."

"No comment." Eli smiled.

"Gotta remember to say 'thanks' to Bill for teachin'ya' that phrase," Buster said as he fired the ball back to the rookie. "Whattya' gonna' do if Haynes throws at ya' today?"

Eli sent a high, arcing toss across the outfield.

"No comment."

"So, the Indians finish this brief, 2-game set in Chicago right where they started it – tied for 5th with the White Sox."

"...and once again Jack, Bobby Feller is the unfortunate victim of the Indians' lack of offense, falling to 22-and-11 on the season. Joe Haynes goes to 5-and-8 with the win – and he accomplished it without throwing at Eli Weaver... no battles by land or sea between them today."

"Speaking of Haynes, it looks like the Sox are having him serve his suspension for that little wrestling match at the Stadium starting with Chicago's game tomorrow. That means Haynes will only miss one start. No word from the Wigwam on when Weaver's suspension will begin."

"That's it for us. Here at Comiskey Park, the Clevelands are now 2-and-10 on this road trip, as the Sox get the measure of the Indians by a final score of 4-to-1."

"We'll talk to you tomorrow from Sportsman's Park in St. Louis. Have a good evening, everyone!"

SEPTEMBER

TUESDAY **3**

Holmes County, Ohio – near Mt. Hope

The Bishop was thankful that his horse knew where he was going. It was late, and the crickets and frogs in the ditches were audibly defining the sides of the dirt road on a warm, humid, late summer night.

It had been a two-hour meeting, and a quite unusual one for those who were teaching on Sunday in the local house churches. The growing concern from one end of the four-county region to the other was one that had never come up before: entire families were showing up to worship more tired than anyone could remember.

From all over Holmes County tonight, the Bishop heard stories that had become familiar throughout the summer: families, from the youngest children to their great-grandparents – not only yawning in the midst of holy services, but actually (and *increasingly*) falling asleep on Sunday mornings... in the presence of *God*.

As the men responsible for the spiritual welfare of their flocks talked, they searched for a common thread.

It has been a strong year for all the crops – corn, soybeans, wheat, and spelt were all doing well. Vegetables were thriving – the roadside stands were filled to the brim. The dairy farms were humming – it seemed like there were more tankers moving up and down the narrow back roads than ever before.

Still, that shouldn't necessarily translate to more tired families, they reasoned.

The work of an Amish farm was constant. From the first milking before dawn, to riding the last hay wagon in at dusk – and then stuffing the haylofts full by lantern light, it was work they rarely complained about, because it was this very work God Himself had called them to.

But... *sleeping* during holy services...?

The Bishop and the elders recognized that the harvest was fast approaching.

Long days got longer.

Tired farmers make mistakes.

Young men – and older men – got hurt. Or worse.

After two hours of conversation and theories that got them nowhere, their only mutual agreement came at the end of the night, as they all agreed to keep an eye on their people, and meet again in two weeks.

Halfway home, he came to the sharp downhill and the hand-built bridge at Yoder's Run – a good place to give Max a drink of water, and a chance to munch some fresh grass before pulling the Bishop's buggy up the last big climb before the last set of gently rolling hills that brought him home.

It was in that small hollow that he heard it.

Human sounds. Yelling...?

He turned to the west and walked up the hill, tilting his head in the direction of the noise.

Happy yelling.

But, so late...?

The Bishop wanted to urge Max out of the hollow, but a hill was a hill, and his Max was Max – old, and a bit ornery – just like him he thought with a smile.

John Yoder's farm was a quarter mile past the crest of the hill. As the Bishop approached the driveway, he slowed Max to a stop.

Again, the Bishop waited. This time, he was much closer than just a few minutes before.

Again, came the happy yells. Yes, the Yoders were up.

But, the house was dark.

Not even a lantern in the kitchen window.

Was ist...? He thought.

The Bishop looped Max's reins loosely around the mailbox post, and began walking up the dark driveway. He stayed in the wheel ruts from the Yoder's buggies where the dirt was nice and soft.

He certainly didn't want to announce his presence by tripping over loose stones and falling on his face – especially now that he was sneaking around on another man's property.

Another happy yell – this time with clapping.

From the barn.

His eyes had now had plenty of time to adjust fully from the English-lighted darkness of Mt. Hope, to the "Amish darkness" of the countryside.

The sliver of candlelight escaping from between the boards of the barn door was what he was focused on now.

But what were they doing in the barn so late on a Tuesday night?

Then – a voice.

But... not John's.

The voice was not natural. It was high-pitched, scratchy.

He got as close to the door as he dared, not wanting to be discovered spying on his own people.

The Bishop carefully took two more quiet steps toward the barn door, and leaned toward the crack to look in.

The Yoders, and his brother's family from next door were in a semi-circle, some sitting on hay bales, others pacing back and forth, and the children – (still awake!) posing with their... baseball bats...?

And the high, ethereal voice spoke again. Everyone in the barn "shushed" each other, and the grownups waved the children in to listen...

"...and here's the 3-1 pitch to Weaver - - swung on and BELTED to DEEP right center – that ball is between the outfielders, and will skip all the way to the wall! One run scores! Here comes a second – and Weaver has turned for third – the relay – the sliiiiiiiiiiiide annnnnnd... SAFE! Weaver is safe at third, and Cleveland's lead is up to 7-to-3!"

"Eli Weaver has a single, a double, AND a triple tonight! WOW!"

The grandparents were smiling and nodding, the men were slapping each other on the back, the ladies were cheering, and the children were swinging their bats, and sliding into piles of hay – then rising, and declaring themselves "SAFE".

A radio.

An English radio in an Amish barn.

The Bishop was stunned.

He backed away slowly from the light coming through the door and made his way quietly back to the road, as the cheers continued from the barn behind him.

Before untying Max and heading home, the Bishop turned and looked back up the driveway toward the Yoder's barn, as the bits and pieces of things he'd seen on his trips into Mt. Hope for the last two months began to make sense for the very first time.

It was at the end of June when he saw the signs in many of the stores in town, proclaiming that they had "FARM RADIOS" for sale.

Then, came the first of July, and the signs were new: "FARM RADIOS SOLD OUT – MORE COMING SOON"

Then, six weeks ago at the English hardware store: "RECHARGE FARM RADIO BATTERIES HERE – CROSLEY, WURLITZER, ATWATER-KENT, RCA"

The Bishop stopped his buggy at three more farms, walked up three more driveways, and found the same thing at the end of each one: a dark house, a candlelit barn, and cheering families.

Listening to English radios when they should have been sleeping in their Amish beds.

As the Bishop fed, watered, and groomed Max in his stall upon finally arriving home, he was already composing a letter to his churches in his mind. It might take him much of the night to write it and copy it enough times so that every house church received one in time for Sunday's service, but he was determined to be waiting to hand them off to the postman when he pulled up to the house tomorrow.

Fifteen minutes later, after he had told his wife he would come to bed 'shortly', the Bishop sat down to write by the light of the oil lantern on his desk.

The Bishop wrote with anger, concern, and... as he calmed down... just a very tiny amount of... pride.

SEPTEMBER FRIDAY 6

"Where were you for breakfast this mornin'?" Buster asked as the ball smacked into the palm of his mitt.

"Out takin' a walk," Eli replied as he awaited the toss back.

Mills snapped the ball back in the rookie's direction. "One more ballgame today and then we get to go home. Y'all ready to go home, son?"

Eli froze for a second as he caught the ball. "Yeah. I'm ready to go home."

"Cleveland, rookie. Cleveland," his coach said.

"How much do we have left?" Eli asked, his mind far away.

"Three weeks," Buster's voice rose, as they both backed up across the outfield to play long toss. "Twenty games."

"Home." Eli shook his head. "Right now, 'home' only means batting last in baseball."

Mills laughed and nodded as he awaited Eli's throw by the left field line.

"Buster, you know what I mean," the rookie said as he sent the ball 200 feet on a line to his coach's glove, "you're from Texas. Cleveland isn't really home. All of us are from somewhere else – Pennsylvania, Kentucky, California... I suppose Feller is going home. He has a house in Cleveland, but he's from Iowa, right?"

"While we're playing this game," Buster said as he fired the ball back, "'home' is where you go when the road trip's over."

Eli shook his head again as he planted his right foot and pushed forward with his return toss. "My home is closer to Cleveland than any of yours. But that hundred miles feels more like a thousand every day."

"Three weeks, rookie. Three weeks."

"...Becker swings and misses, and this game – and this road trip – is mercifully over."

"The Indians lose 9-to-nothing today, managing only 4 hits in the process."

"Even young Eli Weaver fell victim to 'Tribe-itis' today, going 0-for-3-"

"...he's been hitting like a house afire this week, but today-"

"Today Bob, these young fellas look like they decided that the faster our train departs for Cleveland, the faster this 7-city odyssey to every ballpark in the American League would finally come to an end."

THE CLEVELAND NEWS
Best Sports In Town
LIMPING HOME
A Three-Week Disaster
Indians 4-14 On Ill-Fated Trip
By Hal Lebovitz

(Detroit)

The trip was nearly three weeks long and covered thousands of miles by rail.

The scenery as we traveled was pleasant.

The accommodations on the train were first rate. Good food. Comfortable beds. Plenty of light for working or reading into the night.

It was at the destinations where the power went out.

The Indians' 9-0 loss at Briggs Stadium this afternoon in front of 9,281 happy bengal boosters could be explained away. Losses like this happen at the end of a long road trip.

But, what about the preceding two games?

In the 27 innings played in Detroit, Eli Weaver's RBI double in the first inning of the first game provided the only run Cleveland pitchers would see in their support.

Although the Tribe was roused from their slumbers in the top half of innings briefly in St. Louis and Chicago, the rest of the trip provided the type of frustration that can only be generated by a team that knows their season's end is drawing near.

Even the aforementioned Mr. Weaver wasn't immune to Tribe Troubles today.

In the 7th, with Tigers at every base, and facing an insurmountable 5-0 lead, Weaver snagged a liner from the bat of Roy Cullenbine in deep right center field. Whirling quickly, his strong arm uncorked a heave that cleared Cleveland catcher Jim Hegan, and his backup, pitcher Charlie Gassaway – who looked somewhat astonished as the baseball sailed well above his 6'3" frame. Striking the top of the screen behind home plate, the ball skipped into the front row of the upper deck, where a youngster took home an unlikely souvenir. It was the first error of Weaver's career.

George Kell scored from third, Greenberg was waved around from second, and Wakefield got a free trip from first to third, scoring moments later on Webb's single.

The score was now 8-0, but the carnage was not yet complete, as catcher Joe Swift greeted the Indians' third pitcher of the day, Joe Berry, with a solo homer to the upper deck in right field, to account for the 9-0 final deficit.

On this road trip, Eli Weaver went 23-for-77, for a batting average of .298 – fifty points below his season average when the trip began.

As depressing as that may sound, this reporter – looking back over his scorecards for the last 18 games (with one tie in St. Louis) – found that the Indians hit .216 for the trip.

This makes the 19-year-old rookie from Mt. Hope seem Ruthian in comparison.

Cleveland will attempt to salvage some dignity in the final three weeks of the campaign beginning at 3pm Saturday afternoon at League Park.

Allie Reynolds is the scheduled starter for the Indians, and I'm sure The Superchief is hopeful the Tribe's hitting woes reverse with some home cooking.

As the train slowly rolled toward the union terminal, Bob Feller slid into the seat next to Eli.

"Eli… question for you," Feller said. "I know you're gonna' head home for the harvest as soon as we're done playing. But I was wondering if you'd consider coming out on the road with me and some of the boys from around the league. We're going to play across the country, different town every day."

Eli looked confused. "What team? Ours?"

"No, it's kind of an all-star team," Feller said, "me, Bobby Doerr, Mickey Vernon, Luke Appling, Warren Spahn..."

"You'd want me to play with them?" Eli asked.

"You've certainly shown that you can," Feller replied. "A lot of the guys have asked about you. The National Leaguers especially. And, so has the team we're playing against – the Negro League All-Stars – Satchel, Josh Gibson, Roy Campanella, Quincy Trouppe, Larry Doby, Buck O'Neil – they've all seen you on the newsreels, and they'd like to meet you."

"Wow."

Feller nodded. "You've drawn a lot of attention to yourself, kid. Barnstorming is good money, too. Cash on the barrelhead every day. Think it over and let me know."

"I will," Eli said, as the train jolted to a halt, and Feller headed up the aisle to his berth to grab his bag.

SEPTEMBER 7

The West Side Market – Cleveland

He walked.

As the season continued, Eli was seen, honked at by passing cars, waved at by passengers on buses, and gawked at on street corners – by young boys and teenage girls alike.

He had become an expert at 'ballplayer small talk', and had become adept at a fast autograph on almost any solid or flimsy surface: baseball, paper, hot dog wrapper, newspaper page margin, baseball cap, or human skin (forearm or bicep only... please).

On this Saturday morning, he glided through the revolving doors of the Hollenden Hotel and turned toward the river. He found his way to the Lorain-Carnegie Bridge, passing under the gaze of the cut stone Guardians of Traffic, and high above the final winding turns of the Cuyahoga River before it reached Lake Erie.

After a briskly paced mile across the bridge, and walking west on Lorain Avenue, Eli swung open the door of the West Side Market at the corner of West 25th, and entered the great hall.

Butchers with their beef, chicken, and pork. Bakers with breads and desserts. Fishmongers with fresh walleye and perch from Lake Erie. He wandered aimlessly up and down the aisles, at least in this place – and for the moment, relatively unrecognized. Those who shared the aisles with him were not looking for a rookie slugger. They were purposeful and focused on getting the best deals, being on time for the bus, and getting home.

After every corridor in the hall had been walked, Eli exited through one of the north doors, and crossed into the open-air produce market. Every vendor beckoned him toward their stand for samples of various fruits. The vegetable stands were less crowded, except for the vendor at the very end, who was doing a brisk business.

"CORN, CORN, CORN!" he yelled as Eli approached. "So fresh – you can tell by the smell!"

The vendor's son moved quickly to get another bushel out and re-stock the area for the shoppers.

"Hey kid," the vendor called to Eli, "make sure you take some corn home for your mom. It'll taste great with dinner tonight!"

"Looks fresh," the young man said.

"Darn right! Picked yesterday in Amish Country! CORN, CORN, CORN! So fresh you can tell by the smell!"

Eli looked up at the vendor. He was pronouncing the 'a' in Amish with a long vowel sound.

With the smallest touch of a smile, Eli picked up an ear, felt the tassel, and tugged away some of the husk to reveal the kernels inside.

He brought his nose close, took a deep breath, and smelled... home.

"C'mon Mr. Expert, I got a line here." The vendor gestured to those trying to get to his product. "Dozen for a buck. How many you want?"

"None, thanks." Eli stepped back, embarrassed.

"Great," the vendor snapped, "he pulls it open, sniffin' around my merchandise, takin' up space, and doesn't buy a damn thing. Thanks for nothin', kid."

Eli turned and looked at the customers crowding to take his spot.

"It wasn't picked yesterday. Probably Tuesday, maybe Wednesday," Eli said loudly.

"...the hell it..." the vendor stammered.

"That guy about eight stalls down. He's got fresh," Eli said as the customers began heading back down the aisle where Eli was pointing.

Eli Weaver pointed to his nose and looked at the glowering vendor.

"You can tell by the smell... right...?"

"Hey," a few of the shoppers said, "that's Eli Weaver! From the Indians!"

The rookie walked out of the market and looked for the bridge, signing brown shopping bags and butcher paper as he headed back toward downtown.

SEPTEMBER

League Park – Cleveland

It was a sound Eli had not heard before.

It was a sound that he had just created in the crowd. All by himself.

His mind had been drifting all afternoon. Away from the ballpark. Away from baseball.

There was only one other place his mind was going outside of the daily games, and the predictable repetition they brought.

Home.

But at the moment, there was that new sound in his ears.

"BOOOOOOOOOOOOOOOO!!!"

"C'mon rookie, get yer' head in the game!!!"

"You could'a had that one reachin' outta'yer buggy!"

He had to admit, there were so few people in the ballpark, he heard the crack of the bat clearly, and then blinked – found the ball a split-second late, and scrambled back toward the wall. Even with the late start, he was there in time. He just felt it hit the top of the webbing of his glove...

...and drop to the ground.

Eli banged against the wall, stumbled, reached down for the ball, and tripped over himself. Disgustedly, he grabbed the ball, spun, and fired it toward second-

---

"WHOA!!! Look at that one go! Sailing all the way to third while Stephens pulls up at second, and Schultz lumbers home. Now, it's 3-to-1 St. Louis, and Weaver's hearing the raspberries from the few faithful gathered in the right field grandstand."

"His second error in as many games, Jack... in fact, he might be charged with two errors on the play: one for not making the catch-"

"...and the other for another – 'amazing' throw."

Eli flopped down on the bench next to Buster.

"You alright?"

"I guess."

The coach kept staring out at the field and said quietly, "that sure looked like it. Like a guess."

"Sorry."

Buster remained quiet. "We ain't 'sorry' around here, son. We play hard. Every day. If we don't, someone's waiting to take our place."

"Yes, sir."

Mills smacked Eli on the knee. "Two days in a row. Don't make it three."

The rookie closed his eyes, and tilted his head back too fast, banging it against the concrete dugout wall.

He hadn't checked, but he hoped there was a service at Shiloh Baptist tonight.

THE CLEVELAND NEWS
Best Sports In Town
1-RUN WONDERS
St. Louis Wins 4-1 As Wigwam Woes Mount
Tribe Death Spiral Now 15 Of 19

...and... on the facing page of the News:

BROWNS PREP FOR STADIUM DEBUT
New Team – New League
Paul Brown – Searching For Linebackers
"Give Me Eli Weaver" Coach Says
Veeck Laughs – Says "No Chance"

SEPTEMBER

MONDAY **9**

Cleveland

Eli walked into the showroom with Bill Veeck on a sunny Monday morning, the chrome on the new Chevrolets sparkling all around them. As they came around the corner to his office, the owner of the dealership set down his sports section, and rose to greet them.

"Tom Bass," he said, as he extended his hand, "thanks for coming out, Bill – I've been looking forward to this."

"A pleasure, Tom," the Indians' owner replied. "And I'd like you to meet Eli Weaver."

"Definitely a pleasure!" Bass turned with an enthusiastic handshake. "We've been following your season all the way along, young man. Great to have you here in Cleveland!"

"Thanks."

"Tom. Call me Tom. Yes sir, took the family downtown quite a few times this summer. Really enjoy watching you play, son. Just wish your teammates could help you out a little," Bass said, as he pointed to the sports section on his desk.

THE CLEVELAND NEWS
Best Sports In Town
FINALLY A WIN
Indians Score 4 Runs In Doubleheader
Eke Out 3-2 Win Over STL In Nightcap

"We're working on that 'help' every day, Tom." Veeck gestured towards the newspaper. "Don't you worry, in '47 we'll make sure Eli is surrounded with guys in the lineup who can make sure this young man sees some fastballs."

Bass laughed, "Ahh, Bill – you're the baseball man. I'm sure you're going to take care of what happens on the field. I'm a businessman. And I'm interested in how you're bringing so many people downtown to watch a sixth-place team."

Veeck smiled.

"The other week, my wife and kids are cheering for the fireworks, and I'm looking around me at 50,000 people having a great time. Even though we lost the game," Bass said.

"That's the idea." Bill looked Bass in the eye.

"And that's why I called you," the car dealer said excitedly, "I thought, 'If he can get 50,000 down here to see a sixth-place team, what's going to happen when they start to win?'"

Veeck smiled again, "and all those people should be driving Chevys."

Bass nodded, smiled, and looked around his showroom with dollar signs in his eyes. "Let me show you this, young man – the all-new 1947 Chevrolet Stylemaster! Got a few off the truck from Flint this weekend."

Eli stood in front of a gleaming maroon machine with whitewall tires and sparkling chrome front and back.

Bass opened the door. "Hop into the driver's seat, Eli!"

The rookie complied.

"Straight six – plenty of power, three on the tree – nice smooth transmission, and sturdier drive train... hey, we learned something during the war." The dealer laughed. "That radio's great, too. Better reception, and the speakers are a couple inches bigger. Boy, what a great ad it'll make in the scorecard next year – 'Cleveland's Newest Star – On the Field – On the Road'!"

"But-" Eli protested.

"Put your hands on the wheel, son," Bass gestured, "tooling around town in a car like this – pulling into the Stadium parking lot – 'Eli Weaver Drives A Chevy, and You Should, Too!'"

"But-" Eli tried again as Veeck smiled.

Bass slapped Bill on the back. "We'll even give a couple away at the Stadium during the season! Let the fan drive right out of the ballpark in their brand new 1947 Chevrolet! And Eli, your face will be in every ad: 'Why don't you drive what I drive?'"

"But, I can't *drive*," the rookie blurted out.

The dealer waved his hand. "Ahhh, don't you worry about that, son. I know where you come from. We'll make sure that we have one of our fellas here take you out on the streets around the dealership and teach you all the basics. You'll pick it up fast."

Veeck and the dealer patted Eli on the shoulder and headed off to the office to talk business. The rookie sat in the car, a bewildering array of gauges, buttons, wood, leather, and shining metal spread out in front of him.

Was this where his life was going? He had asked himself that question as he wore a suit in the dining cars of trains, as he fell onto the bed in luxury hotels, and as he and his teammates drew the admiring gaze of the young women in the stands at ballparks.

There were more moments – increasingly more – when he seriously thought over this outcome. Staying among the English. Playing baseball. Money. Cars like this.

Rachael would see it.

Would she understand it?

Yes. She would follow him.

He hoped.

Veeck emerged from Bass' office with a hearty laugh and a strong handshake.

"Couldn't pry you out of that car – I knew it!" the dealer yelled across the showroom.

For the next few minutes, Eli signed autographed photos (that did not show his face, of course) of him at the plate, which had miraculously appeared out of his boss' notebook.

A cab appeared in front of the dealership. The owner and the rookie got inside.

"League Park… but, take us along North Park first," Veeck told the driver.

The two rode in silence as the cab swept slowly past some of the most beautiful homes in Northeast Ohio. Veeck asked the cabbie to stop and wait for a moment. The owner and the rookie stood in front of a beautiful Tudor surrounded by neatly-trimmed shrubs, and trees getting ready to change color in just few weeks.

"Eli-" Veeck looked at the young man, "that guy back at the car dealership was serious. He will give you that car to drive and teach you to drive it. And there are a dozen more like him. Remember what I told you about the people who will pay you to hold a bottle of their beer for an advertisement, people who will let you use their appliances, who will give you their suits to wear, and eat at their restaurants…

all because of how far you can hit a baseball."

"It's... more than I can believe," Eli said.

"And these houses we're passing?" Veeck pointed. "Those beautiful apartments near the hill over there? You will be able to live anywhere you wish. Eli, you're hitting .355 right now. There are only a few players in all of baseball who are capable of such a thing. I not only want to ensure that you keep playing here for me, but I want to make sure that this winter we find the right players who can make this team better, and make you even better, because they will surround you in the lineup."

For a young man who grew up around nothing but white houses with black shutters, the idea of owning one of the homes within the sweep of his line of sight was a bit dizzying.

"Eli-" Veeck placed his hand on the rookie's shoulder, "I need to know – soon – not this moment – but soon – whether you will be back with us next season."

Eli shifted uneasily.

"Hey mac," the cabbie called, "the meter's runnin'."

"Hang on. We're coming!" Veeck called. He turned back to Eli. "I know your decision will be a hard one. But I wanted to bring you here today because I want you to see what your future – this future – can look like."

Eli looked down at the sidewalk.

Bill squeezed his shoulder. "That day when I came to meet you, your family, and saw your community, I didn't get it. But, when I saw your family come to Cleveland, when I see all those Amish come to the games in Philly, I'm starting to understand exactly what I'm asking you to leave."

The rookie looked back at his boss.

"But, as hard as that *will be*, I want you to see how good this *could be*."

Veeck smiled. The rookie nodded.

They climbed back into the cab and headed toward the ballpark.

On the Indians' off days, League Park was taken over by the Negro League's Cleveland Buckeyes. As the cab rolled up to the Ticket House at 66th and Lexington, Veeck and his rookie both saw the banners up above the entryway:

BUCKEYES HOME TODAY

WORLD'S COLORED CHAMPIONS

The ticket takers at the turnstiles smiled and waved them both inside.

It only took Eli a few moments to grab what was now a large paper bag filled to the top with his fan mail. He had heard the sounds of bat and ball, and encouragements, and razzing so much in the last three months. But today, even though he wasn't suited up to play, he still instinctively turned toward the sounds of the game, and the fans.

Eli walked up to the upper deck, and then up the ramp, and saw the small ballpark spread out before him.

The green of the grass. The dark of the dirt.

And the speed of the game.

The Buckeyes were playing the Indianapolis Clowns, and the speed – the agility – the athleticism Eli was seeing shocked him for a moment.

Every one of these guys is as fast as I am, Eli thought.

A few minutes later, the rookie added to his list.

Almost all these guys can hit like me, too.

Oscar spotted him in the upper deck on the third base side, and took the steps up, waving and smiling as he approached, and dropped into the seat next to him.

"Hi, Oscar." Eli waved.

"What do you think, Mr. Eli?" Oscar asked.

The rookie shook his head. "These guys are great."

"Agreed," Oscar nodded, "things gonna be changin' soon."

Eli nodded. "Every time I open the newspaper, I'm reading about Jackie Robinson in Montreal."

"And these players...?" Oscar nodded at the field.

"Half of them should be in the majors right now." Eli pointed to the dugouts.

Oscar's eyes narrowed. "Damn right."

It was the first time Eli had ever heard a word like that spoken by his friend from Shiloh Baptist Church. It was also the first time he had seen that look on Oscar's face. What was it?

Anger?

Pain?

Both.

Eli jumped up as a Buckeye outfielder made a spectacular running catch in deep left-center. "What a play!"

Oscar didn't react. He was staring out at the rundown houses along Lexington Avenue past the center field scoreboard.

"Things are gonna be changin' soon," Oscar said again.

"Baseball next year could be very different," Eli said.

Oscar was still looking beyond the ballfield.

"Not just baseball," he said quietly.

SEPTEMBER TUESDAY 10

League Park – Cleveland

Only 2,504 faithful fans saw it. But, the slumping Indians won their second straight, (and only their sixth in 22 games) a 4-2 victory over the Yankees, who came to Cleveland knowing their season-long pursuit of the Red Sox had reached its end.

Eli had gone hitless on the day, but made a perfect throw from the right field corner to snuff out a runner trying for two, and a rally in the process. That earned him the cheers of his biggest fans: The Knothole Gang. The neighborhood children would gather to take turns trying to watch as much of the game as they could through cracks in the sliding metal door in the right field corner. The kids would call for him all game long, and Eli would let them know when he was going to loft some baseballs over the screen and onto Lexington Avenue for them. Before grabbing the streetcar back downtown, Eli would always sign autographs for them – and even get into an occasional stickball game in the alleys near League Park.

Eli's efforts that day also got him a big backslap on the way to the clubhouse from Steve Gromek. The righthander had pitched decently, but without any luck, all season long. At this point, just seeing his record go to 5-14 gave Gromek a bit of relief as a hard year wound down.

As usual, there was a stack of fan mail on the stool in front of his locker, but from ten feet away, he saw what was on the top of the stack.

A letter from Rachael.

DEAREST ELI,

This note is short. Not because I have little to say, but because I want it to make the Monday morning mail in Mt. Hope.

Your fans are growing more numerous by the day here in Holmes County.

The Bishop wrote a letter to be read in every service today expressing his displeasure at how tired everyone is every Sunday morning.

The Bishop feels that the reason for this fatigue is his discovery that so many of our families have purchased "farm radios" and rechargeable batteries.

The Bishop actually came to our gathering to read the letter himself. He seemed to read it directly to your family. Though he did not condemn the radios by name, he made it clear that he was unhappy.

He said, "Now that the tools of the English are in our barns, when can we expect them in our houses?" And: "Is it not better to know how many hundreds Jesus healed from disease, than to know if a right fielder is hitting three hundred?"

None of us could look up at that moment. Except for your little brother Lukas. He jumped up and said:

"Bishop, Eli is hitting .348 after last night! They said it on the radio!"

None of could look at each other, or look up. Your mother did peek, and the Bishop was very red before he asked one of the deacons to pray, and sat down.

Did we all laugh when we got home? Before God, and you, I will admit – yes, we certainly did.

I will not say if I have come to your house for frequent visits in the evenings recently.

But, I will say the many good hits you had in St. Louis and Detroit were very exciting, and made everyone in the family very happy.

Whether you are here or not, it seems you cannot help but create excitement.

EVER YOURS,
RACHAEL

Eli smiled, folded the letter, and placed it back in its envelope.

Then pulled it back out and read it again.

And smiled, and placed it back in its envelope.

SEPTEMBER

League Park – Cleveland

"So, your Bishop ain't a baseball fan?" Buster laughed as he tossed a wobbly knuckleball in Eli's general direction.

The rookie laughed and lunged for the knuckler as it broke. "Guess not."

"How many of your people bought those radios?" Mills asked.

Eli snapped a throw back to his coach. "Well... if he wrote to all the weekly services like Rachael said – I s'pose that'd be the whole county's worth!"

Buster laughed and pushed another knuckleball Eli's way. "C'mon kid, gimme the knuckler – you kinda had the hang of it yesterday."

Eli pulled the ball from his mitt with his fingertips and looked at it in his hand.

"Yeah, you got it," Buster said, "let er'rip."

The rookie smiled and started a cartoon-like full windup with a high leg kick. When he finally released the ball, it was a darn good knuckler – almost no spin, but with a bit of speed. As Buster reached for it, the ball darted downward, and plunked him in the shin. The coach howled in pain.

"Take your base!" Bob Feller yelled in an umpire's tone from a few feet away. "C'mon Eli, quit messing with that nonsense and give him the heater!"

Buster limped over toward the ball with a smile. "Best one yet, kid!"

"...2-nothing Cleveland here in the 5th, and now Bonham has to deal with Weaver again. The Yankee hurler walked him last time, but this time there's nowhere to put him – bases full of Indians!"

"This at bat could decide both teams' fates today, Jack. If Bonham can hold the rookie down, the Yanks are still in the game."

"...and if Eli can get a hold of one, the Tribe will have some breathing room... here's Bonham's first offering – WAY outside for ball one... Weaver doesn't move his feet in the batter's box, but he's got that big bat wagging back and forth. Now, Bonham again – looking in for the sign... and the windup – here it comes... ball two! A little closer, but still not in the neighborhood of East 66th and Lexington."

"Well... he's gotta get one over now – can't afford to go 3-and-0."

"Weaver still rooted in his spot in the box... he's ready. Now Bonham winds for the 2-0 – IN THE DIRT, ball three! Robinson with a great save on that one, saving a run – for the moment, at least. Not many lovers of the game in the ballpark today, but I'm sure you can hear them banging those wooden seats... well, Tiny Bonham... what are you going to throw now...? He looks... he nods... he winds... he delivers... Weaver LUNGES and swings and OHHHHHH, LOOK AT IT GO! WAY UP! WAY OVER THE

SCREEN!! WAAAAAY OUT ACROSS LEXINGTON AVENUE!!! A TRE-
MENDOUS WALLOP!!! 6-TO-NOTHING, CLEVELAND!"

"Jack, I don't think that was a strike! It was well outside!"

"Weaver reached across the plate to get to it!"

"I think Bonham was trying to walk him with the bases loaded!"

"Well – it didn't work, did it?"

"Jack, from where we are in the press box, we could see the kids
scrambling across the street, toward that hedge row. There's plenty of
them searching for that ball, but they haven't found it yet!"

"They might want to knock on the door of those row houses over
there… it's probably in somebody's soup pot!"

"Either way, Tiny Bonham's day is done. He has been excused, and
Cuddles Marshall will be on from the New York bullpen."

"Well, there were rumors all over the ballpark today that Bill Veeck
has been talking with Eli Weaver about a deal for next season… Bill, I
think the kid's price just went up…"

"Thanks a lot, Jack!" Veeck snorted at the radio from the ticket
house in the right field corner.

"And, who might have been the source of those rumors, do you
think?" Ada smiled as she totaled up the ticket stubs collected from
the turnstiles.

"Darned if I know," Harry Grabiner said as he ran his pencil down
the column, adding up the day's take in his head.

"But, he's right," Veeck said. "Eli finishes strong, it might cost us
another five to ten thousand."

Grabiner flipped a page in the ledger to his right. "Looks like pre-
sale for the next two Sundays at the Stadium are both over 35,000…

not bad for a team that's 33 games behind."

"The Red Sox are losing." Veeck smiled as he glanced at the ticker. "We're only going to be 32-and-a-half back."

"That should be good for another 5,000 fans this Sunday." Ada brightened.

"And another ten thousand bucks for the rookie... if these rumors keep spreading," Grabiner said sarcastically.

Veeck's mind was dancing with visions of 1947 glory.

"No comment."

SEPTEMBER THURSDAY **12**

League Park – Cleveland

Buster gestured toward the Red Sox dugout with his thumb. "Well rook, here comes your best buddy..."

"Eli – good to see ya'!" Ted Williams boomed as he headed toward home plate with two bats in each hand. He rested them carefully up against the screen, looping the knobs into the mesh, so there wouldn't be a chance they would tip over.

"Good to see you," Eli paused – his teammates were staring at him, "Ted."

"First name basis?" Boudreau winked at Keltner. "Must be best buddies."

"Go 'shift' yourself, Boudreau!" Williams looked at his teammates and got the approval on his wordplay he was expecting.

"Funny man. You're a regular Fred Allen..." Boudreau shook his head.

Williams still held one of the four bats he'd brought from the dugout. He flipped it, knob to barrel, caught it, and held it out toward Eli.

"Here kid – give this one a try."

"Yer' givin'im your bat?" Johnny Pesky couldn't believe it. "What if he breaks it?"

"First, he's right-handed and he's on the other side of my sweet spot." The Splendid Splinter said. "And second – have you ever seen him hit one off the handle?" Williams looked at all the players around home plate. All shaking their heads.

Eli swung nervously (he knew everyone on both teams was watching), but smoothly. Line drives peppered the left field grass. Then the rookie's reflexes took over on a belt-high toss.

The sound of bat meeting ball changed.

Baseballs began rattling in the bleachers beyond the 375 sign in the left field corner.

"I pick out the billets at the factory in Louisville myself," Williams said. "Sometimes the wood just feels right from the moment you hold it in your hand. Every now and then, I ride out to the forest, and pick out a tree or two when they cut'em down. You can see the tightness of the grain right away – you just *know* when you're gonna get at least a dozen great bats out of a tree when you see that grain."

On his next swing, Eli's hands flew by first, then his wrists completed their turn as his arms followed.

The sound of the bat colliding with the ball was... almost unable to be heard... with all the chatter amongst the players.

"Uh-oh," Williams said, "look at *that* one!"

The conversation stopped as the ball climbed, crossed the left-center field fence over 400 feet away, and then disappeared behind the bleachers.

A couple of the Red Sox offered a low whistle.

"When you make perfect contact," Williams smiled, "it barely makes a sound. Nice swing, kid."

Boudreau caught Eli's eye and nodded toward Williams.

"Aww, let him hit some more, Lou!" The great slugger sounded like a kid who was going to take his bat and ball and go home.

"Thanks..." Eli flipped the bat knob to barrel the way Williams had, and held it out to him. As far as that first name was concerned, he always hesitated, "Ted."

"Tell you what Eli," Williams said as the rookie gave way to the next hitter, "in November, I'll drive through here, and pick you up – take you to Hillerich & Bradsby in Louisville. We'll pick out some good wood and tear this league apart next year!"

"...and the 2-oh pitch from Bagby – there's a ball rifled toward the gap in left-center – Williams checks up, and DiMaggio runs it to the wall! Here's Weaver digging for third... Dom's throw is nowhere near in time, and that hard-hittin' Eli Weaver has another triple!

"Huh. Looks like Ted Williams is flappin' his gums out there as he wanders back toward his position in left-"

"...and Eli Weaver is looking out at him with a big smile on his face! Well, we'll try to find out what that's all about after the ballgame..."

Eli glanced behind the dugout for just a moment, and saw the owner of the car dealership he had visited in the first row behind the dugout. Surrounding him in the box were three other men wearing suits, with shirts open at the collar, and ties loosened.

The car dealer tipped his fedora toward Eli, and nodded slightly. The gentlemen with him raised their bottles of beer.

Eli made a slight nod in their direction-

"All right. One out. Anything in the air, in the outfield, you're tagging up, got it?"

"Yeah."

The Indians sliced the Red Sox lead to a mere 31 ½ games with a 4-1 win.

In the locker room, Tommy, one of the batboys who always arrived just before the first pitch – now that school was back in session – walked up to Eli holding a bat in his hand.

"Eli, this just came over from the Red Sox clubhouse for you."

"Thanks, Tommy," Eli smiled. "And, thanks for polishing my shoes yesterday. It looked like you ran over here from school. You didn't have to do that."

"You're welcome."

"Homework tonight?"

Tommy's face soured immediately. The last thing he wanted to think about at the ballpark was-

"Math."

"Just remember, all division is, is batting averages and earned run averages," Eli winked. "And multiplyin' is the number of ears on a bunch of tassled out corn stalks."

Tommy scrunched his nose at Eli.

"... although you might not need to figure that around here."

"See you tomorrow, Eli."

"You too, Tommy." Eli looked down at the knob of the bat in his hand. There was a note attached. The rookie peeled off the paper and opened it up.

ELI–

I'll bet if you switched to my pattern, you'd be unstoppable, too.

See you in November.

TED

Eli shouldered the bat, then held it out in front of him, looking down the barrel to see the grain lines separated by – maybe a sixteenth of an inch.

He hefted the bat again, then placed it in the back of his locker stall, turning the barrel with Williams' signature away from the eyes of his teammates.

SEPTEMBER SUNDAY **15**

Cleveland Stadium

"I betcha' that's the bat you used in batting practice," Buster said.

Eli was embarrassed that his teammates knew about Ted Williams' gift. "Everybody knows...?" he asked.

"Not too many secrets in a tiny locker room, kid," Mills said as he tossed the ball back to Eli.

The rookie shook his head. "How do you know it's the bat I used in batting practice?"

Buster shrugged, "After you used all the hits in that bat for the rest of the month, what else could he do?"

"All the hits...?" Eli fired the ball back to his coach.

"Superstition." Buster laughed. "Some guys think every bat only has a certain number of hits in it. Once you started sprayin' the ball all over the yard the other day, I saw Ted's face while you were doin' it."

"He looked like you were stealin' his child!" Hank Edwards smiled as Mills threw the ball back to Eli. "It was pretty funny."

"So he gave me the bat?" Eli shook his head.

Ray Mack was playing catch with Edwards, and chimed in. "I bet he thought you contaminated it or something."

Jim Hegan was walking out to the bullpen with Red Embree to warm up. "C'mon, guys. Williams is not superstitious. I have never seen him step into the box and do anything random. He's always in the exact same spot in front of me. Every time."

"J'ever see him step on a baseline goin' on'n'off the field?" Buster said, as he caught Eli's toss.

"What does that have to do with anything?" Hegan snapped. "I step on the lines all the time!"

"Maybe that's why you're hitting .227..." Edwards replied calmly. Everyone in earshot howled.

"Going over today's pitcher in five minutes!" Boudreau called, then walked back down the dugout steps and disappeared toward the clubhouse.

"Anyway," Buster said as he threw back to Eli, "it's obvious 'Teddy Ballgame' likes you – and that's not a bad thing."

"'The Splendid Splinter'," Mack said – to no one in particular.

"Hmm," Mills thought, as he caught Eli's return toss, "how come we never got you a nickname, kid?"

Eli grabbed Buster's return throw. "I don't need a-"

"'The Holmes County Hammer'," Mack offered.

"'The Mt. Hope Masher'!" Felix Mackiewicz said as he headed for the dugout.

Boos rang out from his teammates.

Buster caught Eli's toss. "'The Amish Animal'?"

More booing.

Bob Feller jogged in from his long toss session in the outfield. "'Keen Eye Eli.'"

Someone threw a glove that hit Feller in the back.

Hank Edwards cleared his throat. "My brothers and sisters..." he said in the deep, rolling baritone of a revival preacher.

Everyone stopped playing catch as Edwards pointed at Eli with his bat...

"'Elijiah – The Prophet'!"

The rookie put his hands on his hips and stared at the ground, trying to hold it back, as his teammates laughed.

But, after a few seconds, Eli's shoulders were shaking, too.

"Weaver's got himself a single, a double, and a run batted in already today, and this big Sunday crowd is hungry for more. First pitch – swinging – and a NASTY liner up the alley in left-center! Seerey scores easily. Here comes Weaver around second on the fly! - - Weaver hitting third – and having to DIVE back into the bag as the throw is cut off, and thrown behind him into third... yessir, another TRIPLE!"

"And the A's caught a lucky break, Jack. With no fence here at the Stadium, Chapman just stuck his glove out, and the ball stuck in there. Then, he just whirled and threw without looking, and somehow found his cutoff man!"

"That's just about the only way you can stop young Eli Weaver these days – pure luck. It's 8-1 Cleveland in the 8th.

"And Eli Weaver now has 64 RBI in just a half-season of work in the wigwam!"

"Makes you just lick your chops thinking about what he could do in '47, doesn't it?"

Eli could hear the fans milling, and the vendors calls in the concourse outside the clubhouse. He changed his undershirt, leaned back into his locker, and closed his eyes for a moment before thinking about the second game of the doubleheader.

A SINGLE, A DOUBLE, AND A TRIPLE... ELI'S EVERYWHERE!

"Eli?"

Bobby the batboy handed him a note.

"Some guy in the boxes behind the dugout said I needed to get this to ya' – so, here ya' go."

Eli unfolded the note.

ELI–

My family has been watching you for the last few months, and we think you would be the perfect person to represent our company in 1947, and perhaps many years to come.

We would certainly compensate you well.

I've let Bill Veeck know of our interest, too. He indicated he would be happy to help us.

Keep up the good work!

Could we talk next week?

HERBERT SCHOEN

The Home Corporation

GA1-2323

The rookie slipped the note into his pants pocket, took another deep breath, and closed his eyes as he leaned back into his locker again.

SEPTEMBER ^{MONDAY} 16

Bill Veeck's Office – Cleveland Stadium

0800HRS-CHI
MR.B.VEECK
CLEVINDIANS – CLESTADIUM
W3RDST-CLEOH

BILL-
MUST SUSPEND WEAVER 6 GAMES
SOX KNOW OF OUR DEAL
CHI NEWSPAPERS REPORTING
SPINK TO PROTEST IN SPORTINGNEWS
WILL MAKE IT UP TO YOU
CHANDLER

Ada Ireland had laid the telegram on her boss' desk, and quickly left the room as Veeck slept on the couch in the corner. Her heels must have clicked just a bit too loudly as she crossed from the rug to the tile. Less than a minute later, Bill was fully awake.

"AWWWW, NO! He can't DO THAT!"

She was back in the doorway before he could bellow again.

"ADA!!!"

"Good morning to you, too," she said quietly.

"You saw this?" Veeck wide awake and ready to do battle.

"Chandler? On the phone?"

"YES!" Veeck looked at his secretary, shook his head, and took a breath. "Good morning, Ada. Sorry."

She smiled, "I live to be bellowed at. I'll get him right away. Coffee...?"

"I don't need it to wake up, but yes... coffee," the owner said.

Veeck didn't need to stew more than a minute.

"Chandler's on the line," Ada yelled from her desk. "For some reason, he was expecting your call. Cream...?"

"What?" Veeck paused in his irritation to remember he had coffee coming. "YEAH!"

Bill Veeck stared a hole in the receiver before he snatched it from the cradle of the phone.

"What are doing to me, Hap??? We had a DEAL!!!"

"Good morning, Bill," came the reply from Chicago.

"Three games, Happy." Veeck launched right in. "THREE STINKING GAMES! What happened to all that talk in your office last month?"

"Bill," the Commissioner knew he had to let the owner of the Indians blow off some steam, but he decided to try to calm him down, nonetheless. "I meant what I said. But somebody – either in this office – in the Chicago press – or in the Chicago press through a reporter in Cleveland, got wind of our agreement."

"SO???"

"The reporters called the Comiskeys, Charlie called Spink at The Sporting News, and J.G. called me," Chandler explained. "This all happened last night, and this morning, every paper in Chicago is running a 'sources say' story about the 'integrity of baseball', and the 'honor of the White Sox'."

"We had a DEAL, Happy!" Veeck was nowhere near calm... yet.

"Yes," the Commissioner said. "We did, and we do. It will just need to take a different form."

"Hap, I've got 10 games left," Veeck tried to keep his voice down, "and games 5 and 6 of those 10 are a doubleheader next Sunday that has a pre-sale of 40,000 and climbing. How do I honor my 'rookie of the year' NOW??? Are you planning on suspending him for games 1-2, and 3? Then, 8-9, and 10?"

"What three games were you going to use to complete our deal?"

"8-9, *and* 10!" Veeck was gaining steam again. "The final three games in Detroit! They're not gonna draw flies for those games anyway."

"Bill," Chandler tried again, "I need to keep the peace here. The Chicago press will take this out of my hide for months, and so will *The Sporting News*. Next year has to start calm. Jackie Robinson was the star of the International League this year, and you and I both know that Rickey wants him on the Dodgers opening day roster next spring. I'm getting some annoying rumors from out west about Durocher, and the hoods he's hanging out with, and who the hell knows what you have up your sleeve-"

Veeck laughed into the phone despite his anger.

"I said it in the telegram, and I mean it: I will make this up to you."

"HOW???"

Chandler smiled. "I don't know, Bill. Suppose you try to sign the first negro player in the American League-"

"Now Happy, what would make you thi-"

"Shut up, Bill," the Commissioner said. "I know who your scouts are, and they've been at every Chicago American Giants game for the last two months-"

"All right, all right," Veeck relented, "you got me. I knew I couldn't change this, but you can't blame me for trying."

"Good." Chandler took a breath.

"Still," Veeck wasn't going to let the Commissioner off that easy, "if I lose 20,000 off the gate, I'm probably losing more than $50,000 adding tickets plus concessions. Happy, I need to make some deals this winter if I want to get in the hunt next season, and that $50,000 is just a nice thing to have in my pocket when I call Connie Mack, or the Griffiths to raid their rosters."

Chandler thought for a second. "I've heard some other things from out west. There may be some people out in Los Angeles who might be interested in what you're doing there in Cleveland. Interested in any more minority partners?"

"Always," Veeck replied. "And Weaver's suspension?"

"The next six games," the Commissioner said, "or the last six. Sorry about the doubleheader."

"Dammit." Veeck sighed.

"Thank you, Bill," Chandler said. "I knew you'd – eventually – understand."

Veeck moaned in disgust as he dropped the receiver into the cradle and rubbed his forehead. "Ada..."

"Here's your coffee." Ada tried to be pleasant. "Well. That stinks."

"You were listening...?"

"Of course." The secretary smiled. "What next?"

"Call Eli at the Hollenden," Veeck said with resignation, "and get him over here. He needs to hear this from us first."

SEPTEMBER MONDAY 16

The Weaver Farm – Mt. Hope

The first half of the east field had been harvested the Saturday before, but Elijiah Weaver had stopped at that point because of the huge
boulder about 100 feet from the roadside. Before heading for the barn,
and readying for the sabbath, Elijiah had the team, and his youngest
sons, harvest all the corn for 50 feet around the rock, clearing the space
so that he could deal with it – once and for all – on this sunny Monday
morning, with the first hint of the autumn chill to come appearing in
the vapor as his draught team exhaled as he led them back to the stone.

His brother spoke first as the wagon slowed. "Elijiah, why not leave
this until the harvest is in? The stone's been deep in the ground since
grandfather's day. It can wait."

"Today's the day," the elder brother said. "The ground's got some
give, I've got good help, and-" he smacked one of the Belgians on the
rump, "-a fresh team!"

For the next hour, Elijiah, his brother, and his nephews dug around the huge stone, exposing what he knew was below the soil's surface – a very handy cleft in the rock, with just enough hook to it that his inch-thick ropes would fit around it, and hopefully get enough purchase as his team of three Belgians drove forward.

By 8 o'clock, Elijiah had set the ropes. It looked as though there was enough of the rock's underside exposed to yank it free from the earth, and – if he had the team moving in the right direction – he'd get enough momentum so that the stone would roll once or twice down the slight incline toward the drainage ditch.

In driving his team forward, he never needed to strike them. In fact, he barely had to say a word. Once he had everyone clear, and tension on the ropes, Elijiah's command was simple, and barely audible.

"…hup…"

At that single word, the Belgians strained forward.

Elijiah saw a slight movement from underneath the rear of the stone.

"…ho…"

The halt command was just as quiet, and obeyed just as fast.

For the next hour, the stone's movement was obvious, but not conclusive.

After each effort, Elijiah relaxed his team, always giving them time to gather themselves before the next surge forward.

Meanwhile, the men kept widening the area around the back of the stone, trying to allow as much movement as possible the next time the horse team was called upon.

But, it wasn't working.

9 o'clock soon turned to 10, and frustration was rising.

Elijiah's youngest sons saw the signs of their father's growing anger, and stayed by the Belgians, patting them on the neck between pulls. By this point, their father had turned the commands over to them – as young as the boys were. Children – weighing not even a tiny fraction of the horses at their side – had the animals' trust, and attention.

Now their father had gone to the back of the stone. Enough had been exposed that the boards Elijiah had brought from home could finally be brought into play as levers.

The horses and humans kept up the work in the next hour, as the frustration built. The stone was moving, but any hesitation by the team of horses caused it to rock backward just the same amount it had moved upward and forward.

The mouths of the Belgians had begun to foam. Elijiah knew his time was growing short. Moving this stone was now going to be the lone accomplishment for the day. His team was tired, and he knew they only had one or two good tugs left in them before they'd need to be walked back to the barn.

"Elijiah..." his brother began.

"I know," Eijiah cut him off. He was so tired of this stone bending his plows. Every winter, the freeze and thaw of the Ohio winters would shift the stone just enough that it became difficult to see when driving a team in the spring. Invariably, when March came, and it was time to turn over the earth in preparation for the planting to come, someone – his brother, his cousin, even Eli... even himself if he were completely honest, would lose sight of the stone in the low morning or late afternoon sun, and the sickening sound of steel on granite could be heard all the way back to the house.

Today was the day.

Today had to be the day.

Elijiah gathered the men behind the stone for the final attempt.

While the levers were set behind the rock, he walked toward his youngest boys and told them to listen for his command to start, and his command to halt. They nodded and turned to give verbal encouragement to the team.

Elijiah's advantage now was in brute force. His struggles of the last few hours had brought plenty of help. Buggies now lined the road as neighbors rushed in to add the muscle to the effort.

Unfortunately for Elijiah, that muscle came at a price.

They all had plenty of advice.

When all was in readiness, Elijiah looked his youngest boys in the eyes and nodded.

Within little more than a second, the high-pitched voices of his youngest sons gave the call, the ropes tightened again, and the stone began its slow rise from the hole. This time, its tilt gained even more toward vertical.

The Belgians strained at the ropes.

The stone inched upward.

At that moment, two of the three horses attempted to shift their hooves to gain more traction.

The stone stopped... but held.

Elijiah ran between the levers and got his hands into a ridge on the underside of the boulder. He was not a foolish man, and made sure he had a way of escape in case something unforeseen happened.

Again, two horses shifted almost imperceptibly.

Even though the ropes remained tensed, the stone leaned back just as imperceptibly.

A few of the men along the sides of the boulder released their tension and forward pressure for a moment, and quickly looked at each other, but didn't move away.

Behind the boulder, Elijiah didn't feel the shift. He continued to lift upward, legs planted, knees bent – lifting for all he was worth-

What gave way inside of Elijiah happened quickly. There was no sound he would remember later, but the feeling of what was inside of him coming to the outside was a feeling he would remember for the remainder of his days.

Elijiah fell quietly – with a small gasp, and sank limply to the ground.

The men surrounding him tried to catch their friend as he fell, and let go of the levers.

At this point, seeing that a man was down, some of the Amish men backed away, and the stone began rocking back into the earth.

The horse team was the last to know.

The momentum of the boulder's descent back into the hole pulled them unexpectedly backward as well.

Amazingly, the young boys quickly regained control of the team. But moments later, they turned to see their father on the ground.

Uncle Aaron turned the boys toward him and spoke quietly.

"Boys, get the horses and the wagon back home. Tell your mother that your father has had an accident, and that she should come right away."

The boys heard their father's deep groan.

"We want to see-"

"No. Not now. Go get your mother. *Quickly.*"

Aaron turned to his cousin and pointed toward his buggy. "Get to Johnson as fast as you can. Emil has a truck. Get my brother on those boards, and we'll lay him in the back of the truck when Emil gets here."

"The English hospital?" one of the men asked.

"Millersburg is closest," Aaron replied, and prayed a silent prayer as his brother moaned quietly a few feet away.

SEPTEMBER MONDAY 16

Tower A – Cleveland Stadium | noon

"Six games?"

"Yes Eli," Veeck said stretched out in his desk chair. "Six games."

"Which six?"

Bill frowned. "The Commissioner said it's my choice, but it's a moot point. No matter which games I suspend you for, you'll miss the double-header with Detroit – where we were going to honor you as the American League's best rookie this year."

"And draw 50,000 fans and make lots of money," Harry Grabiner said sadly.

"True. Mercenary, but true," Veeck winced.

The phone in the outer office had begun to ring. Ada crossed to the office door.

"Stop leaning back in your chair," she said, "you'll tip over."

"Yes, dear," Veeck said toward Ada, then looked back at Eli. "It's going to be the last six games – that way, I at least have you for some home games to draw some fans. I'll let the newspapers know that the Comiskeys were behind this, and that should make the papers, and the fans nice and angry with the White Sox next year. We can always play a good 'truth, justice, and The American Way' story when we beat them."

Ada hurried back into Veeck's office and went straight for the phone.

Bill reached to take it from her, but his secretary extended the receiver toward Eli with an expression of concern and compassion on her face.

"It's your mother."

SEPTEMBER MONDAY 16

Pomerene Hospital – Millersburg | 4 pm

"Your husband is quite strong, Mrs. Weaver," the doctor said. "It took quite a bit of anesthetic to get him to relax and sleep. I must say, that was one of the most serious abdominal hernias I've ever seen."

"Will he live?"

"Of course, Mrs. Weaver!" the doctor nodded reassuringly. "He will be back up and working the farm – BUT – not this harvest. By the time he is off bed rest, and on house rest, it will be winter."

The doctor looked to Eli, his hands resting on his mother's shoulders. "This will place you in charge, young man. With a little help, I'm sure your harvest will finish out just fine."

Eli nodded and looked down at his father.

Lying motionless.

His earliest memories were chasing his father to the barn, chasing his father to the wagon to go into town, chasing his father – to tag him with a baseball after dinner on Sunday. Eli has spent his young life in pursuit of his father, trying desperately to keep up with him, and perhaps – on those rarest of days – surpass him... in anything.

Now, Eli shook his head as he stared down at his father – wondering if his pride, his baseball foolishness, had almost cost his father his life.

His mother grabbed his chin until she held Eli's gaze.

"Do not blame yourself, Eli."

"Mother, when I left, he looked so angry, so hurt-"

"He listened to every inning, of every game, every night," his mother said with a small smile.

"*Listened*?" Eli couldn't believe it.

His mother smiled and bowed her head. "We were not the only ones."

Eli's world was spinning a bit now. "You fall asleep at 9, how would you-"

His mother looked with a broad smile. "Because I was listening with him."

Mother and son regarded each other for a moment.

Uncle Aaron nodded. "Do you know how much guilt hundreds of Amish families can produce? Smuggling farm radios into their barns from English stores in Mt. Hope, Millersburg, and Sugarcreek..."

"Rachael wrote me about the Bishop's letter," Eli said.

Bill Veeck pulled the doctor and a nurse aside in the corridor.

The Indians' owner removed a card from his pocket. "Make sure Mr. Weaver has whatever he needs. And don't let the family pay a penny for his care – send all the bills to me at this address. If you need some guarantee right now, I have a few hundred on me..."

The doctor looked at the business card, then up at Veeck.

"Bill Veeck. Of the Cleveland Indians."

"That's me, doc."

He looked at the nurse, beamed, and pointed to Eli. "Then, that's-"

"Eli Weaver."

The doctor looked at the strong young man by the bedside and laughed. "Of course. It's just that there are *so many* Weavers in this area..."

"I'm beginning to understand," Veeck smiled.

"...and Millers, and Yoders, and Steiners, and Horsts... you get the picture."

The nurse, eyes wide, ran to get herself a pen and some paper.

"Mr. Veeck," the doctor began, "you have no idea what it's been like here in Holmes County this summer. Everyone knew the Amish were buying up every farm radio and battery pack in sight. The ones they didn't buy, we were buying. Business in the bars dried up – everyone stayed home to listen to the night games, or hurried home to hear the end of the afternoon games. I'd go out for a walk here in town when I took a break from doing late rounds, and I'd never miss a pitch – I could hear the games up and down every street."

Veeck smiled. The doctor wasn't done.

"For the last few years, the only heroes our children have seen have held guns. Yes, I'm glad we won the war, but Mr. Veeck – how can I say this... I'm not Amish, I'm Mennonite. We don't adhere to the 'old ways', but we still believe in non-violence. This summer, the Amish and Mennonite boys found a new hero. They weren't playing 'war' on the sandlots anymore... they were playing ball again. I think every kid in the county was imitating Eli's batting stance from the photos in the newspapers."

Bill looked at the doctor, then over at Eli by his father's bedside.

"And Mr. Veeck," Bill turned to the doctor – who nodded in the owner's direction, "thank the newsmen for not photographing Eli's face. Everyone in our community noticed, and we appreciated it."

Veeck nodded. "I'll let them know."

The doctor smiled. "It's been a wonderful summer."

"The first of many," Veeck replied.

The doctor looked at him curiously.

"What...?"

"You know this was Eli's *rumspringa*?" the doctor asked.

"Of course."

The doctor looked down, then up at Veeck. "Eli still has a decision to make."

Veeck brightened. "Well..."

"It may not be the decision you'd expect, Mr. Veeck."

"So, you must miss the last six games," Uncle Aaron asked, "for not being violent?"

Eli smiled. "That's the way they've figured it."

Aaron thought a moment. "Then, I think you should go back to Cleveland and play your last games. Then – come back home."

"And leave my father again?" Eli was incredulous.

"Eli – he will not go home from here for a few days. All you would do is sit here. I think everyone will want to hear these last few games. Especially your father."

"But, who will help *you*, who will help *mother*..."

"Before I left, I had word that families were cooking and baking already. Thanks to them, we will be eating well until Christmas." His mother smiled. "Go."

"The harvest-"

Uncle Aaron shook his head. "The Belgians were spent today. They will need a few days to recover. By then, you'll be here, and the feed corn will still be there."

"Doctor," Veeck said, "will you allow a radio by this man's bed?"

"Most certainly."

"Stay with him tonight," Veeck said. "Tomorrow's another off day. I'll head home tomorrow morning if you want to come with me. Or, you can leave Wednesday morning early. Cy can swing by to get you and have you at the park for batting practice."

Everyone in the circle nodded at Eli.

"All right," Eli said softly.

"Just hit some home runs," Elijiah Weaver whispered from the bed... and drifted back to sleep.

WEDNESDAY
SEPTEMBER 18

League Park – Cleveland

"Your dad's okay?" Buster said as he tossed the ball Eli's way.

"I guess so," the rookie replied as he caught the ball and fired it back. "The doctor said it was the biggest... hernia? – yeah, that's the word – he'd ever seen. Said my uncle got him to the hospital just in time."

"And now you got a suspension to serve," Mills said as he threw the ball back to Eli. "Imagine how many games you would have got if you'd actually decked'im."

Eli laughed as he caught the ball.

"Well, at least you get to go home." Mills thought for a second. "You're gonna have a lot of work to do, but you'll be home."

"Yeah," Eli thought out loud as he waited for his coach to return his throw. "I'll be home."

"...not many fans ventured out for this one today – a little over 3,000 by the box office count. And the Tribe has barely been present either, trailing 7-nothing here in the 8th. At least we've had plenty to talk about here in the press box."

"Jack, I don't think anyone quite understands Weaver's 6-game suspension... especially those of us who were in the ballpark for the game with the White Sox on August 17th!"

"And for once, it has done no good to ask Bill Veeck about this mystery... for maybe the first time in his life, Veeck is as silent as the Sphinx."

"Well Jack, here comes the man of the hour."

"Weaver doubled to lead off the second, but was left by his lonesome out there - stranded by his mates who disappeared 1-2-3 in a neat little row. Mickey Hafner has pitched quite a gem for the Senators to this point-"

"-or the Indians have been snoozing to this point."

"-fair enough. Weaver digs in... levels that bat out toward the mound, and here's Hafner's pitch – LINE DRIVE to left-center for a base hit! Spence cuts it off quickly, BUT WEAVER'S HEADED FOR SECOND ANYWAY! Quick throw! Sliiiiiiiiide... and SAFE with **another** double is Eli Weaver!"

"Well Jack, not all the Indians are snoozing at the plate!"

"A kid who's about to be unjustly suspended, with a hustling double, in a meaningless September game, with his team down 7-to-nothing... in the bottom of the 8th... mmmm-mm!"

"Call me crazy Jack, wouldn't it make more sense if the Commissioner's office just kept that kid on the field...?"

THURSDAY SEPTEMBER 19

League Park – Cleveland

THE CLEVELAND NEWS

Best Sports In Town

FELLER'S 25TH IS 5-1 INDIANS WIN

Weaver Suspension Still A Mystery

Miracle: Commish & Veeck Remain Silent

By Hal Lebovitz

(League Park)

It's been a season of hard work for Bob Feller.

"It was a lot harder on the *Alabama*, I can tell you that," Feller said as he stood in front of his locker after yesterday's 5-1 win over the Nats at League Park.

"Here, I just get sweaty and sore. By my gun turrets on the battleship, I smelled like gunpowder. I'll take 'sweaty and sore' any day."

Rapid Robert struck out only 5 on the day, relying on a snappy slider he perfected in the Navy. Feller's famed fastball seems to have diminished in recent weeks.

"With all our pitching injuries, we've been going with Bob every fourth day – sometimes every third day, no matter what," said Manager Lou Boudreau, himself sidelined by injury from the 'player' portion of his title.

"Sure I'm a bit tired," said the All-Star righty, "but I've got all winter to rest."

The Indians actually mustered 10 hits in the contest, and were aided by 2 Washington errors. Jim Hegan banged out 3 safeties, with Eli Weaver and Dale Mitchell each adding 2 of their own.

As for Feller, his historic season is now secure in every way. His 25 wins lead the AL, the 320 strikeouts, and 10 shutouts lead the league by far.

And of course, a no-hitter at Yankee Stadium at the end of April.

"That may be the thing I'm proudest of this season," Feller said. "I had to get through Henrich, Keller, and DiMaggio in the 9th to finish it."

Only 2,441 fans paid for the privilege of seeing another building block for what Tribe prexy Bill Veeck hopes is a year to remember in 1947.

The 66-80 Indians welcome Detroit to town for a Friday-Saturday-Sunday weekend series.

ALL QUIET ON THE WESTERN FRONT:

Meanwhile, the silence remains deafening at the Commissioner's Office in Chicago. "Happy" Chandler has been anything but jolly since newspapermen in the Windy City discovered that the Sox' Joe Haynes suspension of 6-games was being matched by only a 3-game penalty for the Indians' rookie, Eli Weaver.

The White Sox, backed by every reporter in Chicago, badgered Chandler into submission. Now, Weaver's self-defense in front of thousands of witnesses at the Stadium on August 17th merits the same penalty as the instigator.

Every hack in Chicago keeps churning out half-truths, while the Tribe's Bill Veeck and his prized rookie remain silent, and the Commish remains unreachable.

What it means is an early, forced vacation for the most exciting player Cleveland has seen since Tris Speaker.

And that is the truest shame in the situation.

SEPTEMBER

FRIDAY

League Park – Cleveland

Eli was tired.

He didn't know that he was playing in his 85th game in 89 days.

And it certainly wasn't the same kind of tired that came with a day baling hay... or shoeing horses... or cleaning stalls... or a 5am milking session with reluctant cows... or the persistence and regularity of a 16-hour day on the farm.

But he was tired nonetheless.

The game was an hour old. Only in the top of the 3rd inning. But there was a weariness in his legs as he shaded the next hitter a bit toward right-center.

The Tigers had not let Allie Reynolds escape the second, jumping on him for 4 runs on 6 hits in just an inning and two-thirds.

Ray Flanigan – activated because Boudreau had run out of fresh arms in August – lasted just two-thirds of an inning himself. Leaving to a weak chorus of boos from less than 2,000 in attendance, he also walked away from his first major league appearance with an earned run average of 67.50.

Red Embree attempted to stem the tide, but the second pitch he delivered was smashed to the right-center field wall above Eli's left shoulder.

As the rookie sprinted – again – to the gap, he had a split-second to see the ball's trajectory, then turn, adjust his stride to meet the ball, and prepare himself for the ricochet that Buster had taught him just three months ago... metal or wood? Which part of the wall would it hit?

By this point, Eli knew.

He turned his head from the ball's flight to the spot on the wall when he knew it would clang off the metal at the top of the rolling exit door to Lexington Avenue and drop to the dirt.

As the ball fell to the ground, his last glance caught sight of the "340" marker painted to his right.

He reached for the ball as he began his spin and launched another low tracer toward second base.

Eli saw his throw was off to the left of the bag and was gathered in by second baseman Ray Mack.

"What are you doing standing here?" Indians first baseman Heinz Becker smiled as big Hank Greenberg scrambled back to first base.

"That kid's done a lot of damage to us all summer," Greenberg shook his head, "I'm not going to let him gun me down, too."

Now it was 7-0 Tigers, and Dick Wakefield was next.

Embree's 1-1 pitch was a breaking ball – that didn't.

At the moment of contact, Eli's instincts had him on the move again. Within a few steps, he was at full speed, galloping toward the "420" marker in straightaway center.

Centerfielder Dale Mitchell yelled "Metal!" meaning he was looking for the short carom.

Eli adjusted mid-stride, immediately beginning to angle toward a possible carom off the wooden part of the wall at the top, which he quickly recognized was more likely.

As suddenly as Eli had burst to full-speed, he eased up as he once again picked up the arc of the ball headed to the screen atop the giant wall – and then...

The baseball disappeared from view.

The knothole gang outside the ballpark was running and yelling as they chased the prize that meant a free admission to the ballpark if they brought it back to the right field gate.

Why would anybody want to get in here right now? Eli thought.

The rookie passed the veteran Mitchell on the way back to their positions.

Both offered the other no more than a mournful shake of the head.

It was 9-0 Tigers.

Eli had never run as many wind sprints in practice as he had in this game.

And there was still just one out in the third.

And the rookie was tired.

One week into fall, the weather was still summerlike. Eli jogged in after the top of each inning and tried to keep his mind on the game.

His mother had called from the hospital to tell him that his father would be home the next day – Saturday.

And so would he, he thought to himself.

With his mother, sisters, and little brothers consumed with worry about his father's recovery, he decided not to allow them to be concerned with his return at all. Mr. Slapnicka – the English who had first seen him play in June – was back from his scouting duties for the season, and told Eli that he would get him home right after Saturday afternoon's game.

"Weaver! You still in this game?"

"Yes, Lou."

"You're on deck, kid. Let's go!" Boudreau yelled with irritation.

Tigers' pitcher Fred Hutchinson had handled Eli pretty well in their previous meetings, and this at bat in the 4th was no different: curve balls... slow, slower, and slowest – and none of them anywhere close to the middle of the plate. Everything to the outside corner – or just plain outside.

Eli tried to step toward the plate, and yank the ball into left field, but all he did was create the most pitiful of contact sounds, and send an easy bouncer to third baseman George Kell, who snapped his throw to first, knowing that Eli would be running hard no matter what.

In the fifth, Kell smashed his fourth hit of the day into right center.

Eli rolled his glove over, and cleanly picked the short hop. He came up firing as another Tiger sprinted for home plate.

The rookie fired it all right.

Over the screen, and smashing into the wooden platform for Cleveland's radio broadcasters. Bob Neal reached down to grab the baseball. Play-by-play man Jack Graney pulled his handkerchief out of his shirt pocket and waved a "white flag" as the umpires waved another Detroit runner home from third on the error.

Eli saw the broadcasters laughing as they described the play into the large circular microphones in front of them on the platform.

By the time the 5th inning carnage had ended, the score was 14-0 Detroit.

As he walked to the top step of the dugout to choose his bat from the line of bats arrayed in front of the dugout, Eli looked up, and out at the mound.

The Tigers had brought out their own rookie pitcher to mop up.

"Pitching for Detroit... Ted Gray. Gray... pitching for Detroit."

No more Hutchinson.

Eli couldn't wait to get to the plate.

In a 14-0 game.

Eddie Robinson made solid contact but hit the ball straight up. It settled into the centerfielder's glove for the first out.

Eli almost ran up to the batter's box.

But... it was soon obvious that Gray had his instructions from the bench.

Ball one. Outside. Of course.

Gray received the sign. Eli's hands loosened, then regripped the bat as the pitcher's hand came forward.

Ball two. Even more outside.

Eli stepped back and took a practice swing – knowing it might be the only time he might get to swing – today, or tomorrow.

Ball three. This time, a curve. The lefty started it outside, Eli shifted his weight, and the baseball dropped into the dirt where catcher Birdie Tebbetts smothered it.

Eli stepped back again and prepared himself for a walk.

No. He thought.

NO.

Get ready.

He stood back in. Prepared.

As soon as Gray released the ball, Eli recognized the spin.

Curveball.

A hair-trigger later, he recognized the destination – knee-high, at the heart of the plate.

When his hands swept forward, and his forearms turned as one, he knew what was going to happen.

In left field, Dick Wakefield – who had already homered over Eli's head – briefly raised his hands from his knees as Eli connected, but he quickly resumed his position, and did not turn to see where the ball was headed. Even with the left field wall 375 feet away, Wakefield knew the ball wasn't headed anywhere near his glove.

What was left of the 1,650 who had shown up on this Friday afternoon, rose from their seats, or turned as they headed toward the exits, and applauded.

As he descended the dugout steps, scratching the concrete with his spikes, Boudreau – without a smile – tapped on his backside, and his tired teammates mumbled their congratulations.

The score was now 14-1.

Eli sat down on the bench.

And thought about his father, his mother, his sisters, his little brothers, the Belgians recovering in the barn.

And the fields that would need his attention on Monday morning.

And Rachael.

And that sweet little curveball that came right to his bat.

SEPTEMBER ^{SATURDAY} 21

"So, we're not gonna play catch again till spring training?" Buster threw the ball to Eli and shook his head mournfully. "That Commissioner sure knows how to ruin the start of the day."

"No comment," Eli laughed and sent the ball back toward his coach.

"Well, at least Bill taught you somethin' worth somethin'," Mills laughed. "That phrase will always come in handy... you'll see."

Eli saw the group of reporters by the Indians' dugout. "Oh, no... again?"

"They'll probably chase you all the way home." Buster tossed the ball back.

"How many ways can they ask the same question?" The rookie caught his coach's throw and sent it straight back to him.

"How much time you got?" the coach muttered. "Eli, they're gonna keep askin' ya' what ya' think of the suspension in every different way they can think of, till ya' slip up and say what's really on yer mind."

Eli caught Buster's next toss and shook his head.

"So...", the coach smiled, "what's really on yer mind?"

"No comment."

Buster laughed. "You sure ain't a rookie no more!"

"Two out in the bottom of the 6th at League Park, the Tigers still up 3-to-nothing, and here comes Eli Weaver. Weaver's 0-for-2, with a couple of weak grounders to the right side. Trout deals – and there's another breaking ball outside to Weaver for ball one."

"Anything Weaver sees that's near the plate will have to be a mistake, Jack. I think the Tigers are tired of seeing him."

"There's ball two – again outside. 2-and-0 on Weaver. Well, they won't see him anymore after today. The suspension begins after today's game, and will keep Weaver out of the lineup for the last 6 games this season. And, I don't know if anyone in the local papers can write anything else that will throw any light on the situation – Trout winds and fires – yep – ball three, and yep, it's outside... I don't recall us having the crowd count this soon before. Of course, there wasn't much of a crowd to count on this Saturday afternoon."

"2,772 in the park today, Jack."

"Tomorrow's doubleheader, and Wednesday's make-up game against Chicago will be at the Stadium, so this will be the final game of the season – and if you believe the rumors you read in the papers – possibly the final Indians game **ever** at League Park – Dizzy deals INSIDE! And Weaver fouls it at his feet!"

"If he hadn't swung at that, it might have hit him in the hands, Jack! Weaver was so excited to see an inside pitch..."

"Trout won't make that mistake twice. Of course, there's a reason they call him 'Dizzy'... now, the wind, and the 3-1 – WEAVER GOLFS IT TO DEEP RIGHT – HIGH – TO THE WALL – OVER THE SCREEN AND GONE! HOME RUN NUMBER 20 FOR ELI WEAVER!"

"Something for the Knot Hole Gang out on Lexington Avenue to remember him by, Jack!"

"Well... that ball had to be six inches outside, and Eli Weaver decided he wanted it!"

"He sure got it!"

"The Tigers lead is down to 3-1 here in the 6th..."

As Eli jogged back out to right field for the top of the 7th, the small gathering of fans in the grandstand waved and applauded. Walking to his position short of the wall as he tipped his cap, he heard another sound.

The Knot Hole Gang on Lexington Avenue had begun banging on the metal doors the length of the wall. He could hear the kids shouting through the cracks and small holes in the dented metal surface.

"Have a good winter, Eli!"

"See you in April!"

Eli smiled, ran to the wall, and pounded the metal gates back at the kids as they ran from the right field corner out toward centerfield. All along the way, he could hear the kids outside the ballpark cheering with delight.

"One out here in the bottom of the eighth, and here comes Weaver to face Trout again – this time as the tying run at the plate. Conway still standing on first after his leadoff single."

*"Well, they can't walk Weaver, Jack – he **is** the tying run."*

*"On the other hand, Bob – the Indians are still having trouble mustering **any** hits... let alone the **key** hit."*

"Other than Eli Weaver, of course."

"For the last month – missing the injured Boudreau in the lineup –

getting Eli to the bat for the Clevelands every inning would be a rule Mr. Veeck would love to see... here's Trout's first offering – and the few fans in the ballpark boo as Dizzy sends one so far outside, that Tebbetts had to jump up and lunge to his right to snag it!"

*"Maybe Trout **will** put the tying run on!"*

"Dale Mitchell's on deck, and he already has two hits today... here's Trout thinking it over, and taking his stretch – now the 1-0-"

Eli had no idea what was coming after that first pitch, but he knew one thing: if this was his last at bat, it was not going to be a walk.

He saw Trout release the pitch, and his hands relaxed from the moment he saw the spin. Eli could hear the scrape of Tebbetts' shin guards – he spread out quickly to block the ball as it dove for the dirt.

"Ball two."

Eli moved his left foot out of the batters' box, hefted his bat, and stepped back in.

Sometimes catchers notice the smallest of things about a batter that can give their pitcher the advantage. Sometimes, that advantage may last only one pitch, but that one pitch could be the difference between an infield popup, or a run-scoring double to the gap. In this case, Birdie Tebbetts noticed that when Eli brought his left foot back into the batter's box, his toe landed a couple inches in front of his previous spike mark.

He's leaning, the veteran catcher thought.

And now came the decision.

Last time, he jammed the kid with that breaking ball inside. Dizzy made him look silly. The home run was ridiculous – six damn inches off the plate, and the kid 5-irons it over the screen.

This time let's really jam'im, Tebbetts thought.

Fastball.

Dizzy Trout trusted his catcher.

But... fastball...?

Right. Trout thought, sure – I can throw a lamb chop past a wolf...

Is Birdie nuts?

Then the righthander saw Tebbetts' target. His catcher held his mitt up right behind Weaver's hands.

He hit the fastball off the handle. Popup to short. Get Mitchell on the soft stuff. Bottom of the order in the 9th, Trout thought.

He nodded once.

As he brought his hands down into his stretch position, and checked the runner at first, Trout narrowed his eyes at his catcher's target –

In. In. IN.

Bust his knuckles.

At this point, every pitcher since time began makes a decision: commit, or step off. Deliver or reset. Dizzy Trout knew exactly what he wanted to do. He had done it successfully to major league hitters hundreds of times before: jam the hell out of the hitter with a fastball at his hands – make him react to what he initially senses, not where the pitch is actually headed.

The other thing that every pitcher since time began knows is what will happen to the pitch as soon as it's released. It's not part of a conscious stream of thought, it's more of a flash between your ears.

A "yes" or a "NO".

In this case, it was the feeling of letting the ball come off his fingers just a hair late.

The velocity was perfect.

The trajectory was not.

Birdie Tebbetts said after the game that he would swear on a stack of Bibles that he felt the movement of the air as Eli's bat swept through his line of sight.

It was the sound of the contact that most of the few in the ballpark remembered.

There was no loud report, no echo into the upper deck which hung so close to the field at League Park.

It was a sharp, stinging click – the perfect meeting of bat with ball.

It was the speed of the outward – and upward flight – that startled Tebbetts.

Even Eli paused for a second, to watch what he had done...

"IT'S OVER THE SCOREBOARD!!!"

"Dear Lord in heaven..."

"ELI WEAVER JUST HIT THAT BASEBALL OVER THE SCOREBOARD AT LEAGUE PARK!!!"

"It's 460 feet from home plate, Jack!"

"And the top of it is at least 25 feet high!"

"SOMEBODY GO FIND THAT BALL!"

"FIND OUT WHERE IT LANDED!'

"I don't know what to say, Bob..."

"Well Jack, he's hit one out of every other part of this ballpark... why not over the scoreboard?"

"Dizzy Trout is standing in front of the mound, looking to the heavens."

"He's not going to get any help from there, Jack."

"Now the Tigers' hurler looks to home plate umpire Joe Rue for a new baseball."

"That he'll get some help with."

"Well... this game is all tied up at 3, and that home run was another Erin Brew Blast-"

"I think everyone could use a blast of Erin Brew right now – holy mackerel! (laughter in the booth)"

ELI'S '46 FINALE – 2 HOMERS – EACH A COUNTRY MILE! "WHAT WILL HE DO IN '47???"

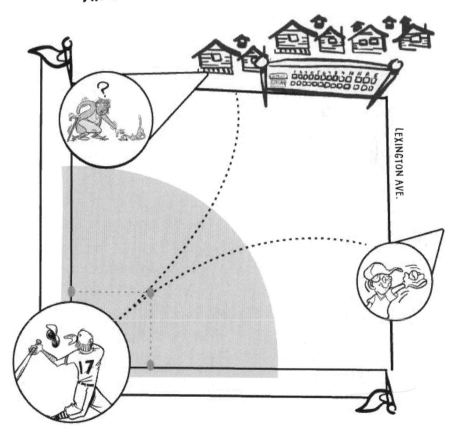

Boudreau punched him in the arm as he jogged down the dugout steps. "You certainly can do some interesting things to a baseball, Eli."

"I think Dizzy saw his life pass before his eyes on that one, kid!" Buster laughed out loud as Eli sat down on the bench beside him.

"If I'd have thrown any more in that first batting practice," Bob Feller smiled as he walked by, "you'd have hit one like that already."

Eli looked out at the scoreboard.

Wow.

That was pretty far.

Eli looked out at the scoreboard again.

3-3 in the 8th.

Extra innings...? Oh, no.

He just wanted to go home.

As it often happens after what seems to be a climactic moment before the end of the game, the *actual* end of the game can get anticlimactic.

In the top of the 11th, it was an infield single, two walks, and a throwing error on a sure double play ball that gave the Tigers a 5-3 lead, and would have sent what was left of the meager crowd home...

But for the fact that Eli was leading off the bottom of the inning.

For Trout, still pitching in the 11th, it was about as good an outcome as he could hope for: the Indians' most dangerous hitter, in a situation where he could do the least possible harm: no tying or leading runs on base. Getting by Weaver – no matter what happened – got him to the part of the order that had done little or nothing all day.

"For Cleveland – Eli Weaver – right field."

Tebbetts – as tired as his pitcher after crouching for 10 innings – knew he had to keep focused for both of them right now. Even so, what do they do with this guy?

Dizzy Trout peered in for the sign, his arm throbbing by his side, and saw –

His catcher shrugging his shoulders, and gesturing with his mitt as if to say, 'whatever you have left, serve it up'.

Trout lowered his head for a moment and thought, 'Well, he can't hit an outside curveball 500 feet... can he...?'

*"We've had a note passed to us here in the press box, that an Indians employee – who looked suspiciously like Bill Veeck – took a member of the ground crew with him to find that last baseball that Mr. Weaver tried to hit to the Terminal Tower. They found the baseball against the back fence of the Brown family – whose home faces East 70th. Their measuring tape gave out about six feet from Mrs. Brown's garden fence, so that last home run by Eli Weaver has been measured at **approximately** 566 feet."*

"And here comes the perpetrator returning to the scene of the crime."

"Eli Weaver is 2-for-4 with a walk. Those two hits are a pair of homers as impressive as any ever hit in this ballpark... and yes, that includes The Bambino. Dizzy Trout stares in, and begins his windup-"

Once again, Eli saw the baseball – and its curveball spin – as soon as it emerged from Trout's hand. His hands leading, his wrists snapping, this time there was an audible crack of the bat throughout the ballpark.

The ball launched into the air again –

"...here's ANOTHER ONE driven deep to left center. Evers is going back – back – back – at the wall – and he MAKES the catch for the first out of the inning!"

"Weaver drove that one a country mile, too – but this time Hoot Evers had just enough room in the deepest part of the park to chase it down."

"Over 420 feet from home plate – but nothing but a loud out to start the Cleveland 11th."

Eli plopped onto the bench next to Mills and stared blankly out at the field.

Trout made short work of Mitchell and Mack, and the game was over.

"...and so, because of a Commissioner who kowtows to a lawless gang of Chicago reporters, Eli Weaver's season will end here today at a nearly empty League Park."

"Because it will take around 475 plate appearances to be eligible for the batting title, Weaver will fall well short. But Jack, when anyone hits .363 over 86 games, that's very significant..."

"Eli, will you stay with the team during your suspension?"

Bill Veeck stepped between his player and the reporter. "We're not done with our appeals yet. Guys, let's not act as if this is over. I don't think it is."

"Aww Bill, the Commissioner doesn't want to make the Comiskeys mad."

"I don't care about the Comiskeys," Veeck snapped back. "I care about the unfairness done to this young man, and by association to his teammates, our fans, and my ownership syndicate."

"Eli, j'ever hit one that far on the farm?"

"No – don't think so," Eli laughed. "'Course, no one back home throws as hard as Trout either."

"Do you have a contract offer for '47 yet?"

Veeck again stepped in front of his young star. "Eli and I have already had a conversation about next year. I hope we'll have a nice Christmas present to tell everyone about in December."

After the reporters had left, Eli emerged showered and dressed, with his duffel bag filled with his plain, Amish clothes. As he set it down, he saw a second duffel – stuffed to the gills.

"What's this?" Eli pointed at the bag.

"Just a little somethin' for the kids back home," Buster smiled.

Eli unzipped the bag and saw a collection of bats, dozens of baseballs, a set of bases, a box of children's caps, and a full set of catcher's gear.

"I figgered they'd like it," Mills winked.

"Well done, Millsy." Veeck slapped him on the back.

"Eli? Just wanted to say goodbye and wish your father the best!" Hal Lebovitz poked his head in the door.

Eli walked over to him quickly and the two went into the hallway.

As they disappeared around the corner, Veeck noticed a full laundry bag stuffed into the back of Eli's locker. The attendants had every other locker cleared at this point, since this was the last game at League Park for the season.

Veeck grabbed the bag and was about to toss it into the pile in the center of the clubhouse, when he noticed how heavy it was. He tugged at the rope and looked inside.

The bag contained all of Eli's "English" clothes – including his socks and shoes, neatly folded and stacked.

Eli wasn't coming back.

Unless he was going to tell the clubhouse boys to send those clothes out to Arizona in the spring.

No.

Eli wasn't coming back.

He heard Lebovitz and Eli talking as they walked back down the narrow corridor to the clubhouse.

Veeck reached into Weaver's locker and shoved what he quickly rolled up in his hand to the bottom of the duffel bag Eli had carried into the room.

"I think Cy's parked on Linwood," Veeck announced.

The clubhouse guys tossed Eli's bags into the trunk of the scout's car, as Oscar ran out from the concourse.

"Take care, Mr. Eli!" Oscar hugged the young ballplayer. "Honor Him, and He will honor you."

"I will, Oscar," Eli smiled. "Tell everyone at Shiloh 'thank you' for me."

"I most certainly will." Oscar raised his hands to heaven.

Bill Veeck looked at his phenom and extended his hand.

"Spring training's in Arizona for the first time next year, Eli," the owner said. "Tuscon. Sunshine, blue skies, cactus flowers-"

"And snakes," Lebovitz added. "Don't forget the snakes, Bill."

Veeck looked at his phenom again.

"Can I visit you at the farm sometime in November?" Veeck nodded. "I have a contract offer that will take care of you and your family very well."

As Eli shook Veeck's hand again, their eyes met. "You're always welcome to visit, Bill."

Cy and Eli opened the doors to the scout's big Ford sedan and disappeared inside.

As the car disappeared around the corner, and began its journey south, Lebovitz stepped off the curb, and stood next to Veeck.

"Off the record Bill," the reporter asked, "what are you going to offer him?"

"Not enough," Veeck answered staring down the street.

With the city left behind, Cy asked Eli, "Hungry?"

The car glided up to the diner, and Cy saw Tom and Helen waving to him.

"As soon as we saw you pulling in, we put your usual on the grill!" Helen said as she burst out the door."

Cy jerked his thumb over at Eli. "You'd better make it two."

Tom walked out to join his wife as she looked at Cy's passenger. "I don't believe we've had the pleasure."

Cy smiled. "Tom – Helen – *that* is Eli Weaver."

The next fifteen minutes were filled with summer night stories of staying open a little late, and gathering around the radio, listening to the games. Morning newspapers rustling as coffee was poured, with breakfast patrons deciphering the box scores and the game accounts. Tom and Helen offered to prepare a basket for Eli's family, but with the lateness of the hour, he declined.

After Eli had signed autographs on menus for all the folks having a late dinner, Cy produced a brand new baseball, and Eli wrote a note of thanks to Tom and Helen, and signed on the sweet spot with a flowing, and very legible script (as Bob Feller had taught him).

It was almost 9 o'clock when the Ford eased up the Weaver's driveway to the sounds of barking dogs, and the commotion of a family ready to celebrate.

Eli went to the living room quickly, and found his father propped up in the easy chair in which he'd been resting since returning home that morning.

"Welcome home, son."

"Father."

Eli and his father were not the hugging type – especially now with Elijiah on the mend, but as they clasped each other's hands, they held on to each other in that way for a long moment.

Eli's eyes scanned the room. He looked at his mother and mouthed the word, "Rachael?"

"Tomorrow," his mother smiled as she mouthed back.

His mother crossed the room and placed her hand on Eli's shoulder. "Mr. Veeck sent that chair for your father yesterday. Here's the note that came with it: 'With kindest regards for a speedy recovery from all of us in the Cleveland Indians family. Get well soon, Elijiah – and thank you for lending us your eldest son this summer. I trust we have returned him in good condition. (signed) Bill Veeck'."

Elijiah motioned to the girls and winked. "Show your brother the 'English evil' that has entered our house."

Eli frowned. His sisters giggled, and ran to the closet, opened the door, and removed the bedsheet to reveal a farm radio with two battery packs.

"You're all ashamed of yourselves, then?" Eli smiled broadly.

"Two home runs today!!!" Lukas and Isaiah yelled.

"There will be many more home runs for you in there." Eli pointed to the large duffel bag on the floor.

Lukas and Isaiah went wild.

Within minutes, the bases and home plate were arranged at the four corners of the living room, and Cy was attempting to tag the speedy youngsters who were sliding into every base with great flourish.

After cookies and coffee, the scout excused himself for a late night drive north.

Eli stepped out on the porch with Cy and left the living room commotion behind.

"I'm not sure how to thank you," Eli finally said as he stared up at the night sky.

Slap put his hands on the shoulders of the young phenom.

"There are two ways you can thank me," Cy said, "one or both may apply."

Eli stared questioningly at the old scout.

"First, you can be the greatest player in baseball for the next fifteen years."

Eli pursed his lips and took a deep breath.

"AND-OR," Cy continued, "you can be a great son, a great brother, a great husband, a great father, and a great teacher of the game you love to these people that you love."

Eli looked up thankfully. "I will, Cy."

"Thank you for using your *rumspringa* on the Cleveland Indians, son." Slap reached out his hand. "You're unforgettable."

"Thank you, Cy."

A handshake. Taillights disappearing in the distance. Then silence... but for the last frogs in the irrigation pond down the hill.

The chime in the old windup clock on the mantle rang eleven times.

Eli leaned his father back in the easy chair.

"Good night, son."

"Do you need anything before I go upstairs?" Eli asked.

"No..." his father said quietly, "go to bed. We'll talk about what order we'll finish off the fields after church tomorrow. It can wait."

"Yes, it can," Eli smiled.

There was a long pause. The insects outside continued their conversations.

"I thought I might not see you again," Elijiah said quietly.

"I thought I might not see you again, either," Eli replied.

Father and son considered each other for a long moment.

They nodded at each other.

Eli climbed the stairs.

As he walked down the upstairs hallway – the familiar boards creaking in just the right spots – he wished his mother and sisters a good night.

Pausing at the room he left to his little brothers, he did a double-take at the door, and exposed more of the wick on his lamp to get a better look.

Sticking out from under the covers on Lukas' side of the bed was Eli's Ted Williams bat, with his brother's arm draped over it and pulled close.

Isaiah was laying on top of the covers wearing a sweat-caked catcher's mask, dusty chest protector, and shin guards that were far too big for him.

At the end of the hallway, his family had fixed him a new bedroom in the sunroom. He placed his duffel on the floor, opened it, and began to pull out his plain clothing piece by piece, as he searched for his bedclothes.

As he reached to the bottom of the bag, his hand felt something different from his clothing – wool flannel.

Eli's hand closed around the cloth and pulled it to the top of the bag.

He placed the Cleveland Indians cream white jersey on his bed and smoothed it as he looked at it in the soft lamplight. For some reason, it looked very different on his bed than it did under the arc lights in Cleveland Stadium.

Picking it up by the shoulders, he flipped the jersey around to see his number "17" on the back. Again, he sat on the bed and regarded it for what seemed like a long time.

Was it worth it?

Would it be worth it to continue? To leave home again?

Eli had no doubt that Bill would come to Mt. Hope whether he asked him to or not. There was also no doubt that Ted Williams would pick him up and drive him to the bat factory in Kentucky if he said 'yes'.

Slowly, Eli folded the jersey, opened the drawer containing his wedding and funeral clothing, and slid the jersey all the way to the bottom of the neatly folded stack, tucking it underneath his plain black pants, and tucking any trace of the uniform from view.

He closed the drawer quietly, and giving up on looking for his bedclothes, Eli leaned back onto his pillow, bumping something with his head in the process.

In the low lamplight, he saw that it was a card from Rachael.

'Eli' was written on the front in her elegant flowing script.

He placed the envelope next to him on the pillow and reached to snuff the wick.

Eli would read Rachael's note, and see her at church, tomorrow morning.

Sunday morning.

The first day of the new week... and a new start.

As Eli laid his head back, and closed his eyes, he heard the sound of a distant steam whistle – and then nothing more.

EPILOGUE

The Budget – Wednesday, November 16, 2012 – page 23

Mt. Hope, OH
Holmes County
November 12, 2011

Along with my brothers and sisters, Libby and I wanted to thank all of you who attended the remembrance of my father, held earlier today at our mother and father's homestead.

To have sent mother on to heaven just a few months ago, and now to have father join her so quickly, has been a shock to us all, but there is a great peace that they are again together.

To hear the stories in recent months of all the things they did for so many in our community of which we were unawares surprised us all – and yet it didn't.

All through the county now, we see homes and hearths, and

barns to ballfields that all bear their loving touch, and their self-less giving to others.

His 85 years brought good to his people, and their 65 years to-gether brought good to our family.

Blessed by 7 children, 23 grandchildren, 48 great-grandchildren, and 2 great-great grandchildren our parents, Eli and Rachael Weaver are resting with Jesus, and we shall carry their name humbly, and with joy.

Elijiah Moses Weaver, Rachael Joy (Weaver) Miller, Elizabeth Faith (Weaver) Yoder, Sarah Miriam (Weaver) Miller, Hannah Peace (Weaver) Horst, William V. Weaver (deceased), and Elvis Buster Weaver, and families.

AFTERWORD

I wanted *Eli* to be a fun story to read.

I wanted Eli's story to have something for everyone.

But... for baseball fans especially – I wanted Eli's story to be *plausible*.

Anyone who has lived near an Amish community would never doubt that a physical specimen like Eli could exist. Having lived most of my life around two of the four largest Amish settlements in the U.S., I can assure you that there are "Eli Weavers" in every township.

In fact, just before writing this final section, I talked to a Mennonite woman (with an Amish background) who looked at me as I outlined the plot, and said:

"Did you base this book on a real occurrence?"

"No. It's just historical fiction. A baseball 'what if'."

She looked at me and smiled. "My father was scouted by the Cleveland Indians in 1946."

I picked my jaw up off the floor.

"A lot of young men were scouted right after the war," she continued, "there were scouts all over the place in those days, looking for exactly the kind of player you described. My dad was a catcher – only 5'8" – but, thick and strong as a mule."

"Did he sign?" I asked.

"Very few ever did," she said. "Home, and the farm were a sure thing for them."

It turned out that Eli was a lot closer to being a real person than I ever believed.

Illustrations

The idea of the book's illustrations were to mimic the 1940's style of sports cartooning. With no digital cameras sporting the ability to fire off a sequence of a dozen frames per second – or the ability to 'zoom in' on a far away play, it was left to the cartoonist in the newspaper's sports department to quickly sketch out a critical moment in the game that was missed by a fixed-lens, one shot at a time camera – and usually altering perspective and reality to get the proper effect.

The 1946 Season

As you may have noticed, I often mention the names of winning and losing pitchers in the story – or hitters who had a particularly good day.

I can assure you – it's all true.

In order to make *Eli* plausible, I needed to have some sort of 'framework' – some way to keep Eli Weaver's exploits realistic.

The American League season of 1946 provided me with a near-perfect scenario:

	WON	LOST	PCT.	GB
Boston Red Sox	43	16	.729	-
New York Yankees	37	25	.597	7.5
Detroit Tigers	33	25	.569	9.5
Washington Senators	30	26	.536	11.5
St. Louis Browns	26	33	.441	17
Cleveland Indians	26	33	.441	17
Chicago White Sox	22	33	.400	19
Philadelphia Athletics	16	42	.276	26.5

Cleveland was tied for 5th, and headed for 6th.

Attendance was lagging.

The Red Sox were comfortably out in front – meaning that none of Eli's heroics would have much of a chance of disrupting the race.

...and, starting the season two months late would keep Eli out of the top echelon of hitters in the AL, since Weaver would never be able to accumulate enough at-bats to qualify for the batting title, or challenge for the home run crown.

To add to my "structure", I enlisted the AL schedule itself.

Should you go to baseballreference.com, and track the Indians through the 1946 season, starting with Eli's first appearance as a pinch-hitter against the Yankees on Monday, June 24th, you will find that every game result, every winning and losing pitcher, and every rainout – remain true to the schedule.

Eli's Stat Line

Here is where the fiction sneaks in.

Eli had to be great – but not 'too great'.

Whenever he had a good day, it couldn't be so good as to make the real final score of the game outside the realm of possibility.

Once again, the real Cleveland Indians of 1946 came to my rescue.

They finished dead last in the American League, hitting .245 as a team.

For me, that meant that Eli would be batting 'exposed' in the lineup, with very little protection surrounding him (especially once Lou Boudreau's aching ankles took him out of the lineup and made him a 'manager only' for a good part of the summer). Eli wouldn't be able to hit too many homers, and he certainly couldn't drive in a large number of runs if no one was on base.

For those wondering, here is Eli's final stat line for the 1946 season:

G	AB	R	H	2B	3B	HR	RBI	BB	K	SB	AVG
86	317	50	115	26	14	21	69	42	33	12	.363

Great. But plausible.

(I'll leave it to the sabermetricians to figure out his modern stats)

Okay... I'll admit to two stats on that line that would destroy the space-time continuum a bit, and I hope you will forgive me:

TRIPLES – Eli's teammate with the Tribe, Hank Edwards, led the AL in 1946 with 16 3-baggers. In order to make Cleveland's offensive output remain as bad as it was, I found it necessary to 'borrow' a few of Hank's triples and give them to Eli. So, yes... Weaver would have bested Washington's Buddy Lewis, 14-13, and led the loop.

STOLEN BASES – Because stolen bases were such a minor part of the game in this era, I held Eli back. With his speed of course, Weaver could have probably pilfered 40 if I'd let him run (that darn 'continuum'). As it is, Eli is in pretty good company in the final totals. And – by the way – Eli was 12-for-12 in steals. (like I said... if I'd let him run...)

1946 AMERICAN LEAGUE LEADERS – STOLEN BASES

George Case	Cleveland	28
Snuffy Stirnweiss	New York	20
Eddie Lake	Detroit	15
Mickey Vernon	Washington	14
Don Kolloway	Chicago	14
Phil Rizzuto	New York	14
Eli Weaver	Cleveland	12
Dom DiMaggio	Boston	10
Taffy Wright	Chicago	10
five tied with		9

Thank You

My thanks to all of you who provided encouragements along the way. And especially to:

John Skrtic for helping me unlock the treasure trove of *The Cleveland News* archives, and to his staff at the Main Branch of The Cleveland Public Library who always allowed me to stay way past my allotted 45-Covid-restricted-minutes. Every time.

Scott Longert – author of many a historical look at the Cleveland Indians of years gone by, who gave me confidence that my history was up to snuff.

Marlin Miller from *Plain Values* magazine. Having grown up Amish, his insight was invaluable on Amish practices.

Isaac Hershberger from *Plain Values* is the designer of the interior of this book. His creative touches were outstanding.

Allen Markovic is the talented cartoonist from Colorado behind the 1940's-style artwork. Thank you Allen, for nailing it.

Anna Zimmerman designed the cover. She does happen to be my middle daughter, and is a designer and photographer living in rural Indiana.

...and most importantly, my thanks to my wife Wendy:

For believing.

ABOUT THE AUTHOR

Mark Zimmerman has been writing since the age of 9.

During his career in advertising, sales promotion, and radio, he has won local, regional, national, and international awards for his creative work.

Mark and his wife Wendy are natives of Northeast Ohio, and have three grown daughters.

Eli – The Phenom's Story is his first novel.

Made in the USA
Monee, IL
22 December 2022

23445895R00229